# EARL OF *Hearts*

# MEARA PLATT

ISBN-10: 1-945767-20-3
ISBN-13: 978-1-945767-20-3

*For Rachel, who shall forever remain in our hearts*

# CHAPTER 1

*Scottish Highlands*
*October 1814*

JOHN RANDALL, THIRD Earl of Bainbridge, reached for his pistol as the howling wind caught the door to MacNaughton's Tavern, flinging it open with a slam that rattled the rafters. All conversation in the crowded establishment suddenly came to a halt as everyone turned to gaze at the rain-soaked stranger standing in the doorway. John tightened his grip on his pistol, wondering what new trouble was about to unfold on this dark and deplorable night.

"What *idjut* would be out in such a storm?" his companion, Jordan Drummond, grumbled, setting down his tankard of ale with a *thunk* on the stained oak table as he reached for his own weapon. But he eased back in his chair a moment later and picked up his tankard once more to resume drinking. "Bah! It's just a scrawny lad."

John gave a distracted nod, his attention now riveted to the new arrival, who was not a lad at all but a slender young woman who appeared to be desperately searching for someone. His heart took a leap into his throat. "Bollocks, what's she doing here?"

*Nicola.*

The wind chose that moment to gust again. It blew the hood of Lady Nicola Emory's cape off her head to reveal the magnificent tumble of her wet, auburn curls and the blaze in her gorgeous, cat-like green eyes. "Better take cover," he said with a groan, his gaze still fixed on the beautiful girl. "She looks angry."

Indeed, Nicola in a temper was a thing to be avoided at all costs. Any man in his right mind would steer clear of her if he valued his life.

John hadn't been in his right mind over Nicola for years now. She'd gotten into his heart long ago and he hadn't been able to get her out no matter how hard he'd tried. But she was his best friend's sister, so it was hands off for him.

Seeing her standing alone, still searching, brought his protective instincts surging to the fore.

What had happened to bring her out on a night like this? He drew back his chair and rose to make his way to her before any of the drunken sots in the taproom approached her.

He wasn't worried about her safety, but theirs. Nicola riled was a force of nature.

She noticed him and was about to start toward him when someone called out, "Shut that door! Dinna ye hear me, lass? Are ye daft?"

Her hands curled into fists. "Shut it yourself, you rum-soaked, tub of—"

"Nicola!" John strode to the door and shut it before a brawl erupted with her in the center of the drunken melee and giving twice as good as she got. For a little thing, she had a stubborn determination and an impertinent mouth, which he'd ached to kiss for longer than he could remember. But that was never going to happen.

Certainly not now.

He'd never seen Nicola this overset. Mingled with her anger was an unmistakable desperation. That worried him. What had happened to leave her so distraught? "Nicola," he said more gently, wrapping his arm around her as he guided her to his table.

She glanced up at him with her big, green eyes, and in the next moment, her entire body crumbled in defeat. She gazed downward and her slight shoulders sagged. Lord, he was an idiot. What she was feeling was anguish, not anger, and that troubled him even more. His stomach roiled. Had something happened to her uncle? He'd always thought the Earl of Darnley was quite fit for a man his age. But the Highlands winds and bone-chilling rains that rolled in from the North Sea could lay a man low. "Why are you here?"

He helped her to slip off her damp cape and settled her at the table he and Jordan occupied. Fortunately, it was in a quieter corner of the tavern. A quelling glance at the curious onlookers had them quickly turning away to stare into their tankards of ale. Good, he wanted privacy, for he was concerned about Nicola and eager to know what had brought her running to him on a night like this.

While John held out a seat for Nicola, Jordan took her cloak and muttered something about hanging it up by the hearth so it would dry.

John cast him an appreciative nod, knowing his companion meant to give him time alone with the girl. His heart lurched once more, for her shoulders were shaking not from the cold but from sorrow. Nicola rarely cried, she simply wasn't one of those simpering, weepy misses. But tears were streaming down her face and mingling with the cold rain on her cheeks. "Answer me, Nicola. What has happened?"

"John." She looked up at him with such an expression of agony etched on her face that his heart shot into his throat again. "I've made a terrible mistake."

He frowned. "What did you do now?"

Her eyes widened in obvious surprise, more than a little hurt by his remark. "Why do you think I did something wrong?"

"You just said you'd made a mistake." He sighed as he raked a hand through his hair. "Never mind, just tell me why you're here and not warm and dry at Somersby's hunting lodge with your aunt and uncle."

She stiffened her spine and tipped her chin up in that mark of defiance he knew quite well. "I refuse to go back to that snake pit."

"Snake pit?" He reached out and brushed back a stray lock of her auburn hair that was wet and pasted to her cheek. He wasn't certain why he did it other than the need to touch her. Her cheek was soft and delicate.

He ran his knuckles lightly along the curve of her jaw, unable to pull away just yet. This was Nicola, beautiful and vulnerable, and at the same time, hardheaded and determined. "The Somersby hunting lodge is one of the finest in all of Scotland. Why won't you go back there?"

She leaned into his touch and closed her eyes. "I caught the Marquis of Somersby with another woman. Oh, John, he's going to announce our betrothal at tomorrow evening's ball and I can't go through with it."

He stifled the urge to cheer. He had no right, for he'd chosen duty over love, taking on dangerous assignments to protect England instead of courting Nicola. He should have been the one to offer for Nicola, but he still had too much to accomplish and could never let on how he felt about her. "Are you certain? You might have mistaken—"

"I didn't. He wasn't just with this other woman. He was *with* her in *that* sort of way. They were in an alcove beside his library. I was on my way there to find a book to read when I heard sounds." Her cheeks flamed a hot, bright red. "I'm such a naive fool. It never entered my mind that he would do such a thing on the eve of our betrothal."

John had never liked Thomas Mooring, the Marquis of Somersby, but he could not blame the man for needing to release his pent-up desire. Nicola was innocent, but also incredibly luscious. Any man would ache to have her. How many nights had he lain in bed, dreaming of her beside him, soft and responsive as he stirred her to passion? "Nicola, sometimes..." *Bollocks.* He did not want to have a conversation about men and lustful urges with the girl.

Or his own lustful urges.

She was his best friend's sister. If he touched her, he would be honor bound to marry her. Not that it would be so terrible, but he was on a dangerous mission at the moment, one he meant to see through to the end. There would be more missions for him when this one was over, perilous ones that were given only to unmarried agents of the Crown. That was the rule when working in this elite unit: marry and you're out. He'd made his choice. He was all in. England needed him more than Nicola did.

He ran a hand through his hair once more in dismay. "Nicola, men have… urges."

She frowned. "You don't."

"What?" The hell he didn't. Right now, he was having a violent urge to throttle her. Did she think he was a eunuch? That his entire body did not roil in agony every time she was near him?

She rolled her eyes. "You've taken offense. I don't mean it that way, John. My point is, if you were a day away from announcing your betrothal to me, would you be satisfying yourself in the arms of another woman?"

She looked up at him, suddenly distraught. "Would you?"

"No." He meant it, too. When he married, it would be for love and there would be no other woman for him but his intended bride.

Nicola cast him a wistful smile. "I knew you'd be faithful. You'd be in love and would treat her with respect and affection. That's the good sort of man you are. The best sort. Any young lady would be proud to marry you. But the Marquis of Somersby is nothing like you. He is an evil viper and he has a dark, odious heart."

Her composure began to crumble again. "So you see, I've made a terrible mistake." She buried her hands in her face and quietly sobbed.

He allowed her a moment before drawing her into his arms to console her. He wanted to continue asking his questions. Nicola could, at times, be theatrical in her descriptions. But he supposed she'd been terribly hurt and more than a little shocked to realize that the man to whom she was about to give her heart was stomping on it by dallying with another woman.

This was just the sort of thing Somersby would do.

For this, and other reasons, John had never liked the man. But he doubted Somersby was evil incarnate. "Has your uncle signed the betrothal contract yet?"

She sniffled. "No, I ripped it up and tossed the pieces into the fire before he could put quill pen to paper."

"And then you ran off into the stormy night?"

She nodded. "I couldn't very well stay under the same roof as that villain, could I?"

John frowned. "You're fortunate you weren't killed by a falling tree or set upon by smugglers or swept away in a sudden flood. Anything might have happened to you."

"I know, but I had to find you. You're the only one who can help me. The marquis will drag me back to his lodge and force me to agree to the betrothal. He wants my dowry. He doesn't want me. I think I knew it all along but refused to admit it to myself."

John leaned back and folded his arms across his chest. He and Jordan had come up to Invergarry a few days ago under the guise of grouse hunting along with the rest of London's elite. But they were quietly working to break up a rather nasty ring of rebels who were financing their operation by smuggling goods through Invergarry. He dared not allow Nicola to interfere with his mission. "I'm sure he won't drag you back or force you to do anything you don't wish to do. Besides, now that you've made your wishes known to your uncle, he'll support you. He won't agree to the betrothal. Nor will Julian ever allow it," he said, referring to her brother, Viscount Chatham, who had been in this elite unit with him until he fell in love with Rose Farthingale and married her.

John trusted very few people.

He liked even fewer.

Julian was the exception. He and Julian were as close as brothers, so he owed it to him to protect Nicola.

He'd died a little inside when her brother had told him of her impending betrothal.

But he had only himself to blame.

Only himself and the torment that had formed him into the man he was.

One who was not fit to declare his love for Nicola.

"You don't understand, John. A simple refusal won't stop the marquis. He has everyone fooled with his charming ways, but he isn't a nice man. He's dangerous and depraved."

John did not know what to do with the girl. She was obviously overset and allowing her fears to run amok.

She stared at his expression and gasped. "You don't believe me."

"Nicola, he made a mistake. That's all."

Her eyes were blazing again. "You didn't see the way he looked at me when he realized I had caught him in the act. There was no contrition. There was no embarrassment or shame. He made no attempt to apologize. Doesn't that speak to the sort of man he is?"

"I don't know. Not everyone reacts the same way when feeling trapped or embarrassed."

"But that's my point. He didn't feel trapped. He made me feel as though I were the one trapped under the force of his arrogant gaze. He frightened me with that look. I don't want any part of him, for I know what he'll do to me once I'm married to him. He'll break my spirit and force me to be a biddable, unquestioning drudge of a wife. He won't be gentle about it either."

John slapped his hands on the table and rose with a groan. His attempts to calm her were only serving to further rile her. "I'll have the tavern keeper send a boy up to the lodge to let everyone know you're safe. There are guest chambers upstairs. I expect they'll all be taken by now, but I'll give you mine. Use one of my shirts for a nightgown. Get out of your wet clothes, and try to have a good night's rest. We'll discuss your situation over breakfast in the morning."

She remained seated. "Why won't you believe me?"

He did not know what to believe. In truth, he was practically senseless at the moment, for the thought of Nicola in his bed, wearing nothing but his shirt against her soft, wet skin, was not helping him come to any logical conclusions.

Fortunately, Jordan returned and set his large frame on the chair beside Nicola's, putting an end to John's attempt to escort her upstairs. "Are ye hungry, lass? Perhaps a bowl of stew to fortify ye."

She smiled at Jordan. "That's very thoughtful of you. I'd like that, Mr. Drummond."

John stifled the flood of jealousy that washed over him when Nicola returned his companion's smile with a sweet and openhearted one of her own. What was wrong with him? Nicola wasn't his. He had no claim to her. Yet his heart was pounding violently in his chest and idiotic thoughts were whirling in that empty head of his. Idiotically possessive thoughts. *Mine. Nicola is mine. No one else can have her.*

But he'd kept silent when he ought to have been courting her.

He'd kept silent when Somersby had shown interest in her.

Nicola blamed herself, but he was the one at fault.

"One of the maids will bring the stew up to my chamber," he said, reaching out to take Nicola's hand. "Come on, I'll help you settle in."

Jordan cast him a questioning look, his beefy hands curling into fists. "Where do ye intend to spend the night?"

"I'm giving her my room. I'll share yours. I can make a pallet for myself by the hearth."

Jordan nodded. "Aye, that'll work."

"Thank you, Mr. Drummond. I appreciate your protecting me, but you needn't worry. Lord Bainbridge has no interest in me other than that of a protective brother."

Jordan arched an eyebrow. "Lass, he isn't your brother."

"No, but..." She sighed. "I would like to go upstairs now. My gown is soaked and I'm chilled to the bone. I don't like the way some of these men are looking at me."

Neither did John.

He cast them a lethal scowl that had them hastily turning away to stare into their tankards once more.

The girl was too pretty for her own good.

She was too pretty for his own good.

He was on an important assignment.

He needed to concentrate on destroying those smugglers.

But all he could think about was Nicola. In his shirt. In his bed.

The storm outside was nothing to the one raging in his heart.

NICOLA ALLOWED HERSELF to lean against John as he escorted her upstairs to his chamber. Fatigue overcame her the moment she rested her head against his big, comforting shoulder. She'd been so tense and overset ever since reaching Invergarry, sensing things were not quite right with the Marquis of Somersby. No doubt her uncle and John believed she was merely being a fickle maiden, but it wasn't that at all.

She would have gone through with the betrothal and the wedding had the marquis been a moderately decent man. She would have vowed to honor and obey him—although she would need to work a little harder on the "obey" part—and agreed to become his wife. Once married, she would have tried her best to make their marriage work. "Thank you, John. I know I've been a bother to you. But I had nowhere else to turn."

"No bother," he said, but Nicola knew he thought of her as an unpleasant boil on his neck that simply would not pop. She did not mean to be a nuisance to him, but it wasn't entirely her fault that she was in this mess over the Marquis of Somersby.

Didn't Somersby have to take some responsibility for his actions?

And that was another thing. The marquis would not permit her to call him Tom or Thomas, but insisted that she always refer to him as Somersby or my lord. They'd never reached the point of amiable familiarity. She'd expected that to come in time, but now knew it never would.

John tightened his grip around her waist as she faltered on the last step. His big, muscled arms drew her close. Perfect arms, but she refused to think about their impressive strength. John did not care for her in that way and never would.

He paused in front of the fourth door on the right. "Here we are."

She said nothing as he opened the door to reveal a cozy fire blazing in the hearth and a comfortable-looking bed that took up most of the small room. John's travel pouch rested on a chair beside the hearth. "Where are the rest of your belongings, John?"

He leaned against the door frame as though afraid to enter his own chamber. Even at this distance, his dark gold hair managed to glow magnificently in the firelight. His eyes were a mix of pine green and lethal gray… yes, that's what they were, a dangerous, haunting green, like the eyes of a predator. A wolf, perhaps. How many times had she lost herself in their vibrant depths? "Jordan's farm is not far from here. That's where I'm staying for grouse hunting season. But we'd planned to spend a few days hunting in these hills since the game is plentiful in this area, so we took rooms here to get an early start in the morning." He nodded toward his pouch. "I have a spare shirt in there."

"Soap and a comb, by any chance?"

He nodded. "Use whatever you need. Ask the maid to help you undress when she brings up the stew."

"Would you mind terribly helping me now? Just a few tugs on the laces and I'll manage the rest. The cold has seeped into my bones."

To her surprise, John suddenly seemed panicked. No, she must have been mistaken. The man had ice in his veins. He was the coolest, most levelheaded person she'd ever known. Nothing ever rattled him, not even the threat of imminent death. She'd seen him in action at her uncle's summer cottage when a ring of Napoleon's spies had come after him and her brother, Julian. "Very well," he said, walking toward her with such obvious reluctance, she wanted to tell him to go back downstairs and she'd fend for herself.

But she was cold and now shivering despite standing beside the fire. Its heat was not enough to warm her, not while she was still in her soaked gown.

"Raise your arm," he said when he reached her side, the request sounding more like a tersely barked order. He bent his head to look at the wet, gnarled lace strings, his breath warm against her neck as he leaned closer. He'd been drinking ale, but the steel glint in his eyes revealed he was quite sober.

Indeed, this was John. Always in control of his surroundings and of himself.

A bolt of heat shot through her as his fingers grazed her waist while unknotting the laces. She tried to hide her response to his touch, but it felt too exquisitely good. It wasn't his fault that he was big and handsome or that she found his touch intoxicating.

Curiously, he always tried to make himself look unexceptional. He wore the most unattractive spectacles, for one thing. But she'd long ago seen through that ruse. His keen eyes and senses rivaled those of any beast on the prowl. Most young ladies in Society considered him a crushing bore. That was the face he showed to all but his closest friends, that of a scholar and a small game hunter who loved the dullest, most esoteric topics imaginable, ones that were purposely intended to have everyone yawning within moments of meeting him.

She wasn't sure why he felt the need to push everyone away.

It hadn't worked with her. She knew the sort of man he truly was. Well, no one truly knew John beyond the few surface layers he deigned to reveal. She'd pierced a few more layers than most, but she still had not come close to penetrating his heart.

She was amazed and honored that he'd allowed her to see in that far. Surely, he must have felt some level of comfort with her.

Perhaps he even liked her a little.

She wasn't sure, for he did not appear to be particularly happy with her at this moment. In truth, she sensed nothing but coiled tension.

"There, done." His voice was raw and husky, sending tingles through her body, which showed how pathetic she was to respond to a man who barely tolerated her out of duty to her brother.

He turned away quickly and headed for the door.

"Thank you, John," she called after him.

He nodded. "Get some rest. We'll discuss what to do about your situation in the morning."

Nicola knew what she was going to do. She was going to pack up her aunt and uncle, and then cut all ties to the Marquis of Somersby.

The only question in her mind was, would John help?

# CHAPTER 2

JOHN AWAKENED AT the cock's first crow, too on edge to sleep any longer. Not that he ever got much sleep. His nights were always fitful, sometimes harrowing, and last night had been particularly bad knowing Nicola slept in the room next to his. He wasn't certain which dreams were worse, the nightmares that had begun in his childhood or the hot, wild dreams of Nicola. He always awoke with an ache from those of her, a burning ache that he wanted to dismiss as purely carnal. But he couldn't, for the girl had a way of slicing through his empty heart.

He quietly rose from his pallet and crossed to the window to peer out of it.

The rain had ended shortly after midnight, and a quick inspection of the road that stretched out from the tavern into the hills revealed it would be passably dry within a few hours. It would only take the heat of the morning sun to dry out the lingering puddles and mud.

His gaze drifted to the distant hills that were filled with rolling waves of purple heather. He loved the Highlands, the heather and thistles, the rowan and gorse growing wild. There was abundant life hidden beneath the blanket of shrubs.

His gaze lifted to the sky and the goshawks quietly circling overhead on the hunt for prey. The clouds gathering over the hills resembled gray-clad clansmen on the march to war, and the wind whistling through the valleys brought to mind the keening wail of bagpipes.

The Highlands suited his temperament, appearing serene on its hard, cragged surface, but scratch below the layers and one would find the wildness simmering beneath. John had learned early on to survive on his feral instincts, much like the wild game that nested in these hills. He'd had no choice. It was the only reason he'd survived.

That was him, the lone survivor.

Those childhood memories still haunted him.

Back then, he'd been too young to protect those he loved, but he was a man now. This was how he awoke to each new day, with a solemn vow to fight anyone who would harm those dear to his heart.

He silently vowed to protect Nicola to his dying breath.

He shook his head and groaned, knowing he was being as ridiculously dramatic as Nicola had been last night. She wasn't in any danger, but if she was firm in her decision not to marry Somersby, there could be some unpleasantness. He would arrange for her and Lord and Lady Darnley to be safely returned home.

After sparing a glance at Jordan, he set about quietly washing and dressing. But perhaps he didn't need to tiptoe about the room. Jordan had remained in the taproom well into the wee hours and was now sleeping like the dead, stretched diagonally across the bed, fully clothed with his boots still on. A thundering herd of horses could have galloped through these quarters and Jordan would not have heard a single hoofbeat.

John could not recall a time when he'd ever let down his guard that completely.

No, he never had.

He left the room to go downstairs for a light repast, but paused first beside Nicola's door. Was she awake yet? He hesitated a moment and then knocked lightly.

He heard Nicola's graceful footsteps moving toward the door. "Who is it?"

"John." He shouldn't have disturbed her at this early hour, but was glad that she was already up and about. He wanted a little time alone with her. He always wanted time alone with her, but never allowed himself to give in to the urge. This was different.

She'd come to him so obviously distraught last night.

"Oh, thank heaven." She opened her door and cast him an angelic smile. "I need your help to tie me up."

"Tie you up?" He quickly dismissed the notion that rushed into his head which was too obscene to reveal to Nicola. "Ah, your lace strings."

She nodded. "My gown is dry but the laces are still a little too stiff for me to manage."

"I'll do it." He stepped into her chamber and shut the door behind him. No one would know. No one would see them. Only the guests embarking on their hunting expeditions would be up at this early hour and most of them were downstairs already. "Did you sleep well?"

Nicola sighed. "No. How about you? I'm sorry you had to sleep on the floor. Between that and Mr. Drummond's snoring, I doubt you got any rest." She cast him another smile, this one more impish. "I could hear his snores through my wall after he came upstairs. I thought a flock of geese had taken up lodgings in your chamber, he honked so loudly through the night."

John shook his head and laughed. "He was a bit loud, but he's sleeping like the dead now."

He forced his hands to slip off Nicola's luscious body the moment he was done. "Are you hungry?"

She nodded.

They made their way downstairs and had no sooner finished a breakfast of oatmeal, bangers, and tea than John heard a commotion at the entry. "Where is she? Tell Lady Nicola she's to come downstairs at once."

John shot to his feet at the sound of Somersby's arrogant voice. "Nicola, get behind me. Seems your husband-to-be is here and he doesn't sound happy."

"I told you last night, that loathsome snake will never be my husband."

He ignored her scowl and nudged her behind him. "You're still angry. The two of you need to calm down and talk this through."

"There's nothing to talk about. He's a monster. He won't listen to me. Besides, I'm not taking wedding advice from you."

John rolled his eyes. "Did you ever hear the adage about not biting the hand that feeds you? I'm trying to help you and you're insulting me."

She stepped in front of him even though he'd been trying to gently push her behind him for her own protection. "Nicola, do as I say."

She cast him the defiant glare that she'd perfected, that pouty-lipped, chin up in the air and sultry, eyes blazing look that made him want to throttle her and at the same time kiss her into eternity.

Lord, the girl was a nuisance.

Her chin tipped up a notch higher. "Talking to him is a waste of time. He won't listen. He means to drag me back to his lodge and punish me for running off. He has a cabinet full of whips of all shapes and sizes."

John growled. "You're making that up."

A rose blush stained her cheeks. "Perhaps. So what if I am? I'll wager that he does. All depraved villains have them. Whips and chains and black masks and lots of naughty leather things that must serve a shocking purpose, although I have no idea what that purpose could be. Not to mention the other wicked instruments of—"

"Where did you hear such nonsense?" He ran a hand through his hair in consternation. "Just get behind me and keep quiet. Can you do that? I'm trying to get us both through this encounter without fists flying."

She nodded and stepped behind him, resting her hand against his back as though needing to hold on to him. "And I don't like the way his lips curl upward in a sneer."

He dismissed her comment as her touch rippled through him. He wanted to tell her not to do that, for his concentration fell to pieces whenever she touched him. "Nicola, wait by the back table where we sat last night. I want you well out of the way while I first approach him."

"Oh, all right. But don't trust him, John."

"Right. Got it. He's a depraved viper." He was glad that Nicola no longer cared for the man and refused to marry him, but was also disgusted with himself for wanting Nicola to be his without any intention of offering for her.

If anyone was a depraved viper, it was him.

The girl deserved happiness and a good man to love her.

"Somersby," he said, approaching the scowling marquis who stood in the entry hall with five rough-looking men. "You needn't worry. Lady Nicola is safe. Mr. Drummond and I will return her to your lodge in a little while. I'm sure her aunt and uncle must be wringing their hands in concern."

Somersby sneered at him, bringing Nicola's words to mind. Whips and chains and toss in a wicked sneer. "She comes back with me now, Bainbridge. Don't interfere or you'll regret it. This is between Lady Nicola and me."

"Are you threatening me? Because I don't take kindly to threats." Gad, had Nicola been right about this arse?

"Where is she?" Somersby raised his hand, about to motion for his ruffians to search the inn, but he must have noticed the lethal glint in John's eyes, and stilled his hand in midair. "Very well, what do you propose?"

"Merely that you speak to her. She was caught unawares last night and was shocked by what she saw."

Somersby nodded. "So she told you."

"She would have sought out her brother had he been here. I was the next best thing. That's all. I am neither condoning nor condemning what you did, nor am I in the habit of gossiping. What matters is how you address the situation this morning. Treating her with kindness and respect will help. She's to be your wife, after all."

"That's right. My wife, not yours. She will never be yours."

*Never.* That one word struck like a knife to John's heart and momentarily stole his breath away. Had he imagined it, or was there a purposeful malice in that statement? A wicked sense of glee in twisting the knife in him?

What had he ever done to offend the man?

Somersby was too busy glancing around and scowling at the small crowd of men now gathered around them to notice that he'd struck deep. Nor did he appear pleased to have these men as witnesses, but John was glad they were present if only to keep the man's temper in check, for he was still riled. "*Mine.* I will not allow her to make a fool of me."

"No need. You're doing an able job of it all by yourself." John knew he should not have goaded him, but the man needed to be taken down a peg or two. He willed himself to remain calm and not curl his hands into fists, but it was no easy thing. He itched to plant the pompous oaf a facer. One solid punch to lay him low. "You're mistaken if you believe Lady Nicola can be threatened or intimidated. You are dangerously mistaken if you believe I will stand back and do nothing to protect her."

Somersby poked him in the chest with his finger. "And you're mistaken if you think to interfere. She is my betrothed. She will be my wife. Do we understand each other?"

John folded his arms over his chest. "She isn't your betrothed yet, nor will she ever be if this is the way you intend to treat her. Put your hand on me again and I'll break it. Put your hand on Lady Nicola and I'll kill you. I think we understand each other very well."

Somersby noticeably blanched at his remark. Good, he wanted to leave no doubt that he'd be watching the marquis. He could tell by the man's nervous glance that he was reconsidering his approach. John smothered a grin, glad that he'd gotten his point across. Even the curious onlookers had hurriedly moved off, obviously not intending to be caught in the crossfire if shots were fired.

"Bainbridge, I am obviously out of sorts. What happened last night distressed me as much as it did Lady Nicola. Of course, I will respect her. She's to be my wife. She will bear my children. She'll be my duchess when I inherit my father's title. I will talk to her. I will apologize to her on bended knee if I must. I'll do whatever it takes to make things right."

John dared not believe a word of his pretty speech, but Nicola must have been listening and did appear to accept what the bounder had just said. She stepped into the hallway and came to his side. "Lord Bainbridge, it's all right. I'll return to Lord Somersby's lodge with him now." She cast both of them a wan smile. "I'm so sorry I worried everyone. How is my uncle? And Aunt Bess?"

Somersby's anger seemed to fade away as Nicola reached his side. "Lord and Lady Darnley are quite distressed, my dear. The sooner we return to the lodge, the better."

She nodded. "I'm ready to go back now. I behaved like a child. Can you ever forgive me?"

A meek and biddable Nicola?

One who was now apologizing to a man she'd called a viper and a monster only moments ago?

John knew her better than to believe his own ears. What was she up to?

"Thank you for everything, Lord Bainbridge," she said, the soft sparkle in her eyes causing his heart to beat a little faster. "Please extend my good wishes to Mr. Drummond. You will both attend this evening's party, won't you? I insist on it. My uncle will be devastated if you refuse."

What? No, he and Jordan were on the hunt for dangerous smugglers. The last thing they needed was to lose a night sipping champagne and listening to Society's elite grumble about how sparse the grouse were this year.

But the short hairs at the nape of his neck were prickling.

Despite Nicola's presently demure appearance, she was going to refuse the marquis' proposal of marriage. Perhaps this was her way of asking for his help in keeping her and her family safe when Somersby's anger erupted. "Of course, Lady Nicola. We look forward to it."

Somersby shot daggers at him with his gaze. "See you tonight then, Bainbridge."

"Count on it, Somersby." *Hell. Hell. Hell and damnation.* He'd have to pack an armory of weapons on his person because the evening was going to turn ugly. So much for catching rebellious smugglers. King and country would have to wait while he rescued Nicola.

He remained in the doorway, his arms folded across his chest and the cool breeze blowing through his hair. The sun was out and beginning to dry the wet roadways. The marquis' carriage kicked up little dust as it disappeared around the bend and made its way toward his grand lodge. His so-called footmen rode behind the carriage, but he noticed one or two of them glance back at him.

He did not like the look of menace in their smiles.

Did they plan to do something to Nicola?

He doubted Somersby would be so foolish as to order her punished in any way. Not when he and Jordan would see her this evening and immediately know if she'd been harmed. Nor would he dare return her to Lord and Lady Darnley with so much as a scratch on her delicate skin. No, he wouldn't dare.

Still, John did not like to think of her alone with that oaf.

He climbed the stairs two at a time and entered Jordan's quarters. "Get up. We have work to do."

"Bollocks, stop shouting at me. My head's about to explode." Jordan slowly rolled to a sitting position and rubbed his hands across his face to wipe the sleep from his eyes and the fog from his brain. "What's wrong? What did I miss?"

John frowned. "Nicola left with Somersby."

That seemed to catch his friend's attention. "And you let her go with that Sassenach horse's arse?"

"I couldn't interfere. She wanted to go."

"Since when has that stopped you?"

John checked the pistol in the hidden holster in his boot, donned his jacket, and grabbed his hunting rifle.

"Ye bloody fool! What are ye planning to do?" Jordan sprang from his bed with a rasping groan and crossed to the door to block him. "I thought you just said you weren't going to interfere."

They were both big men, Jordan a little bigger, but John was more determined. "I won't, unless he stops the carriage and has his men..." He couldn't finish the thought, for it was too gruesome to endure. As much as he detested Somersby, he knew the man would not show his true nature now. And who was to say he would ever harm Nicola? Most men were all bluster. In any event, Nicola was no meek sparrow. "All I wish to do is make certain she is safely returned to Somersby's lodge. Lord Darnley will watch over her after that."

Jordan rolled his eyes. "Very well, give me a moment. We can cut across the foothills and take up a vantage point overlooking the lodge. Let's just hope those smugglers don't get away while we're busy meddling in this marriage business that is none of our concern."

John frowned. "We're not going to meddle, just protect her. She's my responsibility and I—"

"Since when is she yours to look after? Her uncle is the Earl of Darnley. He's more than capable of attending to her care." He grinned at John. "Although I doubt he's fast enough to catch her if she runs away again."

"Stop wasting time with jests. Somersby isn't to be trusted with Nicola. If he lays a hand on her… if he orders his men to…" The words caught in his throat.

Jordan put a hand on his shoulder. "He won't. So don't you do anything rash. I don't know what demons have you by the throat this morning, but you can't let them overwhelm you. Besides, the girl can fight for herself."

"Yes, of course." He knew Jordan was right, but that did not stop the violent tug he felt to his heart. "I'll keep my wits about me. You know I will." He always did, except when it came to Nicola. The blocks of granite surrounding his heart chipped away whenever he was around her.

He didn't like it one bit.

NICOLA'S GAZE WAS fixed on the scenery as Lord Somersby's carriage rolled and bounced its way back to his hunting lodge. A pair of goshawks were on the hunt above the soaring crags, their massive wings outstretched and their heads down as they searched for an unsuspecting rabbit or two to fill their bellies. At the moment, she felt like that unsuspecting rabbit about to meet its untimely end.

Oh, she knew that Somersby had no intention of killing her. But he meant to cheat on her throughout their marriage. Which was why she could not marry him. There were plenty of women who would accept this sort of arrangement. Indeed, most would. He needed to find one of those biddable young ladies to pursue.

Never a coward, she turned to him. "Lord Somersby, we must speak about last night."

The marquis was a handsome man with thick, dark hair and gray eyes that were often turbulent. She'd thought that brooding sort of stormy gray quite attractive, at first. But she now realized that this was all he was, a petulant and brooding marquis who was used to getting his own way in all things and could be cruel when he did not.

While some men took the good fortune of their stature to heart and gave back something in return for the bounty they'd been given, Somersby was not one of them.

"I suppose we must." He nodded and leaned forward. "Your behavior last night was unacceptable."

*My behavior?*

She blinked several times to make certain she was awake and not in the throes of a nightmare. "I beg your pardon? I was not the one caught with my pants down about my ankles."

He did not have the decency to blush. "Has your aunt never spoken to you about… men?"

"Not at great length, but I am not a peahen. I understand quite well what you were doing to that woman… with that… her."

He arched an eyebrow. "Good. Then we are clear."

"On how things will be? Do you mean before or after the marriage? Because I find both possibilities repugnant."

He leaned forward and took her hand in his. She expected his grip to be harsh, but he was surprisingly gentle. "You will be my wife, Lady Nicola. I mean to treat you with respect. But I am a man of hearty appetites. Do you understand what I am saying? I do not wish to satisfy my baser urges on you. I will visit your bed from time to time." He cast her a wry smile. "In truth, I think I will enjoy your impertinent spirit in the bedchamber. But I cannot promise to visit no one else but you. I wish to be honest about it."

She slipped her hand out of his and clenched it into a fist. "Then we are back to where we started. I will not tolerate other women in my husband's bed. We marry for love in the Emory family. We believe in our wedding vows."

He stared at her in bewilderment for an endlessly long moment before suddenly breaking into another smile. "Are you saying that you love me?"

Well, no. She hadn't meant it to sound that way. Indeed, she was going to refuse his marriage offer because she now understood that she would never grow to love him. But he sounded quite gentle and could not be faulted for his attitude when most of Society felt as he did.

She did not wish to hurt him more than necessary when she rejected him. "My lord, we have not been acquainted long enough to be certain of our feelings for one another. But you seem determined to carry on with your… entanglements… much as you do now, and I am saying that our marriage will not stand a chance of surviving if that is your decision. I want a man who is faithful and who values me. I am not going to be anyone's broodmare, no matter how fine the stable in which I'm kept might be or how plentiful and tempting the carrots tossed my way as placating treats may seem."

"I see." He took his pearl-handled walking cane and thumped it against the roof of the carriage.

Nicola frowned when he did not follow up with a command. Instead, he settled back against the fine leather squabs and folded his arms across his chest. His smile was no longer charming but cold, and it held the unsettling hint of malice.

Her heart began to beat a little faster. "Why did you bang on the carriage roof just now?"

"No reason. Must I explain my every action to you?"

"No, but it did not appear to make any sense to me."

"It is my signal to my driver to take more care. We seemed to be hitting more ruts in the road than necessary. I would not like you returned to Lord Darnley with bruises all over your body. He might believe I placed them there."

Was she reading too much into his words? Was this a shielded threat that he would beat her if she questioned him after they were married? She shook her head and sighed. "Very thoughtful of you, my lord."

There was no point in pursuing the discussion since she'd made up her mind about him and needed to develop a workable plan to get herself and her aunt and uncle away from his hunting lodge with as little fuss as possible.

He leaned forward and took her hand again. "Somersby Hall is not such a terrible stable, and the jewels I shall gift to you as my wife are quite pretty carrots. You shall have everything your heart desires as my marchioness. Give me fine, strong sons, and daughters as beautiful as their mother, and you shall have my respect, my discretion. My generosity."

"But never your love." She nodded. "So why choose me? I can be replaced with any of a dozen other young women with dowries as fine as or finer than mine who will not question or challenge you."

"No. There is only one of you, my dear. It must be you and you alone. No one else will do for my purposes." His lips twitched as they turned slightly upward at the corners. His eyes had a turbulent, but unreadable look to them.

*My purposes.* This was no confession of love. What was he going on about then?

Her stomach sank into her toes. *Mother in heaven.* He was using her to hurt someone.

Her brother? Her uncle? She had to find out what he meant to do.

# CHAPTER 3

JOHN DECIDED NOT to wait for his companion, who was taking too long to ready himself. They weren't dressing for a bloody London ball or Covent Garden theater, but merely intending to race up a few hills to keep an eye on Somersby's carriage until Nicola was returned to the arms of Lord and Lady Darnley.

Impatient to be on his way, John went to the tavern's stable to retrieve his mount, Valor. He called for one of the grooms to saddle his horse, a new purchase from Jordan's prime stock, for Jordan was a breeder of renown and Drummond Stables had an excellent reputation throughout Scotland, England, and even Ireland where horse breeding was serious business.

Although John had only recently purchased Valor, he'd already trained the horse to respond to him and even taught him a few useful tricks. Indeed, all of John's plans had been going well until last night. Foil a rebel plot, catch a few smugglers, and acquire a prime horse. Perhaps bag a few grouse in the bargain. Not bad for a few weeks' work.

It would have been all good if not for Nicola storming back into his life.

He crossed to the stall and patted Valor's nose. "Ready for a little exercise, my restless fellow?"

The black gelding was built for power and endurance, much like the chargers bred for battle in medieval times. Valor was a beautiful beast and John looked forward to teaching him more tricks, especially those to use if they were ever in a scrape and had to make a fast getaway.

He had yet to train Valor to use his hooves as weapons, but that would come next. The beast had an impatient nature and was already stamping and kicking, eager to be led out of his stall and taken for a long run.

"Larkins? Bigwell? Anybody in here?" When neither groom responded, John shrugged it off. They'd probably gone off with the group of hunters who'd gathered around him and Somersby a short while ago. He set his rifle against Valor's stall and crossed to the tack room to fetch the saddle himself.

He was about to grab it when he heard several men enter the stable. Something about them put him instantly on alert. They moved silently, something no group of hunters would do, for they'd all be chattering away, boasting of the grouse they were sure to bag this morning. Their hunting dogs would be barking beside them in noisy anticipation.

No dogs.

No excited barks.

No jovial boasting.

John removed his spectacles, tucked them into the pocket of his jacket, and then slipped behind one of the rear stalls. It offered him a good vantage point while waiting for these strangers to come into view. But instead of moving toward him, they closed the stable doors, effectively shutting him in with them and keeping everyone else out.

Very little sunlight had spilled in when the door had been open. Now, the entire stable was wrapped in darkness.

No matter, it gave him the advantage.

His eyes quickly adjusted to the lack of light.

He did not need to see these men to know they were Somersby's hired scum. Nor was it hard to guess their intent. They had purposely trapped him in here to beat him senseless. Perhaps they meant to kill him. *Bollocks.* He ought to have taken Nicola at her word. Was she safe? Would Somersby dare harm her?

He should never have allowed her to return to that villain's lair.

"Lord Bainbridge," one of the ruffians who'd accompanied

Somersby this morning called out with gloating malice. He lit a lantern and set it atop a dusty worktable. "Come out, my lord. We need to have a little talk."

John did not respond, but the man must have seen his shadow cast in the lantern's dim, orange glow. He gave a bark of laughter and slowly began to walk toward John, his footsteps cautious as they crunched on the straw that littered the floor.

The man's confederates shuffled behind him, and as they approached John, their leader motioned for them to surround him. Despite having him outnumbered five to one and the stable doors securely shut, their movements were hesitant and halting.

Good. They were afraid of him, as they ought to be.

Their boots scuffed along the dirt floor and he heard one of them curse when he tripped over a loose floorboard.

Had they harmed Larkins and Bigwell? No wonder those grooms hadn't responded to his call. "And what are we to talk about, gentlemen?"

One of the men now stood between him and his rifle that was resting against the wooden slats of Valor's stall. The man was apparently unaware that he'd set down his weapon. Still, it was out of reach and of no use to John at the moment. But he still had the pistol hidden in his boot if it proved necessary to shoot his way out. The odds would turn in his favor if Jordan ever got himself down here.

Five assailants in all. He could take down two. Jordan could take down two. And there was always one coward in the group who would hang back and then run off to report their failure to Somersby.

But Jordan wasn't here yet.

*Bollocks.*

As the boldest assailant took a step toward him, John noticed the blacksmith shovel clenched in his gnarled fingers. "Our master was concerned that ye hadn't heard his warning."

"I heard it loud and clear," he said, watching each man as they completed a circle around him. No doubt, they believed they had him trapped.

"Very good, m'lord. But we just want to make certain ye never forget it." He raised the shovel and swung it hard, managing to strike John on the shoulder with a glancing blow. He'd been aiming for John's head, but John had parried to avoid it.

John grabbed one of the other assailants and hurled his scrawny body into the man with the shovel, grunting in satisfaction when the two fell in a heap at his feet. But they'd be up in a moment, and two others were coming at him, attempting to grab his arms to hold him down.

Where was Jordan?

He could do with his help about now, for these were big fellows, even for hired muscle.

He kicked one hard in the groin, then grabbed a bridle that was dangling on a nearby beam and slammed it into the other man's face. The man cried out in pain and grabbed his nose as blood began to spurt from it. But their leader and his scrawny companion were back on their feet and charging at him, so he had no time to enjoy his small victory.

As John reached out to grab the scrawny one and toss him again, the fifth man suddenly found his courage and heaved a barrel at him, managing to catch him on the hip. That threw John off balance long enough for the assailant with the shovel to land another glancing blow, this time to his ribs.

John was not a man of violence, but neither did he believe in meekly accepting his fate. He kicked the fellow hard in the gut and then wrestled the shovel out of his hands, easily accomplished as the air rushed out of his assailant and left the man unable to breathe. He then struck his scrawny companion under the chin with the shovel, satisfied when the man keeled over with a whimper.

Breathing hard himself, John glanced around in satisfaction. He'd put all but one of them out of commission. Shovel man was on his knees still trying to catch his breath. The scrawny one was writhing on the ground and holding his possibly broken jaw. Of the first men he'd taken down, one was still clutching his inflamed balls and the other still crying over his broken nose.

The coward who'd tossed the barrel at him was nowhere in sight, but the stable door was now flung open, allowing sunlight to stream in. John knew the whimpering scum had run back to Somersby.

He turned back to the leader of this rabble, who did not seem quite as brave as he had been a moment earlier when he'd held the iron shovel. John now had it. "Tell Somersby if he sends you idiots after me again, I'll have his guts for garters."

"Ye'll be dead," the man growled and withdrew a pistol hidden beneath his jacket.

John groaned. "Put it down before I kill you."

"Ye have it the other way around, m'lord. I'm going to—"

John swung the shovel down on the man's hand with enough force to break it, and probably had broken it judging by his shriek of pain. The pistol discharged, its shot landing harmlessly in the floorboards.

Jordan strode in just then, carrying the unconscious fifth man over his shoulder. He dumped him on the ground beside his writhing companions. "What's going on?"

"Took you long enough," John grumbled.

His friend shrugged. "You did all right for yourself. What shall we do with these gents?"

"Tie them up for now. I'm in no hurry to return them to his lordship. They rode in behind Somersby's carriage, so their horses must be tethered somewhere nearby. Let's collect them, too."

"You aren't seriously considering returning the men and their horses to Somersby, are you?" Jordan arched an eyebrow. "Because I have a better idea. I'm known in these parts. Just say the word and the magistrate will lock them away for as long as you wish."

"I like that plan." John grinned. "The fewer men left to protect our marquis, the more likely he is to behave himself for the duration of his stay."

"Are you going to mention this to Lady Nicola?"

He shrugged. "She doesn't need to know just yet. She's already overset."

Jordan's eyes rounded in surprise. "The lass ought to be told. This isn't a question of boasting about your valor, but of her own safety and that of her family. Those men were sent to break bones.

Namely yours. And mine, if I got in the way."

"I know." John sighed and ran a hand across the nape of his neck. "Let's take care of these gentlemen first and then ride over to Somersby's hunting lodge. If I sense danger, I'll take Nicola and her aunt and uncle out of there at once."

"If?"

John was still rubbing his neck, for he was angry and frustrated and worried about Nicola. "Somersby is the sort of snake who sends others to do his dirty work for him. He won't get his hands soiled. If he truly wants to marry Nicola, he'll behave himself for now. But knowing Nicola, she is making her own plans to leave as we speak. They have friends staying in the area. She'll be safe enough with them. We'll escort her and her family to those neighboring friends, if necessary. But that's the extent of our involvement. We have rebel smugglers to catch. Oh, and we'd better find the two grooms, Bigwell and Larkins. I'm not sure what Somersby's men did to them to get them out of the way."

"Do you think they were bribed?"

"I don't know." But a quick search of the stable revealed the two men had been hit over the head and dumped into one of the rear stalls. John was relieved that they were alive and hadn't suffered much worse than a lump on the head. They'd have a splitting headache for a week, but hopefully nothing worse.

It took most of the morning and into the early afternoon before Somersby's men were taken into the magistrate's custody and placed in confinement. The magistrate, a burly giant of a man with bushy, white hair and a heavy brogue that John had trouble following, took to his task with enthusiasm. Dougal MacLean was his name, and he was no lover of these "Sassenach invaders," as he called Somersby and his ruffians. "Lord Bainbridge, I'll hold these troublemakers for as long as ye need me to hold them," he assured, giving John a hearty slap on his sore shoulder.

John suppressed a yowl. Perhaps the man swinging that shovel had landed more than a glancing blow. He'd have the bruises to show for it before the day was out.

He and Jordan rode back toward the tavern, taking a roundabout route that took them past Somersby's hunting lodge.

Although they were to return this evening, John still needed assurance that Nicola had not been harmed.

Somersby probably hadn't touched her. He would not dare put a hand on her yet.

But what if he had?

John put the notion out of his head before it drove him mad.

However, a little twinge of worry kept creeping in. Nicola was defenseless. What could Darnley do to protect his niece? He wasn't a young man.

*Have I failed her?*

"Be careful," Jordan said when they reached the outskirts of the hunting lodge.

"I'm always careful." John dismounted before Jordan could offer up another lecture. He cut through the hedgerows to steal closer. Dark thoughts continued to whirl in his head, and although he felt quite certain he'd put enough fear in Somersby to make him behave, John still needed to know that Nicola was safe and would remain so even after she refused to marry the man.

"Uh oh. I recognize that look." Jordan groaned. "We're merely on a scouting mission for now. Remember that, John. Ye can't storm into the marquis' hunting lodge like a wounded boar with a spray of porcupine quills up its arse and take off with the lass."

"No, I'll wait until the party. It's the best time. Somersby can't do anything about it while half of London Society is watching."

Jordan groaned lightly. "This is a mess. Somersby's going to come after you with a vengeance. A few broken bones won't be enough. He'll kill you this time."

John was already feeling sore from the glancing blows he'd received to his shoulder, ribs, and hip from his earlier fight. But that only served to firm his resolve. "Let him try. I look forward to gutting the bastard."

Jordan's expression turned thoughtful. "Don't do anything rash. Never forget that Lady Nicola will be caught in the middle of this fight."

"When have you ever known me to act without deliberate care? Protecting Nicola is my first priority. I'll beat the stuffing out of Somersby if he dares threaten her. I'll keep her safe." John curled his hands into fists. "The thought of her under his roof for even another hour turns my stomach."

Nicola came into view just then, strolling in the garden on the arm of the marquis. She seemed to be without a care in the world, her tears and heartbreak of last night all but forgotten.

Jordan continued to study him with concern. "The lass does not appear to be in any danger. Somersby's vindictive, no doubt. But his anger seems aimed at you, not at his intended. Jealousy does things to a man that he might not ordinarily do."

John grunted in frustration, for he'd taken the measure of the man and knew exactly what sort he was. "He's a ruthless, possessive cur."

"And you're not?"

"There's a difference. I'd never purposely hurt an innocent."

Jordan sighed. "Just promise me that you'll be careful. Assess the situation before you act."

"I always do."

"Och, but your senses are addled when it comes to the lass. And we have an assignment to finish." He sighed again in the face of John's silence. "Very well. If she truly is in danger, then do what you must. If it comes to that, we'll escort her and Lord and Lady Darnley to my cousin's estate in Moray. They'll be safely out of the way with Graelem and Laurel."

John nodded, for Graelem Dayne, known as Baron Moray, would protect them. Few men would ever dare cross him. His wife, Laurel, was a beautiful young woman, but just as fierce. "Then we'll return here and pick up the trail of those smugglers again."

"Assuming they're still around."

"That's a risk we'll have to take." He'd deal with the consequences if his mission failed. Assuming there would be any consequences. In truth, there was little Prinny could do to him, for he was one of the Crown's best agents. Likely nothing serious would happen.

Nicola and Somersby were now joined by Lord Darnley and his wife. While the two men walked ahead, their heads bowed in earnest conversation, Nicola and her aunt locked arms and leisurely strolled behind them as though neither had a care in the world.

This made no sense. Nicola was not the sort to be hysterical one moment and then happy as a cat in cream in the next.

What was happening?

What was he missing?

⁂

"NICOLA, I FORBID you to go through with your mad plan," Lady Darnley said, moving to block Nicola from leaving her bedchamber once they'd returned from their walk. "We're supposed to be resting before this evening's party. What if you are caught? Pretending that you are searching for your lost locket will fool no one."

"Do you have a better idea?" She attempted to dart around her aunt and scamper out the door, but her aunt proved to be an immovable barrier and Nicola was not about to forcibly push her out of the way. "Please, Aunt Bess. I must do this."

"Child, you are attics-to-let. We shall speak to your uncle Darnley and make hasty preparations to leave. That's *all* we shall do. Somersby won't dare make a scene."

"You're wrong. He'd dare anything once he realizes I won't marry him."

Her aunt sighed. "Nicola, leave this matter to me and your uncle. Go about the rest of the day as planned. We may not be able to leave before tomorrow morning. So, I want you to act as though nothing unusual is going on. You must look your best for this evening's party, no matter what unfolds."

"It isn't enough," she insisted. "I have to search his study. We must have something to hold over him or he'll do his worst. Why won't anyone believe me? Somersby is a wicked man who must be stopped. I think my plan is excellent. If I'm caught, what's wrong with telling him that I've lost my locket and am hunting for it?"

Her aunt rolled her eyes in obvious dismay. "Everything is wrong with that excuse. Is he supposed to believe that you lost it in his private study? A room you've never entered before and have no right to be in now?"

Nicola stubbornly tipped her chin up. Perhaps her aunt was right, but she needed to do something. "I'll tell him that I thought one of his servants might have found it and brought it to him for safekeeping. Please, Aunt Bess. We must find out why I'm the one he is determined to marry. We know it isn't for love."

She spoke the last with a hitch of pain that her aunt noticed at once. "Oh, my dear. I understand your feelings are hurt, but few couples ever marry for love. Your brother and Rose are the exception, not the rule."

"So are you and Uncle Henry. You love him."

"I do now, but I detested him at first." She shook her head and chuckled. "He was handsome as sin when he was younger, but insufferably arrogant. I cried for days when told I was to marry him. I even ran away. Fortunately, he was as stubborn as a donkey and would not give up on me. That same sort of man will come along for you. Just be patient, Nicola. He's out there waiting to open his heart to you."

Nicola gave her aunt a hug. "Thank you."

If only it were true, but she doubted anyone would ever care for her that deeply. Certainly not John.

"He is out there, Nicola. Just be patient," her aunt repeated.

Nicola shook her head and laughed. "Patient? We all know that will never happen." But her laughter quickly faded. "Aunt Bess, Somersby means to hurt someone we love. What if it's Uncle Henry? Or Julian? We can't allow them to come to harm. We must uncover his plan and fight back."

Her aunt and uncle were loving guardians. They had taken her and her siblings in with open hearts after their parents had died. She knew they would risk their own lives to protect any of their nieces and nephews, which was why Nicola had wanted to search Somersby's private papers on her own. But her aunt was too sharp and had caught on to her plan immediately.

Her aunt gave her an affectionate pat on the shoulder. "Very well. If we're to steal into Somersby's study, then I had better get my pistols. We may have to shoot our way out if we're caught."

Nicola's eyes rounded in surprise. "You carry loaded pistols?"

"Always. And they are at your service. Your uncle keeps two hidden on his person at all times, too. Just say the word."

"Thank you. I hadn't expected…"

"We may be old, but there's life left in us yet. In truth, your uncle has been feeling out of sorts lately. This adventure is just the thing to revive his spirit." There was a twinkle of determination in her aunt's eyes, almost as though she were looking forward to a fight. Nicola had heard tales of her aunt and uncle's exploits in their youth, but it was hard to imagine any of it was true. They were a sweet, white-haired couple who doted on their nephews and nieces, hardly the sort to fight bare-fisted, or clash swords, or shoot anyone.

Yet, her aunt had just told her that she'd run away from her own wedding and had fought her uncle as he'd dragged her to the altar. They had also been complicit in her plot to abduct Julian… for her brother's own good, of course. He had married Rose because of it, so all had ended happily. No one was ever meant to get hurt.

Nor did anyone get hurt.

But this was different.

Her aunt stepped away from the door. "Stay close to me, Nicola. We'll grab my pistols and then make our way to Somersby's study."

Nicola was eager to start the search. The man was hiding some deep, dark secret, but what was it? Finding that out would give her the upper hand in their dealings, which were bound to be unpleasant. If he had concocted a plot against someone close to her, she was going to foil it.

But who was the object of his loathing? Her uncle? Her brother? Someone not related to her?

She did not like being used as a pawn, and if he thought she'd meekly accept her role, he was sorely mistaken. Proof had to be in here somewhere and she was going to find it. Then she'd hand it over to John. He'd know what to do with it.

Yes, John would help.

He'd take over and keep them out of the nasty affair as best he could. Despite her aunt's bravado, she and her uncle were no longer young and spry. They might be injured if any shooting was involved. "If we do find something," Nicola said in a whisper as they stepped out of her bedchamber and peered down the empty hall, "we shall quietly hand it over to John and let him do what is needed. Agreed?"

Her aunt frowned.

"Say yes, Aunt Bess. This is as daring as we ought to get. I don't want a direct confrontation with Somersby, not while we're in his home. If that means I must agree to the betrothal to throw him off the scent, I'll do it. Once his sordid dealings are brought to light, we'll be able to end the betrothal with little consequence to my reputation or uncle's purse."

After what seemed an interminable length of time, her aunt gave in and nodded. "Agreed. Do you have any idea what we're searching for?"

Nicola sighed in relief. "No, not specifically. A clue as to the identity of the person he means to hurt. Anything that smells illegal. Anything, really. Just promise me that you'll be careful, Aunt Bess. This is a dangerous undertaking and we aren't even certain what we'll find or what we're up against."

"I'll behave. But I want the same promise from you, Nicola. And if we're going to pretend to be searching for a lost locket, then you had better not have it dangling about your neck. It's the lamest excuse you've ever concocted, but I can't think of any better at the moment." Her aunt turned her around and unfastened the clasp to the necklace she was wearing. "I'll hold on to it for now. This way, if you're caught, I can pretend I've found it." She tucked it into the sleeve of her gown.

They walked downstairs and made their way toward Somersby's study without incident. No one was about. The servants were in the front rooms busily preparing for this evening's party. The other guests were resting in their chambers.

Nicola was about to enter the study, but her aunt held her back a moment. "Child, must I teach you everything? Knock first. If he's in there, he'll know immediately that we are up to something if we steal in unannounced."

Her aunt was right.

Nicola sighed and knocked on the door. "No answer." She knocked a little louder, just to be cautious. "I think we are clear. Let's go in. Search through all his business papers first. It seems a logical place to start. But be careful to put everything back in its proper order. He mustn't know we've been going through them."

Her aunt followed her in. "What a shame about the marquis. He's such a nice-looking man. Too bad he turned out to be such a toad."

Nicola cast her a mirthless smile. "Let's hope he is nothing worse."

"Indeed." Her aunt pulled out one of her hairpins and straightened it flat. "You sort through his papers. I'm going to look for a locked drawer. Or a secret drawer. Or a locked secret drawer. Those are the best. They always contain the dirtiest secrets."

Nicola's eyes rounded in surprise. "Aunt Bess, tell me truly. Were you a spy in your younger days?"

Her aunt ignored her, too busy searching under Somersby's desk. "Aha, what do we have here?"

Nicola heard the click of a lock and then a soft thud as something fell to the floor. She crawled under the desk with her aunt. "It's a book. No, a diary of some sort. Maybe more of a ledger, for these appear to be financial entries of a sort."

"A diary and a ledger all in one? We've just struck gold." Her aunt's eyes brightened and she had a satisfied grin on her face. "Those always hold the best secrets."

"But I can't make out any of the words. It's in a code of some sort." Nicola's expression turned thoughtful. "What do you think he's hiding?"

# CHAPTER 4

THICK CLOUDS OBSCURED the stars, and the night held the crisp chill of impending snow as John rode to the Somersby lodge. The glow of lanterns in the distance and the scent of smoke from a hickory fire helped guide him toward the imposing house. He and Jordan rode in silence, the leathery creak of their saddles and the soft clip-clop of their horses' hooves upon the cold, hard earth being the only sounds to fill the air. But as they approached the lodge, the sound of laughter and general revelry reached their ears.

"We won't be staying long," John told the young groom who had run up to attend to their horses when they reached the lodge. "Keep our mounts at the ready."

Jordan cast him a frown. "Och, I'm still not certain I like this plan."

"Why are you grumbling? We've put Somersby's ruffians out of commission. If I know Nicola, she's already made plans to leave. We are only here to make certain Somersby doesn't attempt to stop her. We may have nothing to do but enjoy the party."

"I'm not grumbling," Jordan muttered. "Scots never grumble."

John laughed.

He tossed the lad a coin to make certain their horses would be at hand if they needed to make a fast escape, and although he may have appeared casual, he was busy taking everything in. Only two footmen stood beside the front door to attend to guests arriving in carriages. The carriages, he noted, were then taken by their drivers to a rough-hewn building just down the road. No doubt it was the lodge's own carriage house. The conveyances would be held out of the way until their owners called for them.

"Only two footmen," John muttered as he and Jordan entered the lodge.

"I noticed. I'll scout the card room," Jordan said. "You take the salon. I'll join you in there shortly."

John was immediately swallowed up by the crush of guests as he entered the salon, but since he was taller than most, he was able to see over their heads with relative ease. He needed to find Nicola. The party was well under way and she had to be here… somewhere.

He began to walk through the room with no obvious purpose in mind.

"Bainbridge, how was your hunting today?" said an acquaintance who was also an avid sportsman.

"Good, Willoughby. I bagged five." Of course, the five were Somersby's men and not game birds, but it had been a good result. Those scurrilous villains had been well and truly caught by him and Jordan, their intended prey.

He continued his casual stroll, his gaze resting on every young woman with auburn hair, but none of them were Nicola. Where was she? He eased upon spotting Lord and Lady Darnley chatting with friends in a corner of the salon.

His jaw clenched when he realized Nicola was not with them. *Bollocks.*

Where was she?

He hid his concern, for he was being followed by several of Somersby's footmen. They must have been instructed to keep a close watch on him. Perhaps they'd been told to lure him out of the room and finish the job their cohorts had failed to accomplish.

Jordan caught up to him as he was about to approach Lord Darnley. He slapped a beefy hand on John's shoulder to hold him back a moment. "Most of the staff is made up of locals. Maids. Butlers. Even most of the footmen are local boys. I've had a word with a couple of them. They won't be helping Somersby if there's a fight."

John nodded. "I only counted four in here who stick out as hired ruffians. We can take them down easily. Those other five who came after us today were the worst of the lot, so far as I can tell. Now that they're simmering in the magistrate's prison, we ought to have a fairly easy time of it. But I haven't seen Nicola yet and that worries me."

"Och, John. She must be here and unharmed or Lord Darnley would have grabbed that ancient battle axe hanging over the hearth and buried it in Somersby's head by now. The lass may have a big temper, but she's a little thing and not easily seen in a crowd."

John knew his companion was trying to reassure him. What he said made sense, for Lord and Lady Darnley were quite protective of their niece. But those dark, haunted thoughts were stirring in John's brain once more and he found them hard to hold down. "I'll see if she's in the music room. Somersby might have led her onto the dance floor for the opening quadrille."

A harpist, fiddlers, and a pianist were seated in a corner of the music room playing a lively tune. Most of the furniture had been pushed back against the walls or simply removed to create room for dancers. Beyond this room was the dining hall. When he didn't spot Nicola on the dance floor, he sauntered into the dining hall on the chance that she might be in there.

The main table held trays of wild game and fish, and a massive roast boar on a silver salver dominated the center. Along the back wall were smaller tables laden with desserts. The marquis had spared no expense to celebrate a betrothal that would never be.

"Nicola, where are you?" John muttered under his breath, deciding to return to the salon in the hope she was there now. She might have run upstairs to fix her gown or change her necklace for another. There were any number of innocent reasons for her absence.

But he knew Nicola.

She was up to something.

He was about to take another casual turn around the salon when he noticed her slip in through the double doors that led onto the terrace. Had she been outside the entire time? In this cold weather? He knew Somersby had not been with her and was likely searching for her as well.

He watched Nicola make her way toward her aunt and uncle, and caught the almost imperceptible nod she cast them upon reaching their side. "Damn it, Nicola," he muttered under his breath.

What had she done?

He waited to the count of ten before making his way through the crush of guests. This would hardly be considered a large crowd by London standards, but it was a sizeable gathering for these parts. Only formal Highland clan gatherings drew larger crowds.

John knew most of the people here, for as the Earl of Bainbridge, he was a sought after bachelor and invited to all the best parties, despite his attempts to put everyone off. Several acquaintances called out to him, but he merely acknowledged them with a curt nod.

He dared not take his eyes off Nicola.

Not that it was a chore for him to fix his gaze on her.

Indeed, it was too pleasant a task by far.

She now stood chatting amiably with her aunt and uncle and several of their Upper Crust friends. Her beautiful eyes were sparkling with mirth and her auburn hair was done up in a casual riot of curls that perfectly framed her heart-shaped face. A few soft tendrils caressed her slender neck.

She looked radiant, managing to shine brighter than any candlelight's warm glow. His gaze drifted lower. He couldn't help himself. The girl had a body that could stop a man's heart.

*Bollocks.*

He shook his head and silently berated himself for allowing his thoughts to wander.

John was only halfway across the room when he saw Somersby come to her side and hold out his arm to escort her to the music room for a dance. She smiled at him. The pair appeared blissfully happy.

Jordan put a hand on his shoulder. "You have that look again. Promise me you won't do anything foolish."

"Protecting Nicola is not foolish."

Jordan's grip tightened slightly. "Does she look like she needs your protection?"

"I don't know."

"Don't know? Or don't want to admit that she's changed her mind and intends to go through with the betrothal? Perhaps you don't know the lass as well as ye thought."

John ignored the comment. He admittedly was on edge about Nicola's upcoming betrothal. Eaten up inside about it, truth be told. But it wasn't because he was jealous. Well, he was jealous. Almost to the point of madness.

But this was about Nicola, not him.

She wanted out of this betrothal.

She had done something to ensure it would not take place. Why else would she have slipped in from the terrace and nodded to her aunt and uncle?

She had set a plot in motion and just acknowledged it to her conspirators. Or had he gone completely mad because he wanted to believe that Nicola would not marry Somersby?

When the dance ended, Somersby returned her to Lord Darnley's side. John took the opportunity to greet her and their gazes finally met.

He knew at once, felt a jolt to his heart at the slight falter in her smile.

He had been right. She was in trouble and asking for his help. "Good evening, Lord Bainbridge. I'm so glad you are here."

He bowed over her hand. "Wouldn't have missed it, Lady Nicola."

"I'm so pleased." He felt the tension in her slender fingers as he lightly grasped her hand. Her smile was fragile and forced. "Are you enjoying the party?"

Somersby emitted a low, feral snarl to interrupt their conversation. He drew Nicola closer to his side, obviously marking his claim to her. "How dare you show your face here, Bainbridge."

John arched an eyebrow. "Lady Nicola invited me. Or have you forgotten? Perhaps you thought your *friends* had taken care of me."

"What have you done to my footmen?"

"Footmen? That is a charming way to refer to your hired scum. You'll never see them again. Assaulting an earl is a serious crime. And don't forget that we're in Scotland now. Neither your influence nor your bribery will work here." He noticed two of the nasty-looking footmen they'd spotted earlier now making their way through the crowd. "Tell your dogs to back off, Somersby. If they set a hand on me, I shall kill you. Are we clear?"

"There's obviously been a misunderstanding, Bainbridge." The marquis gave a flick of his hand and his footmen stopped and slowly began to back away. He had them well trained, just as one would train hunting dogs. "They are only here to protect me. If you give me your word of honor that you shall not strike me, then they won't harm you."

"I'll make a bargain with you. Give me no cause to strike you and I won't." He grabbed a champagne glass off the tray of a passing servant and held it up in a seemingly casual toast. "Care for a dance, Nicola? I believe the musicians are about to play a waltz."

Somersby's face turned red. "Keep your hands off her. She's mine."

"Not for another hour, I believe." He held out his arm, knowing he should not be goading Somersby as he was doing now.

Nicola frowned at him. "I don't think it would be appropriate, Lord Bainbridge. But I'm glad you've made it to our party. Is Mr. Drummond here as well?"

"Yes, he'll join us in a moment." He supposed Jordan had backed away to secure the perimeter of the room on the chance that more of Somersby's ruffians were called in.

Nicola breathed a sigh of relief. "Good. I look forward to seeing him again."

Somersby stood silently beside Nicola, but there was a lethal look in his eyes. John knew that look well. He'd seen a similar expression on the face of the cold-blooded man who'd killed his parents.

Somersby wanted him dead.

Merely because Nicola had run to him yesterday? He wasn't certain of the reason why and did not care.

What mattered was Nicola.

What did the marquis intend for her?

Nicola was worried about it, too. He could tell because he knew her well, for he'd been friends with her brother for years and often spent holidays with Julian and his family. Nicola was the younger sister who worshiped her big brother and—by association—him, too. She always wished to tag along wherever they went.

She was the little girl who would put her skinny elbows on the table and hang upon their every word whenever they spoke of their adventures. She would steal downstairs when she ought to have been asleep, eager to spy on their late night card games or rounds of billiards.

For some odd reason, he could always sense Nicola's presence and would give Julian a silent warning that they had innocent company. Which meant only the mildest curses allowed, if any. And no talk of women, certainly never about those they'd slept with or meant to sleep with shortly. No talk of their Crown activities, for certain.

What was Nicola worried about? She was all grown up now, no longer the child he'd harmlessly indulged. But she was still innocent when it came to men.

He'd slit Somersby's throat from ear to ear if he ever stole her innocence. It wasn't merely a matter of completing the act of joining their bodies. Her innocence could be stolen in so many ways. By breaking her spirit. Teaching her to fear him. Raising a hand to Nicola.

John would kill Somersby if he ever did that.

Lady Darnley coughed and stepped between him and the marquis, for the hatred between them was palpable and caused the air around them to sizzle like a bolt of lightning about to strike. She obviously meant to distract them before they came to blows. "Poor Nicola has lost her favorite locket. You know the one, Bainbridge. The one you and Julian brought home as a gift for

Nicola from the Scarborough fair."

"Of course, I remember it." He arched an eyebrow, for he'd never given her any such gift nor ever been to that fair. "Her favorite."

"I'm quite distraught about it," Nicola said. "I'm sure it must have fallen in Lord Somersby's garden, but I'm not certain where. Perhaps in one of the flower beds. Or in the pond. It might have fallen when I tripped over that old tree stump at the foot of the garden walk. I'll look for it first thing in the morning."

One of Lady Darnley's friends who happened to be passing by and caught some of her conversation cast her a sympathetic glance. "I'm certain Somersby will find it for you. If he can't, he'll buy you a very pretty replacement."

"A diamond-studded replacement," another of their friends intoned, casting Nicola a knowing smile.

John frowned. Since he and Julian had never been to that fair nor had he or Julian ever bought his sister a locket, what was Nicola telling him?

Lord, he was a dolt. She and Rose used to hide messages within knotholes in trees. She'd hidden something in the tree stump for him to find. *Bollocks.*

That's why he hadn't seen her earlier.

She'd been out in the garden, planting it inside the tree for him to find.

What had she put in there?

And how much time did they have before Somersby realized she'd stolen this thing of importance from under his nose?

After a suitable time had passed, John made his way through the crowd toward the terrace doors. He moved slowly, stopping to greet other friends and acquaintances. Jordan happened to be standing quietly beside those doors, his back to the wall while he nursed a scotch in his hand.

"I'll have one of those," John said, asking one of Somersby's footmen to bring him a glass. The man seemed to be lingering beside him and Jordan, no doubt instructed to listen to their every word.

John had no intention of dulling his mind with spirits, but this was the plausible excuse he needed to send the man off on a useless errand and out of earshot. "Nicola's hidden something in a tree stump in the garden."

"A secret message? Asking for our help? She doesn't appear to be in distress."

"She's scared. Somersby's having us watched. I need you to create a distraction while I retrieve it."

Jordan grinned and curled his hands into fists. "It will be my pleasure."

John scanned the crowd for another glimpse of Nicola to be certain she was safely in the company of her aunt and uncle. "I'll slip out while everyone's attention is on you."

"I always love a good brawl at a party. Here goes." He shouldered his way through the crowd.

It wasn't long before John heard the clatter of a tray hitting the floor, soon followed by the tinkling sound of shattered glass. "You Scottish bounder! You knocked that tray onto me on purpose," the bellicose Lord Whitney shouted and took a swing at Jordan. No doubt this was why Jordan had chosen him as the target. The man had a short fuse, especially when drunk as he obviously was now.

A roar sprang from the crowd and everyone rushed forward to see the fight that had just erupted.

John silently stole out through the terrace doors, but he'd hardly made it down the steps into the garden before someone quietly called his name. He heard soft breaths and light footsteps behind him. "John, let me show you where I hid his book. There isn't much time. You need to grab it and ride away as fast as you can."

"What book? Nicola, so help me…" That usual feeling came over him, the one where he wanted to throttle her and at the same time kiss her into eternity. He took her hand instead, wanting to keep her close as she led him hurriedly toward the gnarled remains of an old tree. "Damn it, Nicola. What's in that book?"

"I'm not sure. Lots of foreign names, as well as dates and numbers. It's written in code so I couldn't make any of it out. It was hidden in a secret drawer that he kept locked."

John groaned. "A secret drawer?"

She nodded impatiently. "Yes, that he kept locked," she repeated. "Aunt Bess was helping me search and she found it. Don't ask me how she knows about such things or how she managed to pry the lock open without breaking it. I think my aunt and uncle led secret lives in their younger days. I'm tame compared to them."

"Tame? You are reckless to a fault." But he kept hold of her hand and gave it a light squeeze. "Go back inside. Stay close to your aunt and uncle. Pretend you don't know anything. Somersby will blame me for the theft and come after me."

"I know you'll lead him a merry chase." She spoke in a breathless whisper as they continued through the garden and finally reached the old stump. She reached into its hollow trunk and withdrew what appeared to John to be an elegantly bound book. She stuffed it into his hands, reached up on tiptoes and kissed him on the cheek. "Godspeed, John. Don't worry about us. My aunt packs pistols."

The light press of her body against his sent a jolt of excitement through him. He wanted to take her into his arms and kiss his way down... he'd leave that thought for later. Someone was coming. "Hush, Nicola."

He grabbed her hand once more and hastily led her to a nearby thicket to hide. The sharp branches, he realized, were cutting into her skin. To her credit, she made no protest. Not a sound, although it had to hurt. He removed his jacket and wrapped it around her shoulders, hoping the sturdy cloth would offer some protection.

"He came out here, my lord. I'm sure of it," one of Somersby's footmen said, scanning the surrounding shrubbery for sign of him. But it was dark and one could hardly see one's own hand. The marquis and several more footmen were now standing beside the tree stump, unaware of what had been hidden there only moments ago.

"Damn it. Find him." Somersby let loose with a string of curses. "I want Bainbridge dead."

"But, my lord. The plan... we can't do this. He's an earl."

"Do you dare question me? I don't care about any agreed upon plan. Kill him and toss his body into Loch Linnhe or it'll be yours that's tossed in first. Let the currents sweep him out to sea."

John put a finger to Nicola's lips to signal her to be quiet. He needn't have worried. He doubted the girl was able to breathe, she was that scared. He drew his hand away and wrapped his arm around her trembling shoulders.

She rested her head against his chest and nodded.

Although Somersby's footmen held their lanterns high as they conducted a sweeping search of the area, he and Nicola managed to remain hidden in the shadows. The marquis was about to leave his men and return to the lodge when another of his hired ruffians came running out, calling to him in panic. "The book is missing."

Somersby clutched his heart in that moment. "No. It isn't possible."

"Your betrothed is missing, too."

Somersby snapped. "Find them! Find them and kill them both! What are you waiting for? Don't let them get away!"

*Blessed Mother.* What was in this book?

Nicola glanced up at him, her eyes wide with fear.

John waited a moment longer to be certain they were alone in the garden, then he eased her away from the thicket. "You're coming with me."

"Where?" she asked, trying her best not to stumble in the darkness as he dragged her toward the stable where his horse remained at the ready. He wanted to take Jordan's horse for Nicola, but that would leave Jordan trapped. Besides, Nicola was not a good enough rider to manage a gallop on horseback in the dark of night, not on a horse she'd never ridden over terrain that was not familiar to her.

He had no choice but to have her ride with him.

"We're going to Inverness and from there to Edinburgh. I'll leave you with the Royal Scots Dragoon Guards. You'll be safe in their hands."

"You're going to leave me there?"

John ignored the plaintive tone in her question. "Somersby is desperate to recover this book. I don't know what it contains, but I suspect it is something important to the Crown. If so, I'll need to get it to London and into the hands of the Prince Regent as soon as possible. I can travel faster on my own. But first, I need to make certain you are safe. The regimental commander will protect you while I'm gone."

"But he isn't you, John."

"Damn it, Nicola. I can't take you with me. I'll come back for you as soon as I've handed the book over to the royal authorities. I promise."

"You won't forget?"

He wanted to laugh out loud. Forget this girl who now filled his nightly dreams? He wasn't certain just when he'd gone from loving her as a sister to loving her in a completely different and carnal way. But one thing was certain. He'd always loved her. "No, I won't forget."

He motioned for her to be quiet and told her to stay behind the stable while he climbed into the hayloft to make certain none of Somersby's men were lying in wait for them. He'd be able to see all that was going on in the stable from his vantage point.

Two of Somersby's men were hiding near the stalls.

He crept behind the first man and quietly knocked him out. He did the same to the second man. Only the young groom remained. Would the frightened boy call out in alarm? John tossed him another coin. "I won't hurt you, lad. Bring my mount to the rear of the stable, then count to twenty and run off to report my escape to Lord Somersby."

"Oy don't 'ave to tell 'im a thing, m'lord. You can clobber me, too. One good wallop to knock me out. Please m'lord. It'll be easier that way."

John had never struck a child before.

Nor would he ever.

Not after… he shook out of the haunted memories. "Sorry, lad. Can't do it. Here, I'll tie you up and gag you. Never mind about bringing my horse around back. Courtyard's clear. I'll do it myself. Tell him you heard me say something about catching a boat at Fort William."

John knew he'd wasted precious minutes, but he worked fast to bind the boy's hands and was rewarded by the look of relief in the lad's eyes. "As soon as he rides away, I want you to find Lord Darnley and tell him that I have his niece and she's safe with me. Make certain none of Lord Somersby's men hear you or you'll be putting us all in greater danger, even yourself. Understand?"

"Aye, m'lord."

"Good." He gagged the boy, then quietly led Valor to the back of the stable where Nicola was waiting. He lifted her onto the saddle and quietly cursed himself for the fire that shot through him the moment his hands circled her waist. "Hold tight to that book," he said, making certain she was securely perched in front of him as he mounted behind her and swallowed her in his arms.

She nodded and clutched the book to her chest, giving a little gasp when he suddenly spurred Valor to a gallop.

Despite the wintery chill now in the air, John felt as though his body was engulfed in flames. Nicola's soft curves were plastered to his hard chest. Her sweet roses and apples scent mingled with the scent of the pine and heather that surrounded them.

He ought to have been shivering with cold.

He ought to have been shivering with fear, for Somersby and his men could not have been more than a few steps behind them.

But all he felt was an odd contentment. Nicola was in his arms, almost lost within his jacket that was still wrapped around her like a blanket. This was where she belonged. With him. "My aunt and uncle," she said, raising her voice slightly to be heard above the wind.

"They'll be safe. Jordan will protect them."

She laughed lightly. "No, John. You needn't sound so pained. I know you're worried about them, but they can take care of themselves. What I mean to say is that my aunt and uncle will protect Mr. Drummond. The marquis won't dare harm them, not while so many of their Society friends are watching. I doubt he even cares about them now. He's desperate to find us. Do you know what's in this book?"

He shook his head and groaned. "Something illegal, possibly treasonous. Something that I was sent here to investigate. If he's involved, it will get him hanged. What possessed you to do something so reckless?"

"I am not reckless. I'm... I don't quite know what I am. But Somersby said something to me on the ride back from MacNaughton's Tavern that alarmed me. He doesn't love me."

"That's alarming."

She frowned at him. "My point is I think he's using me to hurt someone close to me. I had to find out who. Can you blame me for wanting to protect those I love? I don't know what else is in this book, but I hope it reveals the identity of the person he's seeking to destroy. It could be my uncle or Julian. I can't imagine who else values me enough."

"You'd be surprised."

She snorted. "Doubtful. This is my third season and I'm firmly on the shelf."

He drew her up hard against him. "Nicola, there is someone out there who loves you more than anything in this world, who cares for you more than he cares for his own life. Trust me. He's out there."

"John, you are a terrible liar. But thank you."

He made no comment in return, for he'd said too much already.

They rode in silence for several more hours, heading northeast toward Fort Augustus and traveling as fast as they dared in the dark. Once there, he'd have to find a boat to take them up Loch Ness to Inverness. The boat would have to be big enough to carry Valor, for he wasn't leaving this beautiful horse behind. While he trusted the locals to return the powerful stallion to Drummond Stables where he or Jordan could pick him up later, there was no telling what Somersby would do if he got his hands on the majestic beast first.

John slowed Valor as they rode over an uneven hillock, concerned that he might stumble and injure himself.

The terrain was rugged in this area.

The crags were plentiful and dangerous.

They were riding along the Fraser border, familiar territory to him, and John debated whether to forgo the boat and remain on horseback, turning south toward MacPherson land. He and Nicola could spend the night at Cluny Castle, the ancestral home of one of his school mates, Malcolm Gordon. If Malcolm was in residence, then perhaps he could leave Nicola in Malcolm's care while he rode on alone to London without going to Edinburgh first. He'd make much faster time without her. And staying on as a guest at Cluny Castle wouldn't be a hardship for Nicola. She would have a hot meal at least twice a day, a hot bath whenever she wished, and a soft, clean bed to sleep in every night.

No, he decided almost at once. Malcolm was a scholar, not a fighter. He wouldn't know how to protect Nicola if Somersby forced his way in.

In truth, John wasn't certain he could leave Nicola behind even if Malcolm was capable of fighting off Somersby and his vermin.

His heart would not allow it.

Nicola was his to protect.

Could he leave her in Edinburgh with the regimental commander?

He gathered her more securely in his arms, for their tense escape had exhausted her and she appeared to be falling asleep, lulled by the steady, loping stride of his horse. He'd worry about what to do with Nicola once they reached Edinburgh. Logically, he knew that she would be safe and well guarded there. He knew that it was wisest to ride off on his own to deliver the ledger into the Prince Regent's hands.

But he was never logical when it came to Nicola.

Valor suddenly lurched forward, jolting John out of his musings and almost unseating him from the saddle. "Damn."

The stallion recovered immediately, but appeared to be favoring his front right foot slightly.

"John, what's wrong?" Their near fall had shaken Nicola out of her sleepy haze and she cast him a worried look.

"Valor must have stepped on something sharp or gotten a pebble lodged in his shoe." He dismounted and helped her to dismount while he quickly checked the extent of the damage to his horse's hooves, especially that front right hoof. "We'll have to stop in Fort Augustus and find a blacksmith to tend to him. It shouldn't delay us too long. I'll need a little time to secure our passage on a boat to Inverness anyway."

He breathed a sigh of relief upon finding nothing wrong, but he had the horse trot in a circle around them a few times to be sure he was in no lingering discomfort.

"He seems fine." John turned to Nicola. "Let me help you back into the saddle." He still intended to stop at the blacksmith shop. No harm in making certain Valor hadn't been injured.

Nicola held onto his shoulders as he lifted her up.

He climbed on behind her and drew her close, trying to convince himself it was only because Nicola needed the warmth of his body. It had nothing to do with his fiery ache for her. No, nothing to do with him.

Nothing to do with his heart. "We're about an hour's ride from Fort Augustus. We'll get there shortly before sunrise, but we may have to wait around until the shops open. You need warm clothes. Sturdy boots and stockings." He would purchase a woolen cloak or heavy scarf for her, as well.

Her teeth chattered as she nodded. "Yes, I'm cold."

"You must be hungry, too." He'd look for an inn or tavern to secure a hot meal for both of them.

"Famished, but anything will do. We can eat while on the run, if we must." She attempted to stifle a yawn, but it didn't fool him.

"I can see that you're exhausted," John said. "Rest your head on my shoulder. Close your eyes and try to sleep. I have no food to give you or blanket to keep you warm. But I can offer you my shoulder as a pillow. It may not be the most comfortable—"

"It's perfect." She turned slightly to snuggle against him. She was now facing him and her breasts were lightly pressing against his chest.

Had he not been holding her close for hours, he would have shot out of his saddle at the heavenly touch.

Had Nicola noticed the quickening beat of his heart?

He was responding and it wasn't even direct contact. His jacket was still wrapped around her, providing an added layer between them. But it did not seem to matter. He felt her against him.

He felt her softness.

He felt her every lush curve.

Mostly, he felt her chipping away at the thick stone wall

surrounding his heart.

He held her tightly against him as she began to drift off to sleep, wanting to protect her from the worst of the bitter cold. It was a bone-seeping chill. She had to be half frozen in her thin, silk gown.

She'd never once complained.

His lips twitched in the hint of a smile when he heard her light snores a short while later and knew she'd given in to her exhaustion. He was glad she'd managed to fall asleep. They rode on without incident and John breathed a sigh of relief when the town of Fort Augustus came into view shortly before sunrise. "Nicola?"

Her eyes were closed and her breaths were soft and steady.

He bent his head slightly and kissed the top of her head. "I'm glad you're alive, brat."

She gave a sleepy purr. "Did you just kiss me?"

"No, brat."

She purred again, a soft, kittenish sound that stirred him in places that should not be stirred while she was pressed so tightly against him. "It felt like a kiss."

"It wasn't. You'll know when I kiss you."

"I will?" She smiled against his chest. "John, promise to do it soon."

"Go back to sleep, Nicola."

Bollocks, what had he gotten himself into?

# CHAPTER 5

JOHN CAST HIS gaze skyward and gave muttered thanks when he found the blacksmith shop open. They'd reached Fort Augustus shortly before dawn and he wasn't certain how early the townspeople stirred. Early, he realized, hearing the sound of wagons and wooden carts rattling over the cobblestone road. This was a seafaring town. Several fishermen were up and about, setting off to catch their trout and salmon from the local streams. Boatmen were already sailing out to sea in search of bigger catch that would keep them out for days or weeks until the hulls of their vessels were weighed down by fish to sell.

All that mattered to John was that he did not have to waste time pounding on doors to obtain the goods he needed. Several shopkeepers were already in their shops, preparing to open for the day. Innkeepers had lit their fires and were serving their patrons a morning meal. The scent of eggs and sausages and freshly made bread tickled his nostrils and made his mouth water.

He left Nicola at the blacksmith shop while he hurried down to the dock to secure a boat for them. The air was warming, but the loch remained cold. The clash of hot sun striking cold waters created an eerie mist that rose above the white-capped waves and crept over the vessels moored in the harbor like smoky wraiths waiting to steal unguarded souls.

John strode along the wooden pier, taking in all the sights and sounds and pungent smells. His senses were heightened, as always. He was on the alert for Somersby and his men. But all seemed calm. Several women were talking and laughing as they set up their stalls beside the dock to sell their fish. He heard the groan of anchor ropes as they eased and strained against the ships that floated on the gently lapping waves.

His own footsteps sounded loud to his ears, but few people seemed to notice him as he made his way along the dock in search of a boat to carry them to Inverness. It did not take him long to find a willing captain, a burly, leathery-skinned Scot by the name of Alexander Grant. He gave the man a few coins as a deposit. "I'll be back within the hour."

"Take yer time, my lord. I ain't in no rush." He closed his beefy fist around the coins and grinned.

John returned to the blacksmith shop to fetch Nicola. Their next stop was at one of the local inns for a meal. They'd take whatever was available. He did not care if it was last night's stew or salted pork or week-old, smoked kippers. Anything hot would do. Oatmeal was a popular Scottish fare meant to warm a person's blood and nourish his bones.

Nicola was in need of that, for she was little and slender, and not used to this hardship.

Her stomach was rumbling.

So was his.

They settled in the common room of one of the more pleasant-looking inns. John ordered a hearty meal for both of them and allowed himself a moment to escape from their worries. Valor was shod. Boat hired. Food now brought to them piping hot and smelling heavenly. All that remained was to obtain suitable clothes for Nicola.

He hoped the ladies' shops would open by the time they finished eating.

"John, this food is delicious," Nicola said, taking another spoonful of the hearty leek soup they'd decided to order. The tavern proprietor had delivered it to them with a loaf of bread that was hot, crusty, and steaming, it was that fresh out of his oven.

John eased back in his chair, his attention divided between Nicola and the window that afforded him an unobstructed view of the street. He was always on the lookout for Somersby and his men, his pistols always at the ready. "Don't eat too fast. You'll make yourself ill."

She smiled up at him, her big, green eyes wide as she spared him a mere glance before digging into her soup again. "I'll try not to. But I'm so hungry and everyone is staring at us. What must they think?"

He shrugged. "Does it matter?"

She blushed. "It does to me. We are alone, no chaperone in sight. I'm dressed in a delicate, silk evening gown that would not keep a mouse warm on a summer's day, and I have your jacket wrapped around my shoulders. You must be half frozen."

"I'm fine." Riding for hours with Nicola's body pressed against his had generated enough fire inside him to keep him warm even under the full blast of an icy winter storm.

She sighed. "I suppose I'm foolish to worry about our lack of a chaperone when I was the one who got us into this mess."

"None of this is your fault." He sopped up the last of his soup with the warm bread until there wasn't so much as a drop left on his plate. He had a cup of tea and then washed it down with ale. "Are you ready? Let's find you some warm clothes to wear."

She smiled at him again.

His heart shot into his throat.

He was in trouble.

He hadn't slept all night and Nicola had managed maybe thirty minutes. They were on the run from villains intent on killing them. They hadn't washed, and they'd just devoured their food like vultures feeding on a boar carcass. Yet, he'd never felt more content. Nicola's smile was sweet and beautiful and all he could think about was how splendid she looked, and how badly he wanted to hold her in his arms again.

He shook out of the thought as they rose to leave. While most of the locals appeared merely curious, some were frowning at him and Nicola. He understood why. These Scots were moral, churchgoing people with a pride in their heritage and a dislike for all things English. A few of them were old enough to have been alive during the Jacobite uprisings. For most of them, their parents or grandparents would have lived through those unsettled times and told them stories about it. He suspected that more than a few old-timers were still hoping to resurrect Bonnie Prince Charlie and start a new rebellion.

The smuggling operation he'd come up here to investigate was also linked to a possible rebellion plot. But talk of overthrowing the king was mostly taproom chatter and those who did the chattering were often so deeply in their cups that they could not stand up without their legs giving out from under them.

John wouldn't know how it felt to be drunk, for he'd never allowed himself to lose control. But he did understand the looks the men were casting Nicola, for that sleepy slant to her eyes and the lush curves of her body made her look sultry and at the same time temptingly innocent. "Nicola," he said in a whisper, leaning close so that his lips almost touched her ear, "if anyone asks…"

"Asks what?"

"Just say you are my wife. Lady Bainbridge. Newly wed. Just married in London last month. It's important. They're likely to run us out of town otherwise. Or do worse."

"Such as hurl stones at us?" She nodded. "They must already be wondering what we are doing here at this hour and in these inappropriate clothes."

"They are. I don't want to make matters worse."

She nibbled her lip. "Let's go then. Just a quick stop at one of the local shops to pick up something suitable for me to wear and then we can be on our way. I'll change into the new clothes once I'm in the boat. The sooner we're gone, the better for both of us. I won't rest easy until we are well out of Somersby's grasp. As it is, it will take him less than a minute to find out we passed through here should he decide to search north."

He covered her hand with his own to reassure her.

Nicola quickly chose a sturdy gown, boots, and stockings at a nearby shop that sold woolens. She also selected a tartan shawl and a clan tartan for him. "John, you must have something to keep you warm while we're on the water."

He wanted to protest, for they'd spent too much time in town already. They were running for their lives, yet she was worried about him catching a chill. He grinned, somehow liking the fuss she was making over him. He'd closed himself off so completely for most of his life and wasn't used to these little gestures of concern. "Are we good? Anything else you need, Nicola?"

"Perhaps a comb and some soap?"

He nodded and turned to the shopkeeper, a bright-eyed, older woman by the name of Mrs. Fraser. He supposed half the townspeople went by the name of Fraser and the other half by Grant since those were the major clans in the area. "Would you by any chance have these items?"

There was little on display in the front of the shop but shawls and scarves. However, every time the friendly, older woman went into her back room, she came out with exactly what they needed. "Och, indeed. A few lovely combs and several lovely, scented soaps, my lord," she said, casting him a knowing smile.

He also bought ribbons for Nicola's hair, and then they waited for Mrs. Fraser to wrap their purchases. With packages in hand, they hurried to the blacksmith to retrieve Valor before heading to the boat.

To John's relief, Valor walked up the gangplank without fuss. The horse's hooves made a light clip-clop against the wooden slats. Nicola had gone aboard first, and it was her coos and petting that calmed Valor and got him safely on deck.

Nicola turned to John and graced him with a gentle smile once Valor was secured. "That went well."

John laughed and absently drew her into his arms as they pulled away from the dock. He hadn't been thinking, just acted because it felt natural. Nicola did not seem to mind, so he made no move to step away.

Nicola sighed and rested her head against his shoulder. "Thank you," she said softly.

"I should be thanking you." He wrapped her more securely in his arms, for the boat was beginning to pitch and roll with greater force now that they'd pulled away from the dock. They stood together, her back pressed to his chest, both gazing at the town that would soon disappear from view. The mist began to surround them and would soon swallow them up completely in its shrouded folds.

She turned her head slightly to glance up at him. "Why would you thank me?"

"I think the ledger you found might contain the information Jordan and I came up here to uncover. It would have taken us weeks to figure out what you managed to put in my hands in a single day."

She turned fully to face him. "Aunt Bess is the one who deserves the credit."

He sighed. "She would never have been snooping around Somersby's lodge without your urging. Promise me you'll never do anything so foolish again, Nicola."

She gave an indignant huff. "It wasn't foolish. I had to do something to protect my family."

"It was dangerous. You might have been killed." Their luck had held so far. Even Valor appeared to be responding well to the roll of the waves and the tip and sway of the boat. However, the boat wasn't very big and Valor, who was penned in on the deck, would be easy to spot from shore once this morning haze lifted. "We're not out of danger yet."

He thought once more of the young boy he'd tied up when they'd made their escape a few hours ago. Could he be trusted to direct Somersby and his ruffians westward? John had to believe the lad would, but he was also concerned that Somersby would see through the lie and harm the boy. His stomach began to roil and his anger mounted at the thought that an innocent child might come to harm for doing him a favor.

No, the lad was quick-witted and could take care of himself.

Still, John resolved to quietly ask after him when he returned to Invergarry to tie up whatever loose ends remained from his assignment.

His thoughts returned to Nicola, who was once again leaning back against his chest, comfortably nestled in his arms as they watched the curtain of mist descend between them and the town, causing it to disappear from view. They still had a long way to go to reach Edinburgh, and he wasn't certain he had sufficient funds to get them there without Nicola enduring more hardship. In truth, she still hadn't complained and was not the sort who ever would.

He decided to call on his connections in Inverness as soon as they arrived. They could help him secure additional funds, and he hoped those funds could be raised quickly, for he dared not spend an hour more than necessary in that coastal town. He would be recognized and could not risk the news reaching Somersby.

He and Nicola would have to travel at a fast pace, but there was no reason to deprive Nicola of all comfort.

After a few moments, she eased out of his arms. "I had better change out of my gown."

He nodded and cast her a tender grin. "Need help?"

She blushed. "I'm afraid I will. These elegant gowns are not designed to be easily slipped on and off. I don't think I can reach these pearl buttons down the back."

While Captain Grant and his crew, comprised of his two sons, Hamish and Malcolm, busied themselves with the sails, John helped Nicola climb down into the hold. The stairs were steep and the hold was dark and empty. It smelled of rotted fish. "Oh, dear. I hope I don't smell as foul as that."

He chuckled while lighting the small lantern hanging on a peg near the ladder stairs. "I fear we shall both be a little ripe by the time this boat reaches its destination. But I'll settle you in a quiet inn once we dock at Inverness and order a hot bath to be brought up to our room."

"Our room?" Her eyes widened in surprise.

"I dare not leave you alone, Nicola. And we will be refused everywhere in town if the innkeepers believe we are traveling together while unmarried. It won't matter whether I order one room or two. This isn't London. No one here will turn a blind eye to our 'sin' even if I slip them a few extra coins."

She began to nibble her lower lip in consternation. "Speaking of coins, how much do you have left? You've spent on the blacksmith, our food, my clothes, and this boat." She shook her head and sighed. "I didn't think to carry a purse on me. That was a stupid oversight on my part."

He came to her side. "I would not have taken your coins."

"John, that's ridiculous. You'd rather see us sleep out in the cold than take anything from me? I would have loaned the sum to you. I know you would have paid me back. Not that I would have required it, but you would have insisted."

He gave her cheek a light caress. "You don't have a purse on you. I'm almost out of funds. No point arguing over this. I have a few errands to run as soon as we reach Inverness. The first will be to secure a loan. The next will be to book passage for us on the next boat to Edinburgh. We won't have long to wait, hopefully no more than a few hours, assuming the weather holds and the boat departs on time."

"And if the weather doesn't hold?" she asked, staring up at him with her sleepy, slanted eyes. Her full, sensual lips were lightly pursed and beckoning.

He turned her so that she was facing away from him before he gave in to the urge to kiss her. "We'll get you a horse and ride to Edinburgh together. Stand still. Stop fidgeting."

"I'm not fidgeting."

"You are. You jump every time I touch you."

"I can't help it. Your hands are cold. Be careful. Don't rip the buttons."

"Any more orders?" he grumbled. Did she think this was easy for him? Undressing her and knowing he could never touch her intimately. "Most women like it when I put my hands on them."

She gasped. "You've done this with other women? Of course, you have. I... I..."

Lord, she sounded heartbroken. He cursed himself for a bumbling fool. Somersby had cheated on her and she was still bruised over it. "None that ever mattered."

That was an even stupider thing to say. He quickly undid the last two buttons and then put his hands on her shoulders, stroking them gently with his thumbs. "Nicola, I'm nothing like Somersby. There's no question I'd be faithful to the woman I love once I declared my intentions."

"I know." She slowly released her breath that ended in a quiet sob. "Do I matter to you, John?"

*More than the moon and stars.*

*Hellfire. Hellfire.* "Of course. Julian will have my hide if I allow any harm to come to his little sister." He should have released her and moved away. But he could not bring himself to let her go.

The gown had fallen off her creamy shoulders, exposing her bare back and shoulders to his view. It should have slipped to the floor, for silk was light and supple. But Nicola was clutching it tightly to her bosom… her gloriously ample bosom that would fill the cups of his palms. "You know that isn't what I'm asking, John."

Her gown would slip off with a gentle tug. That's all it would take to strip it off her. That's all it would take for him to lose control and break every promise he'd ever made to himself. He'd vowed to find the men who murdered his parents. He'd vowed to exact revenge on them. He'd vowed to destroy evil wherever he found it. He'd vowed never to put those he loved at risk. "Don't, Nicola."

To admit that she mattered to him would make him vulnerable again and he'd vowed never to allow it to happen. Nicola was his weakness. His hunger. His yearning.

She released another ragged breath. "Do I matter to you?"

He needed to let her go. Why couldn't he let her go?

The lantern light shone on her thick riot of curls and illuminated their beautiful reds and browns. He wanted to pull out the pins holding up her hair and watch the fiery strands fall in a wild tumble around her soft, creamy shoulders. He wanted to plunge his hands through the silky length of that lush mass.

He wasn't certain he could maintain his control if she turned around.

*Don't turn around, Nicola.*

*Don't turn around.*

The gown slipped lower.

"John…"

He growled low in his throat.

She turned around.

# CHAPTER 6

NICOLA HADN'T A moment to catch her breath before John's lips descended on hers and she was captured in his crushing embrace. Oh, dear heaven. This is what she'd dreamed of, to be swept into John's arms, to be kissed and loved by him with all the passion in his soul, a passion he took such great care to hide.

But he wasn't hiding it now.

Nor was he being coy and giving her a mere peek at another layer. No, he had opened himself wide and was baring his heart and soul to her. She could respond with no less. No hiding any of herself to him. She would allow this kiss to lead wherever it may, for she'd wanted him so badly all these years, never understanding why her body cried out for him.

Only him.

She ached for his touch.

Needed his touch.

Needed his heart.

And yet, she'd almost settled for something less.

John gave a sexy growl as he deepened the kiss, taking possession of her mouth and demanding no less than possession of her soul in return. There was an animal intensity to the press of his lips on hers, to his sensual touch, a feral power that surrounded her and carried her in its forceful grip.

She wanted to release the gown she'd been clutching, for she wanted nothing between them now. But John would not allow the cool silk to slide down her body and pool at her feet. Even as his kiss turned wilder, hotter, he refused to lose control. He refused to take more than this splendid kiss from her.

She felt his building passion, felt the heat flowing through him just as it was flowing through her, felt the coiled tension in his muscles. Yet he took care to be exquisitely gentle with her. She knew he would never hurt her. This was John, a man always struggling to control his raw desire, for he was as much a protector as he was a hunter, and protecting her mattered more to him than anything else.

*She mattered to him.*

She had her answer.

*Thank goodness, she mattered.*

But she sensed that it would break his heart if he were forced to admit it to her.

She ran her hands along the muscled length of his arms and then circled them around his neck to draw him closer. It felt important to hold onto him, somehow to make him understand that this was right, that she would never betray his heart if he allowed her in.

She doubted this first kiss was enough to convince him.

There would be others, she hoped. For now, she would take all that he was willing to give and simply enjoy the moment. How could she not enjoy? Mother in heaven! The man was built of granite. All of him, from his massive shoulders anchored to muscled arms and broad chest. His taut, lean waist and powerful legs.

But it wasn't merely his physical beauty that attracted her. John was so much more than a handsome facade. He was a man of valor. All those he protected slept peacefully because he watched over them. It was no coincidence that he'd thought to name his stallion Valor.

To be noble. To honor and protect. This was John, the valiant knight who'd give his life for right and justice.

She pressed against him to soak in the heat of his body and reveled in the touch of his rugged hands as he ran them across her back and then brought one forward to cup her breast. Fire exploded within her, a hot burst of molten desire that flowed like lava through her body.

He wasn't gentle, but neither was he hurting her. He could never hurt her, even though he was unleashing his pent-up desire and perhaps a little anger that she'd pushed him into revealing more of himself than he'd ever intended. Anger aimed at himself and not at her.

He drew his mouth from hers and began to kiss his way down her body, suckling the wildly beating pulse at the base of her throat.

Starlight exploded before Nicola's very eyes. "John, oh…"

But the soft release of his name suddenly brought him to his senses. He groaned and shook his head as though wanting to take back what had just happened. "This cannot be. Nicola, I'm sorry. This cannot be."

"But it was. It did happen. I'm not at all sorry." She placed her hand against his cheek, fully aware that she stood beside him with her gown about to slip off her body and leave her bare. It would have slipped off by now if not for the strength and tenderness of his arms that were still wrapped around her. "You said I'd know it when you kissed me. You certainly proved that true. It's all right, John. I'm not asking for more than you are ready to give me."

He kissed her palm with the same fierce gentleness as their first kiss. "That's the problem. I can't give you more. Not now. Not yet."

She nodded. "But you will in time."

"I don't know, Nicola. Perhaps not ever."

She refused to believe him. He'd just given his heart to her with that kiss. Reluctantly, to be certain. However, to force him to acknowledge what he'd done seemed wrong when he was so obviously tortured by what he perceived as weakness in himself.

He kissed her on the forehead. "You must be cold. Let's get you dressed."

He turned away, his gaze now fixed on the ladder stairs as though they held endless fascination. Sighing, she slipped out of her delicate gown and quickly folded it before placing it carefully beside the package containing her new purchases. She donned her new linen undergarments, and then the woolen gown and stockings. The gown had been boiled in a plain, brown dye, but when John turned back to help her lace it up, one would think it had been a shimmering, gossamer fairy gown, for his eyes lit up.

He almost smiled, but stopped himself in time. "It fits."

Nicola struggled to hold back tears. She'd loved this man all her life. Yet, until this very moment, she'd had no idea he reciprocated the feeling. He'd never let on, always guarded himself. Even now, instead of feeling happy about the kiss they'd shared, she could see that he was angry and frustrated with himself. He considered their kiss a sign of his weakness.

Would he ever accept that love was the answer to his torment? Could he kiss her like that and not love her? He'd said he was nothing like Somersby. In her heart, she knew that he wasn't. But neither was he ready to declare his feelings for her.

She held her breath as he leaned close, his hands lightly grazing her body while he tied the row of laces that she could not reach herself. "John…"

"Don't ask me about the kiss, Nicola."

"Why not? Am I supposed to pretend it meant nothing to either of us?"

"It was an unfortunate mistake."

"No, it wasn't. Don't you dare make less of it."

"Then I won't. But don't you dare believe it changes anything."

It had changed everything, but she wasn't going to argue with him while they were running for their lives. "I think I'll brush out my hair and knot it into a braid," she said, licking her lips and trying to keep her heart from breaking.

She sighed as his warm breath tickled her ear. His taste was now on her lips, the masculine warmth of his mouth mingled with the bread and ale he'd washed down earlier with his soup. The taste of him lingered and made her hungry for more of him.

He was no longer inclined to talk, so she kept up her own chatter because she'd cry otherwise. The kiss they'd shared was not a mere "anything." He'd opened his heart to her and if that was not a sign of love from this man, she did not know what was. He obviously hated himself for his moment of weakness and was now fortifying his barriers against her. "Um, the wind is strong on the water and nothing else will hold my hair in place but a braid."

"That's a sensible idea." He drew away and rifled through their packages until he found the new comb and ribbons.

She took the comb and chose a ribbon of forest green velvet that would not clash with the color of her hair or gown. To her surprise, he turned away and fixed his gaze once more on the stairs. "John," she said, not bothering to hide her irritation. He wanted to forget the kiss ever happened. She wanted to remember it forever. "I'm fully dressed. Why the sudden need for propriety?"

He muttered something unintelligible under his breath. She realized he was still angry with himself for giving in to his desire, but she had enjoyed their moment and was not going to be shamed into denying it. "We are running for our lives. If Somersby and his men catch up to us... the point is, we may not survive this chase. I'm not going to die wishing I had told you how I feel about you. I suppose my feelings for you are obvious now."

Indeed, how much more obvious could she be? She would have allowed her gown to slip to the floor and not been ashamed to stand naked before him. He was the one who held it up to maintain her propriety even while he kissed her with scorching passion. "Don't make me feel lesser for it. Please, John."

His back was still turned to her, so she could not tell what he was thinking.

But it felt as though he was scowling fiercely.

"I'll help you climb back on deck when you're ready. Just call out to me." He took the stairs as though still being chased by Somersby and his men. Or chased by demons that he was desperate to outrun.

Perhaps he was merely running from her.

Perhaps he would always run.

She wasn't going to worry about that now, for his kiss had revealed the truth.

She mattered to him.

JOHN CLIMBED ON deck and stood beside Valor, stroking the stallion's neck as he gazed across the loch waters. The mist had lifted and only remnants of its cloudy haze remained in spots along the shore. He allowed the gusting wind to blow over him and cool him down. Him. Not the stallion. He was the one whose blood was still on fire.

Nicola had a way of smashing through his barriers. For years, he'd been able to hide the effect she'd had on him because they were never left alone. But being on the run and forced into close quarters with the girl was a disastrous combination.

This was only the beginning. They had several days of travel before reaching Edinburgh, assuming Somersby and his men did not interfere with their plans and force them to take another route. But there was no sign of him or his hired ruffians yet. He'd been watching the distant shore for riders.

Nor was there sign of a boat following them.

"John," Nicola called to him, popping her head out of the hold. She struggled to clamber out while holding onto the skirt of her gown and at the same time trying to keep the wind from whipping several loose strands across her face into her eyes.

He lifted her out with ease, holding onto her waist to steady her as the boat rolled over the waves. She held onto his arms and smiled uncertainly up at him. "Thank you."

She looked pretty with her hair bound in a loose braid down her back and her body draped in the simple woolen gown that she filled out to perfection. "How do your boots fit?"

"They're a little stiff, but I'll manage." After a moment, Nicola blushed and moved to the railing to look out over the water.

John held back, folding his arms across his chest as he watched her. Captain Grant approached him. "Pretty wife, m'lord."

John nodded.

"Newlyweds?"

John nodded again. "A month."

He wasn't eager to chat with the captain, but he'd referred to

Nicola as his wife when first engaging the captain and his boat, and he was not about to change his story. He had hoped the old Scot would mind his own business, but perhaps he was having second thoughts about helping him and Nicola. After all, the man had his sons with him and did not wish them to think he was aiding in the ruin of an innocent young lady.

Nicola was quality and it showed.

John did not blame the man if he was having second thoughts about carrying them to Inverness. They were traveling without baggage or servants. They had no carriage. Just one horse they shared. It was obvious they were on the run; the only question in the captain's mind had to be the reason for their running away. John had no desire to embellish their lie, but he had less desire to be tossed off the boat.

He was about to fabricate a few more details when Nicola's cry of alarm put an end to their discussion. "John, look! On the shore."

"Damn." Somersby and his men hadn't been fooled for long. They were on the road to Inverness, obviously riding hard to intercept them. But at the same moment Nicola spotted them, they'd spotted Valor penned on deck. John quickly drew Nicola away from the railing and then turned to the captain. "Those men are dangerous. Sail this boat to the opposite shore. Now."

"But m'lord."

"Captain Grant, those men will kill us all. You and your sons will not be spared. My wife will not be spared." Lord, he'd referred to Nicola as his wife and it felt so natural and easy. "I know you suspect that it is her family riding to stop our elopement, but I assure you, it is nothing of the sort. Let us off now. We'll never make it to Inverness alive."

As though to prove his point, the riders on the shore began to fire their weapons at the boat. Fortunately, their shots fell short, but the captain needed no further convincing. "Hamish, Malcolm! Keep down, lads." He grabbed the rudder and steered the boat toward the southern bank of the loch.

John sighed in relief, knowing they would gain another few hours' lead on their pursuers, who hadn't the means to cross this body of water but had to ride around it. They'd need all the advantage they could gain, for their route on this side of the loch would not be an easy one. Inverness was out of the question now. They had no choice but to ride southward through the mountains. Once over the mountains, the trails would become open roads, but it would be days before they reached those flat, well-traveled paths.

Perhaps days before they ate hot food, for he would not dare light a campfire. The smoke from any fire would be seen from a distance and its scent would travel for miles.

He glanced at Nicola.

The girl was pale and frightened, but her resolve was strong. She would do her best not to slow him down, but Valor would be weighed down by her extra weight. At least she was slight and slender. Nor could John ride at breakneck speed while holding her in front of him in the saddle.

Captain Grant drew his vessel up beside an old dock that appeared ready to fall into the water. Most of the boards were splintered and several had fallen off completely. John hoped the dock would hold under Valor's weight, but to be safe, he jumped off the boat and tested the remaining boards. "Come, Nicola. It will hold you."

He wanted her safely off first, for her clothes and boots needed to remain dry. He and Valor were not likely to be so fortunate. He helped her off and then carefully led Valor, moving slowly and testing every step. The dock creaked and swayed, but held. "Thank you, Captain Grant," Nicola called out as John was about to lift her onto the saddle.

"Good luck to ye and yer husband, m'lady. Godspeed."

John wasted no time in riding into the mountains and out of sight of the loch. He'd have to rest Valor from time to time, but there were many streams in the mountains. Water would be plentiful and so would the sweet, meadow grasses. Valor could graze to his heart's content. Sustaining himself and Nicola was the problem. They had no choice but to survive on the meager bread and cheese he'd brought along. However, they might pass a croft or two, or a small village, along the way. He'd restock their provisions whenever the opportunity presented itself.

The day had turned sunny and the sky was a deep azure as they made their way through the mountain foothills. The air was warming and now held little chill. He hoped they'd make significant progress, for the good weather was not likely to hold for long and he wished to put as much distance between them and Somersby as he could.

Despite the danger they faced, John's sense of contentment returned. Although he and Nicola spoke little, he felt comfortable with her. Perhaps it was because he'd known her ever since she was a little girl. But it was more than that, for he'd known many women over the years. With Nicola, he felt as though he was with someone who understood him as no one else did or ever could.

He was thankful that she did not appear to resent him for the kiss that should never have been. Yet, she had every reason to be angry with him over his behavior.

He was still angry with himself, certainly angrier than she'd ever been.

Perhaps that was what Nicola's brother Julian had meant after he'd fallen in love with Rose Farthingale, that John would know when the right woman came along for him. That John's heart would recognize her and there was nothing he could do about it.

He'd never felt like this with anyone but Nicola.

He'd known her for years and always saw her among her family, playing with her younger siblings and yet also at ease with the elders. They were six siblings in all, Nicola the eldest among the girls. Their household was chaotic and joyful, and they'd welcomed him into their home.

Nicola had always treated him as though he belonged, even when he was taciturn and surly, which he was often. But she never took offense.

Whenever he looked at her now, he saw warmth, love, comfort.

"We'll have to stop every few hours to rest Valor," he said, clearing his throat and trying not to sound like a man who was falling in love. To be precise, trying not to sound like a man who'd already fallen deeply in love. "Let me know if you need to stop sooner."

"Thank you, John. But it won't be necessary. I'll manage." She turned slightly to glance at him as they rode. "I think we ought to read through Somersby's secret book whenever we rest Valor. The more you or I can retain in our memory, the better."

He nodded. "I had planned to do just that. Let me sort through it first. I've had more experience in these matters than you. I'm more likely to decipher it faster and know what's important."

She pursed her lips, obviously not liking his suggestion. "I found it. And I'm not a ninny. I'm good with puzzles and know how to keep accounts."

"I'm speaking of experience with smugglers. I have no doubt of your cleverness. But since you've never been a smuggler, I don't think you'll understand all the references or their significance."

She glanced at him again. "Are you saying that simply to mollify me?"

He cracked a grin. "No, I'm saying it because it's true. You're one of the cleverest women I know. Far more intelligent than most men, too."

"Nicely said, John." She cast him an impish smile. "But you've never been a smuggler either."

"I have, but only in service to the Crown."

Her annoyance with him seemed to melt away, just as the mist had melted off the lake waters earlier in the day. "Truly? What did you smuggle? Can you tell me about those missions?"

He saw no harm in passing the time this way. He'd confide some of his earlier adventures since they were several years in the past and not likely to put anyone in danger if a name or two slipped out. "Which would you rather hear first? The mad monk of Ballymena? Or the harlot of Honfleur?"

She shook her head and laughed. "They both sound intriguing. What were each of them smuggling?"

"Irish whiskey was the mad monk's contraband. The harlot was actually a French countess who traded any French products she could put her hands on. Lace, perfumes, wines."

Nicola frowned. "But those seem harmless enough. Why assign you to bring down their operations?"

"They each took their profit and put it toward bringing down the English monarchy. Had they kept their ill-gotten gains for themselves and lived purposeless lives of luxury, they would have attracted no one's notice. But their wealth was used to purchase weapons, train mercenary soldiers, and generally stir hostilities. The mad monk was building an army of Irishmen to invade England. The countess was working for Napoleon, supporting his spy operations."

Nicola turned slightly in the saddle once more to look at him. Her eyes were wide and she was obviously eager to hear more. "John, how did you disrupt their plans?"

"The mad monk was easy. We set him up so that it would seem I was a sympathizer to his cause. English soldiers gave chase one night and cornered him in one of the smuggler's caves. I 'happened' along and rescued him from capture. Instant trust. I was able to penetrate his circle of rebels to the highest levels and bring them down."

"I still don't understand." She nibbled her lip in contemplation. "Did they have no issue with your English accent?"

"They might have, had they not believed I was Irish."

Her eyes rounded in surprise and she gasped. "You pretended to be Irish? Your accent must have been very good to fool everyone."

He nodded. "It was."

She smiled and rested her head against his shoulder. "I knew it would be. You are remarkable. And how did you fool the French countess? By pretending to be French?"

He laughed lightly. "No, my French is good, but my accent is not. Irish mercenary was my role."

"Irish again," Nicola murmured. "What don't I know about you? Did you grow up in Ireland? It seems obvious that you did, for it is no easy thing to fool a native speaker and you managed to have the mad monk and his cohorts completely taken in."

He shrugged. "I spent time there."

She turned in the saddle again to gaze up at him. "But something terrible happened there. Didn't it?"

He cursed silently, wishing he hadn't spoken to her at all about his missions. That was a mistake on his part. But Nicola had a way of putting him at ease and making him let down his guard. She understood him almost better than he understood himself.

In truth, he wasn't complicated.

He wanted revenge on the man who'd killed his parents and left him for dead. He wouldn't rest until he'd found the villain and exacted his vengeance. It should have been easy enough to pick up that old trail even now, for it had been a brutal crime against an English emissary and that emissary's wife, and not something the Irish locals or those on his father's staff would ever forget.

John had spent his life training for this confrontation. He was now a grown man in the service of the Crown. He was an earl, no less, and had the highest connections. But he'd been surprised by the difficulty he'd encountered in gathering information. Everyone he spoke to, English and Irish, used the same excuse. They couldn't recall, for the deaths had occurred over twenty years ago. He understood that, but to have nothing at all? Not so much as a kernel of a clue. That was troubling. It spoke of conspiracy. It spoke of a purposeful cover-up.

Nicola put her arms around his waist and rested her head against his chest. "You'll tell me when you're ready. I'm sorry if I distressed you."

"No, brat. You didn't."

The worst part about seeking revenge was the possibility that he'd never achieve it. The villain could be dead by now. The thought that a cold-hearted murderer might have died a natural, peaceful death tore John up inside. He'd carried this dark rage inside of him for all these years and meant to unleash it on the culprit when he found him.

Nicola lifted her head off his chest and looked up at him again. "Your heart is beating so fast, it's pounding a hole through your chest."

He frowned at her. "You're mistaken."

"Very well, dismiss my concern. But I'd like to point out that I found Somersby's secret book in the matter of a day. So why won't you trust me to help with whatever else is obviously troubling you?"

"I don't need your help," he said, his jaw clenched with tension. He did not want Nicola anywhere near that investigation. He wasn't going to do the decent thing and turn his parents' killer over to the authorities. He was going to rip the man's heart out and toss it to the carrion birds to eat.

She squirmed on his lap, shifting her position to better look him straight in the eye. "You don't *want* my help. That is very different from not needing it. I think you do need me badly." She emitted a breathy sigh. "I wish you'd let me in. I know I can help you."

"How? By meddling and getting yourself killed?"

"Would it be any worse than the predicament we're in now?"

He supposed not, but this was his quest for vengeance. His alone and he was not going to risk Nicola's life to achieve it. "I'm torn apart with worry over you, brat. I need to keep you safe. Just let me do that."

She shifted once more, now turning her back to him, unaware of the turmoil she was causing him with her every little movement. "Very well," she said, the hurt evident in her voice. "But I am not a lump of clay. I have feelings and protective urges too."

"What does that mean?"

"I don't know yet. I've never had to face death before. But I'm not a coward. If I have to risk my life to protect you, I'm going to do it."

He grabbed her by the shoulders and turned her to face him. "Over my dead body."

She frowned at him. "If that's what it takes to protect you, then… yes."

# CHAPTER 7

"THE HELL YOU will," John said with a growl. "Let's set some ground rules, shall we? Rule number one, I protect you. Rule number two, I keep you safe. Rule number three, you keep hidden if there's any danger. Rule number four, you *don't* protect me. Rule number five—"

"What if you're outnumbered and I can help? Am I supposed to sit by quietly and watch you die?" Men could be such dolts sometimes.

"Yes, and you can close your eyes. Then you won't have to watch me die."

Nicola chafed at his words. "That isn't funny. Don't ask me to do nothing at all. It isn't in my nature and I'll never agree to it."

He hugged her a little tighter to him. She wasn't certain whether he'd drawn her closer out of annoyance because she was riling him or out of his obviously protective instincts. His need to keep her safe seemed to run so deep within him, it was as though his soul would die if any harm came to her.

No, that was ridiculous.

He growled again, and although he was angry with her, that low, throaty sound stirred her heart. He meant it as a warning, but to her it was a mating call.

He tugged on the reins to slow Valor down as they began their climb into the mountains. "Do you see me laughing?"

"I understand the seriousness of our situation. I'm not suggesting that I will do anything reckless." She doubted he would believe her since he thought her stealing Somersby's book of accounts was the height of folly, and now he was stuck having to keep her alive while getting that book to the proper authorities.

"Then do as I say. I mean it, Nicola." There was something in the way he now held her, as though wanting to take her into his heart and keep her tucked in there forever. Was this how he felt whenever he was on assignment? Did his need to protect run as deep with everyone he was charged to watch over? Or was she different?

"Warning taken, John. I know Somersby will be relentless in his pursuit of us. I'm more than a little scared of what might happen if he finds us. Terrified, actually."

He eased his grasp on her. "Good. Stay that way. If he finds us, you need to keep out of my way and let me handle him."

She nodded.

They rode in silence a while longer and Nicola allowed herself to be distracted by the scenery, marveling at the splendor of the rough pines and tall oaks that soared to the sky and blocked most of the sun from the forested paths. They crossed crystal blue streams that flowed over pristine rocks and rich, brown earth. Green and amber grasses grew in abundance along those stream banks.

They were safest while keeping to the forest, for the thick vegetation hid them well. But they would also have to cross large expanses where they would be forced out into the open, exposed to anyone's view from as far as the eye could see. Crossing barren hills and open meadows was the most dangerous part of their journey. Although those hills and meadows might look beautiful in their sweep of purple heather, they offered no protective cover. Their low shrubs would never hide them.

As the sun began to dip below the trees, John drew Valor to a halt beside a stream. He dismounted and then helped Nicola down from the saddle, holding her by the waist until he was certain she'd recovered her footing. "There's an old military trail that runs near Aviemore. We'll make better time once we pick it up."

"Do you think Somersby knows of it?"

John nodded. "Likely. Part of any smuggling operation is to get the goods distributed as efficiently as possible. Old roads that are little used and remain in relatively good condition are what any smuggler would favor."

"Then why are we using it?"

"Because he will be looking for us on the main roads. He knows that's where we'll make the fastest time, and that's where he'll ride to find us."

"He saw us go into the mountains."

"Yes, but he doesn't believe I'd be so foolish as to take you over those mountain peaks. There's a road that runs eastward we could have taken about three hours ago, one that skirts Inverness and takes us a little south of it to Cawdor and Nairn. That's where he thinks we're heading, into Shakespeare's MacBeth territory where we can pick up another boat to sail us to Edinburgh, perhaps even London."

While Valor drank from the stream and began to graze upon the nearby grass, John sliced a few chunks of the bread and cheese he'd removed from his pouch and handed some to Nicola.

She accepted the food gratefully. "Thank you, I'm famished."

They sat on the trunk of a fallen pine, and when they'd finished their meager fare, John knelt beside the stream and cupped water into his hands to drink. Nicola was surprised when he offered her the water first, then realized that this was John behaving true to form. He thought of others before he ever thought of himself.

She smiled at him and drank the offered water. Only then did he take some for himself.

"Um, John... I need to take care... um, personal matter."

He laughed, understanding what she was trying to say. "You'll find privacy over there." He pointed to a row of bushes not far from the stream. "I'll stay here. Don't take too long."

She hurried away, for the call of nature was persistent. She finished quickly and then washed her hands in the stream. The water was cold since it came down from the mountains, but felt bracing when she splashed some on her face and neck as well.

When she returned to John's side, his big frame was stretched out on the grass. His eyes were closed. He was on his back, his head resting on his arms that he'd crossed behind his head to form a pillow. Shrugging, Nicola sat down beside him.

He eased one eye open and shifted slightly to hold out his arm to her. "Come here, brat. Valor needs another twenty minutes or so to rest and we ought to do the same."

She nodded and scrambled to lie down beside him. If not for the threat of death hanging over them, she would consider this was a moment of heaven. For years, she'd longed to be in John's arms. Here she was now, resting her head on his chest as he held one arm around her shoulders to draw her close to the heat of his body. "John, shouldn't we be reading that book of accounts instead of sleeping?"

"No, brat. It will take us about a week to reach Edinburgh over land. What's more pressing at the moment is to lose Somersby and his men."

"But you think he's following a false trail into MacBeth territory."

"Yes, but I can't be sure. He will consider every possibility. His own life is at stake and the lives of all those involved in his operation. He won't be alone in hunting for us. I don't know how many men he can muster to track us down, but he'll be dispersing them throughout Scotland in order to cover every potential route."

"But we have the advantage for the moment. Right?"

John nodded. "Right, he has to guess where we're headed, and with every new choice, every crossroads he reaches, he has to give up a man or two to follow that possible trail. He expects us to end up in Edinburgh or London, but he can't be sure of that either. Nor will he know whether we've hired another boat or will continue over land. There are several roads leading into Edinburgh. I expect he'll have men positioned at each entry point with orders to shoot us on sight. He'll have men watching the docks and the regimental headquarters. He'll be desperate to stop us before we speak to the regimental commander."

"All the more reason for us to ride straight to London."

He gave her shoulder a light caress. "And give him more time to find us and that book? We're two riders on one horse and have little food or money between us. He can ride on open roads while we have to keep to mountain trails. He'll call on unsuspecting friends and give them some lie about us. Perhaps that I've abducted you, that I'm crazed and dangerous and must be shot on sight."

Nicola sat up abruptly. "No one would dare shoot you. I would tell them the truth."

He looked at her and shrugged. "It won't do much good if they've already shot me."

"John, you're as well-known as Somersby. No one is going to harm you. The notion is ridiculous."

"Fine. Then stop fretting and don't ask me any more questions."

He held out his arm to her again.

She sighed and settled against the muscled line of his body. Although she was tired, her mind was too active to sleep. Or so she thought. The next thing she knew, John was lightly shaking her to wake her up. "What? I must have..." She blinked her eyes open and saw the elongated shadows across the forest floor. "Has it only been twenty minutes?"

John shook his head. "An hour, to be precise. You were sleeping so soundly, I didn't have the heart to wake you."

"Oh, John! I'm so sorry."

"Don't be. We all needed that extra time and can make up the lost half hour at any point. We'll reach Aviemore early tomorrow. Somersby will likely have his men posted there as well."

"They'll see us."

"That's why we can't risk riding into town. We'll forage on the outskirts, hopefully find something to eat. Perhaps a chicken left to roam wild, abandoned by a crofter who gave up on farming the land. The terrain is rugged up here and there ought to be more than a few abandoned crofts along the way."

"Do you think we might sleep in one? I hope we come across one tonight. I know we can't light a fire, but at least we'll be protected from the wind."

He helped her to her feet and then lifted her onto Valor's back before climbing up behind her. "We'll see. I'd like to get another three or four hours of riding in this evening. There's a valley that runs between these mountains and we need to cross it by night. There's no cover for us in daylight."

Nicola settled back against his chest. John's body was becoming familiar to her. She loved the size and strength of it and knew that she'd never tire of being in his arms. But it was foolish to wish for their time together never to end. There was no question that it would end as soon as they reached Edinburgh… or London, if he could be persuaded to take her there instead.

What would happen once he delivered Somersby's book to the Prince Regent? Would he ever admit he cared for her? Would he consider courting her? They'd be safe once the book of accounts was in royal hands. Somersby and his cohorts would have no time to plot revenge while on the run from the British army.

John could then court her if he wished. But she knew deep in her heart that he would return to taking on dangerous missions for the Crown.

He'd push her away and pretend she did not matter to him.

She would lose him once they reached London.

Was there any way to win his heart before then?

JOHN FELT A shiver run up his spine. He and Nicola had slept in the forest last night and had now been traveling for several hours when he sensed they were being followed. He'd learned to trust his instincts and always rely on them, so he knew for a certainty that someone was on their trail. But those same instincts told him it was not Somersby, for the marquis was not a patient man and would have made his move by now.

So who was following them?

He maintained an easy, loping pace until the trail turned sharply to the right and put them out of sight of their trackers for a moment. As soon as they'd passed the bend, he quickly dismounted, grabbed Nicola by the waist to take her off Valor, and then led them off the narrow path toward a copse of trees that was thick enough to hide them all. "Stay here," he said with quiet urgency. "Keep Valor calm."

Nicola's eyes rounded in alarm. "John—"

"No questions now. I need you to keep hidden." He hurried back to the trail with knife in hand, prepared to take on whoever rounded the curve.

Within moments, several stragglers came into view. "Well, I'll be damned," he muttered and stepped in front of the lead horse. "If it isn't Red Sammy Fraser. What are you doing in these parts, you old horse thief?"

The portly Scot swung his leg over and slid off his aging mount with surprising agility for a man his age and size. "Bainbridge? Don't tell me I've been wasting my time following ye these past hours. We heard the shots yesterday and saw Captain Grant's boat suddenly veer toward that broken down dock. Where's the girl and that magnificent horse that came off the boat with ye?"

John had dealt with the canny Scot in the past and trusted him as far as any man could ever trust a reiver. It was the other three men he didn't know and had no reason to believe wouldn't harm him or Nicola. "The girl happens to be my wife and she's pointing a rifle at your heart, awaiting my word to shoot."

It was an outright lie, but Sammy's companions would not know that.

Sammy took off his tam and ran a hand through his thick, white hair that had once been a blazing, fiery red, thereby earning him the nickname of Red Sammy. "Ye're married, lad?" He arched a snowy eyebrow in surprise. "Couldn't have been long ago."

"Only a month. Married in London. Came up here to hunt and enjoy the scenery, but we got into a bit of trouble."

Sammy glanced at his companions and all four of them grinned. "Those shots we heard," Sammy said with a nod. He glanced toward the copse where Nicola and Valor were hidden. "Ye saved m'life last year and I won't be forgetting that any time soon. Tell yer wife to set down her weapon and come greet yer old friend." He then turned to his companions. "The horse and girl...

er, lady, are his and that's the way they'll stay."

He turned back to John with a sad shake of his head. "Too bad. That's the finest bit of horseflesh I've ever seen in these parts. But I give ye my word, laddie. Ye and yer wife and that magnificent beastie of yers shall have safe passage through the mountains. Ye'll be on yer own beyond Loch Avon though." He cleared his throat. "We had a bit of a misunderstanding with a regiment of Scots dragoons a few months back and seems they've put a price on my head."

John winced. "What did you do this time?"

"Ain't never harmed no one, if that's what ye're thinking. But we misappropriated a wagon they were delivering to Braemear. We thought it carried casks of ale. How were we to know it carried their payroll?"

John groaned. "You stole from the royal exchequer? Sammy, not even I can help you out of that scrape. But I'll see what I can do. Are you willing to return what you stole?"

"Don't need yer assistance, m'lord. But thank ye for the offer." He turned back to his three companions once more and scowled at them. "Get off yer horses and come pay yer respects to the man what saved yer father's life, m'boys."

John arched an eyebrow in surprise. "These are your sons?"

Sammy nodded. "Archie, Malcolm, and the youngest is Angus."

The boys, who were all lean and strong in appearance, did not look too pleased about their father's command. Upon closer inspection, he saw the family resemblance. Sammy had likely been a handsome man in his younger years, but harsh Scottish winters, too much home-distilled whisky, and a fondness for treacle pies had not been kind to his body.

Archie was the eldest and served as spokesman for all three sons. "We appreciate yer saving Sammy's life, Lord Bainbridge. He speaks highly of ye, so ye need have no fear of us. We don't steal from our friends."

John smothered a grin as he tucked the knife he had been holding back into his boot. Sammy and his sons were reivers, which meant they'd steal from their own grandmothers if the opportunity presented itself. They wouldn't blink an eye before stealing from family, friends, or neighbors. However, he had no choice but to take them at their word, for saving their father's life was no small thing to them. "I'll fetch my wife."

He hoped Nicola had overheard their conversation and understood that while he trusted Sammy and his boys to some extent, he did not trust them entirely. He wasn't certain what they would do if they ever found out she was not married to him. Not that they would do anything immoral. No, his biggest fear was that one of those lummoxes would decide it was time to take a wife for himself and choose Nicola.

If they were stupid enough to steal a royal payroll, they'd be stupid enough to steal a young woman, no matter her aristocratic connections or her objections.

He strode to the copse. "Nicola... my love." Lord, it felt so right to call her that. "Er... it's all right. You needn't be afraid. These men are friends of mine. They are eager to meet my bride."

He took her by the hand, unable to bring himself to release her while in the presence of Sammy and his sons. Friends such as Sammy could never completely be trusted. The old Scot owed him a favor and took that debt seriously, but that debt would be repaid once he'd given them safe passage through the mountains.

What would Sammy do then? John wasn't certain.

In truth, probably nothing sinister would happen. John was grateful for his assistance and knew that these Frasers would not hesitate to protect him and Nicola from Somersby's men. After all, Sammy did have somewhat of a code of honor.

"A pleasure to meet you, gentlemen," Nicola said, casting them a smile that could not help but win them over with its heartfelt sweetness.

Nicola was a beautiful girl. He'd always thought so, but never more so than now. She needed no elegant gown or expensive adornments to enhance her looks. The simplicity of her clothes and casual style of her hair brought out her natural beauty and allowed it to shine through.

She was dressed in a drab, brown woolen gown. Her long hair was braided and tied back with a ribbon. Her eyes drooped slightly from fatigue, and her cheeks and nose were pink from the chill in the mountain air.

Sunlight filtered over her. To John, she glowed like a creature of magic, a wood sprite or exquisite faerie.

He tore his gaze away from Nicola and turned to Sammy and his boys, grinning as he noted their gaping mouths and wide eyes. Indeed, Nicola was casting her magic over Sammy and his lads. They were struck mute by her beauty and could not form the words to respond to her greeting. Angus was the first to recover his wits. "Good day to ye, Lady Bainbridge."

Sammy chuckled. "I can see why ye married her, laddie. Got yerself a prime stallion," he said with a longing glance at Valor, "and a prize filly." He grinned in approval at Nicola. "Didn't think Bainbridge would ever marry, but ye must have struck him like a bolt of lightning. What man could ever resist a pretty thing like ye?"

"Thank you, Mr. Fraser," Nicola said sweetly, but she nudged a little closer to John's side, for Sammy was doing little to hide his admiration of her. Neither were his boys.

John gave her hand a gentle squeeze to assure her that he would keep her close. "Sammy, my wife is tired and hasn't had much to eat. Do you—"

"Say no more, laddie. Ye'll be our guests this evening in our home. We ought to reach it by nightfall if we don't dawdle." He turned to his sons. "Mount up, lads. We're having company this evening."

John lifted Nicola onto Valor and climbed on behind her, settling her against his chest and wrapping one arm around her waist to hold her securely to him. They'd been riding like this for two days now. He ought to have been used to her nearness. But he wasn't.

He couldn't get enough of Nicola.

His physical ache was nothing to the ache in his heart.

Young Angus had not taken his eyes off Nicola since she'd stepped out from the copse of trees. Sammy noticed his son's look of adoration as well. He rode up beside John. "Seems odd that yer wife is wearing no jewels and her gown is rather plain."

Nicola stiffened in indignation. "We're on the run for our lives, Mr. Fraser. My fine gowns and jewels were left behind in Invergarry." She drew a breath to say more, but John gave her another subtle squeeze in warning. While Sammy looked like an oafish dissolute, he was one of the smartest men John had ever met and his instincts were as good as his own.

The way Sammy and his boys were eyeing Nicola gave him more than a little cause for concern. There was only one way he was going to keep these damn Frasers from claiming her for one of them.

He had to leave no doubt in their minds that she was his.

He had to claim her for himself.

The Scottish way.

# CHAPTER 8

NICOLA DID NOT understand why John was scowling at her. Not that she could see him scowling, but she sensed that he was. What had she done now? She'd been on her best behavior since going on the run, and had hardly spoken a word in all the hours since they'd met Sammy Fraser and his sons. Perhaps he wasn't scowling at her, but was worried that they were being led into a trap. "John," she started in a whisper, but he gave her a little squeeze that she understood to be a warning to be quiet.

So she said nothing more, merely remained squirming tensely in his arms.

His body felt tense, too.

"We're not far from Sammy's village now," John said as the sun dipped low on the horizon. The hour was late and the path had grown dark, for they were once more in the mountains and the tall pines obscured any sunlight that might have reached them. Certainly no moonlight or starlight would ever penetrate here.

There was an eerie quiet to the night. The only sounds Nicola heard were the occasional snorts and whickers from their horses. Not even the clip-clop of their hooves could be heard upon the soft carpet of fallen pine leaves.

They'd had to wait until nightfall to cross another open meadow, and then make their way over two small mountains before coming upon a village of no more than a dozen homes. From what Nicola could see, they were mostly rough-hewn cottages and none of them were stately. But the scent of roasted meat from an earlier supper lingered in the air along with acrid peat smoke from hearth fires.

Nicola's stomach growled.

She was hungry enough to devour anything that moved in front of her and did not succeed in devouring her first.

John sighed. "There's one thing we must do before we eat."

She frowned. "What's that?"

He said nothing for a long moment. "Just follow my lead. Do as I do. Repeat what I say. It is important."

She had no idea what he was talking about, but nodded. "Very well. Care to give me a clue what's going on?"

"No. Just do as I tell you."

They drew their mounts up before the largest home among this circle of otherwise small, rundown houses. Someone was awake, for there was movement inside and suddenly a light emanated from the window. Whoever was watching them had lit a lantern and was now hurrying to open the front door. "Och, ye old scoundrel," a sturdy-looking woman of about five and thirty years chided Sammy as the door flew open with a loud groan, sounding as though it was about to come off its hinges.

Sammy dismounted and gave the woman a hearty kiss on the lips. "Maeve, m'love."

The woman tugged on his ear and then put her hands on her hips to mark her irritation. "Don't ye dare sweet talk me, ye rascal. I thought the soldiers had finally captured ye. What kept ye away for so long this time?" Then her gaze traveled to Nicola and John. "What have we here?"

"Friends of mine, Maeve." Sammy hastily made introductions before striding inside and bidding them all to follow. The woman was not his wife, for Sammy's sons did not call her their mother, and Angus muttered something about her being Black Sammy's widow, and Black Sammy was an arse who did not treat his women right, so Maeve was much better off warming Red Sammy's bed as she had these past ten years... even though Black Sammy had only been dead nine years.

Nicola's jaw dropped open.

Fortunately, she had no need to say anything. Sammy was now explaining their plight to Maeve. "Lord Bainbridge is a good friend of mine. He and his... *wife*... are in need of our assistance. But first, they're in need of food and a fire to warm them. They've been on the road for a spell."

Oh, dear. He'd stressed the word "wife" as though he did not believe she and John were married, which they weren't and never would be if the matter were left to John.

Yet, Nicola felt the comforting warmth of John's arm around her shoulders. In the next moment, John put both hands on her shoulders and gently turned her toward him. Then his hands slipped from her shoulders to claim her hands. They now stood facing each other, although she had to tip her gaze upward to meet his, for he stood a head taller than her, perhaps a bit more. John was a big man.

And his jaw was twitching, not quite in spasms, but noticeably to her familiar eye. He did not look at all pleased.

"What's wrong?" she asked in a whisper.

His gaze upon her turned surprisingly tender. "Sammy's looking for proof."

She frowned. "Of what?"

"Our marriage. He doesn't believe we are husband and wife."

She tried to feign outrage, but it was hard to do when their so-called state of marital bliss was a lie. "How do we prove it?"

"Like this." He cupped her chin in his hand and tipped her face up. At the same time, he closed his eyes and lowered his lips to press them lightly against hers. She responded as any woman kissed by John would, melting into a limpid pool at his touch. She was acutely aware that Sammy, Maeve, and Sammy's sons were watching.

Although his kiss was purposefully gentle, she would not call it tame. He was tense and straining like a stallion, eager to set his rampant desire free. She felt the same, now certain she'd been born a hussy, for she felt no shame in responding to him in front of spectators. After an appropriately long moment, he drew away and smiling, caressed her cheek with his thumb. "I declare before these witnesses that I have taken Lady Nicola Jennifer Emory as my wife before man and God. She is my Lady Bainbridge for now and ever more."

Ah, she understood what he was doing and cast him a return smile. He was maintaining the pretense to keep her out of the clutches of Sammy's boys, who had not stopped ogling her since they'd first set eyes upon her. "And I declare before these witnesses that I have taken John Randall, Earl of Bainbridge, as my husband before man and… God. He is my Lord Bainbridge for now and ever more."

She prayed silently for forgiveness, for it was one thing to mislead these men. She did not trust them as far as she could spit. And yes, she could spit as well as any man. But to lie to the Good Lord did not sit well with her. Hopefully, He would understand her desperation and know she'd never lie without compunction unless her life and John's were in danger.

Sammy grumbled as he slapped John on the back. "I was sure ye were lyin' to me, lad. Guess I was wrong. Ye're a lucky man. I hope ye appreciate her and treat her as finely as she deserves." He turned to Nicola. "Ye must be a saint, lass. Or an angel to put up with the likes of him."

She shook her head and laughed. "Then you know him well, Mr. Fraser."

"Call me, Sammy." He eyed her speculatively. "Ye look soft and gentle, but ye seem to have him well in hand, so I suspect there's a good dose of strong will and Scottish stubbornness in ye."

"I am most certainly strong-willed and stubborn, but I'm afraid I'm not Scottish. My family is English. I hope none of my ancestors ever did you harm."

Sammy shrugged. "Likely they did. Some fierce battles took place up here, ending with Culloden Moor. But I think while yer men were off fightin', some of our men were off wooing the Englishwomen who'd followed them up here. Lass, that red hair and yer blazin' green eyes give ye away. There's a Scot lurking somewhere in yer royal blue bloodlines."

"My hair is auburn, not red. And my—"

John stepped between them before matters got out of hand, for accusing any of the women in Nicola's family line of infidelity was typical of Sammy taking matters too far. The old bounder wouldn't see it as an insult, for declaring her a Scot was, to his way of thinking, a great compliment. "Obviously, that's why I fell in love with her at first sight," John said, casting Nicola a wink. "My wife is her own person, whatever her ancestry, and she won't hesitate to take a fist to your nose if you don't stop goading her, Sammy."

Maeve clucked and tsked in agreement. "Behave yerself, Red Sammy. His lordship has proved they're wed so leave them alone. Yer sons will have to find their wives elsewhere. And it wouldna hurt their prospects if they washed more often. They're handsome lads, but who's to notice under all that filth?" She took Nicola and led her to a stool by the fire. "Make yerself comfortable, m'lady. I'll put on some stew to warm."

Nicola liked the no-nonsense woman and admired the way she maintained control of four obviously stubborn men. She may not be mother to Sammy's sons, but they obeyed her and responded to her as though she were. "Thank you, Maeve. Please call me Nicola. It seems ridiculous to maintain formality, especially after the kindness you've all shown us."

As she'd taken her seat beside the fire, John had moved to the fire as well. Was it merely to warm himself? She did not think so. John was still keeping close to her. She did not understand why. They were pretend married now and the Frasers had believed their lie.

She sighed. It was only a small fib, a necessary misstatement given under dire circumstances.

*Lord, forgive me.*

Truly, it had felt wrong to lie to Maeve, but she did not have quite as much guilt about lying to Sammy and his sons. They were unrepentant rogues, and Angus in particular had not stopped staring at her. Perhaps that was what John had noticed also.

"M'lord," Sammy said once they'd eaten their stew and washed it down with a surprisingly good homemade ale. They were all seated on sturdy benches around the dining table. Maeve was busying herself serving Sammy and his boys with second helpings, for they had announced they were still hungry and demanded more. "Yer pretty wife looks ready to fall asleep on her feet."

John nodded and cast him a wry grin. "Unlike us scoundrels, she isn't used to a harsh life. She's never been on the run before."

Nicola muffled her yawn. "I'd hardly call your hospitality harsh, Mr. Fraser. You've been most generous with us and I thank you."

"Och, I wish I'd had a girl and not just pigheaded sons. The pleasure is all mine, I assure ye, Lady Bainbridge." He slapped his hands on his knees and grunted to his feet. The wooden bench groaned as he eased off it.

Sammy then playfully caught Maeve about the waist and drew her up against his portly frame. "Maeve, m'love, would it be all right to offer yer cottage to these lovebirds for the night? I'd suggest that his lordship sleep here while ye ladies retire to yer cottage, but ye can see his lordship wants her warm body beside him and isn't about to agree to any arrangement that doesn't have her in his arms. So, ye can stay with me tonight, and everyone's happy," he said with a wicked grin. "Ye look like ye need a little warmin' up yerself and I'm just the man to oblige."

Maeve hit him across the head with the wooden spoon in her hand. "Ye big oaf. Is that any way to talk in front of Lady Bainbridge? Look, the poor thing's blushing. Och, lamb. Ye must ignore Red Sammy. But ye and yer husband are welcome to my cottage. Ye ought to be safe enough from outsiders this evening."

"Thank you, Maeve. I appreciate the offer. You see, I've quickly grown used to having Lord Bainbridge by my side and would not like to spend even one night apart."

Sammy and his sons guffawed and John looked surprised.

Sammy gave him a hearty wallop on the back. "Seems the lass can't get enough of ye. Hungry for ye, she is. And by the look of ye, it seems yer even hungrier for her. I thought ye Uppity Ups did not like to share beds." He shook his white-capped head and sighed. "Archie will show ye the way. It does m'old heart good to see a young couple in love. But ye mustn't wring him dry, m'lady, or he'll be useless tomorrow. We have a long ride ahead of us and

I plan to have us on the road before the cock's first crow."

Nicola breathed a sigh of relief once she and John were brought to Maeve's cottage and finally left alone. John had brought his weapons along with him, and they'd been given a lantern to see their way around the small place. Nicola could instantly tell that Maeve was a fastidious woman. Although small and sparse, her one-room home was neat and nicely maintained.

There were feminine frills, some pretty dishes on display. Lace runners on a few, small tables. Lace curtains. These little details had been lacking in Sammy's abode. Although his cottage was much bigger, it had suffered from the lack of tender care by the rowdy men who lived there.

Sammy and his boys were not the delicate sort, certainly would never think to dust shelves or wash floors or not slam doors.

They were not the sort to decorate with lace either. No, they would smuggle lace, for certain. But never keep it for themselves.

"John, what happens next?" She did not know what he had in mind for sleeping arrangements, but whatever he decided was fine with her. She was tired, practically dead on her feet, and wished nothing more than to close her eyes. All the fight had gone out of her when he'd taken her hands in his and declared he was her husband.

Her lips were still tingling from his gentle kiss.

Their marriage was a lie, but John had spoken those words with such gentle affection that the lie had sounded splendid to her ears.

"We'll have to share Maeve's bed." He took her hand in his, sounding more remorseful than pleased. "I'm sorry, Nicola. But they'll grow suspicious if we don't sleep together, and then that whelp, Angus, will be claiming you for his own."

She laughed lightly. "All these seasons on the shelf and suddenly I'm the belle of the Highlands ball."

He frowned at her. "You were always the prettiest girl wherever you went. You're the one who chased the men away."

"Until Somersby." She slipped her hand out of John's grasp and put it to her lips to stifle a sob. "Oh, John. I don't want to think about him tonight. How could I have been so stupid? How could I not see the man he was?"

"No one saw it, Nicola." He placed her hand back in his and led her behind a curtained area of the cottage that served as Maeve's bedchamber. The bed was small, hardly big enough to hold one person. Perhaps it would fit two people if they snuggled tight. John was big and broad shouldered, but she was fairly slight in build.

Besides, she and John had been pasted to each other for days. Surely, they could manage to spend the night squeezed together.

In truth, it would be heaven for her.

He stayed her hand when she started to remove her shawl. "Don't undress. Just take off your boots. We may have to make a run for it if Somersby or his men show up."

She nodded, turning away slightly to hide her disappointment.

She was ready to strip down to nothing for this man, but his mind was on his duty and not on laying claim to her body even though she was his pretend wife. And now he wasn't even looking at her, but was striding to the window to peer out into the blackness.

"Bollocks," he muttered, striding to the door to make certain the latch was secure. He then lifted Maeve's table, which was made of thick, sturdy oak, and set it firmly against the door.

"What are you doing?" That table appeared to weigh as much as a horse. Yet, John had lifted it as though it was nothing.

"Sammy's boys are curious."

She gasped. "Were they peeking in?"

He nodded. "Still are."

"What?" She raced to the window and saw their shameless faces grinning back at her. "How dare they!"

John caught her by the waist as she made to open the window to punch the closest of Sammy's sons in the nose. "They mean no harm."

"No harm?" Her hands were still curled into fists and she was furious. That John managed to remain calm only brought her anger to a boil. "They need to be taught a lesson."

She reached for the window again, but John held her back. "Enough, Nicola. We need them on our side, not turning us over to Somersby."

"But they're your friends. They wouldn't dare… would they?"

He finally released her and ran a hand through his hair in obvious consternation. "Red Sammy's an odd duck. No telling what he might do if you insult his boys, even if they are misbehaving."

"Well, they're not going to gawk at me all night." She hung her shawl over the window like a curtain and heard their grumbles. "I'm going to bed."

She stalked back to their bedchamber—oh, goodness! Had she just thought of it as that? *Their* bedchamber?

John cleared his throat. "I'll join you shortly."

She sank onto the straw mattress and tugged off her boots. "What are you going to do in the meanwhile?"

"Decipher Somersby's book, especially the ledger entries."

"Me, too!" She forgot her anger and her eyes widened in anticipation. "Bring it here. We can look at it together."

"No."

At times, John could be as infuriating as Sammy's wayward boys. "No?" She rose and came to his side as he dug through his saddle pouch to retrieve the book. "How can you deny me? It's my book, since I'm the one who found it."

He arched an eyebrow, looking quite wickedly handsome as he smiled at her in wry amusement. "You're the one who *stole* it, to be precise. So let me do my duty and memorize as much of it as I can as long as we have it."

"As long as we have it? What do you mean? Don't we need those ledger entries as proof?"

He nodded. "I'm trying to get it safely to London, but if Somersby catches us, I plan to trade your life for this book."

Warmth flowed through her in a slow, soothing wave. This was John being protective again. Saving her life was foremost on his mind. Oh, how she wished that little ceremony he'd performed in front of Sammy and his family had been real. She would have been so proud to be John's wife. "All the more reason why I should be the one to read it and memorize what it contains. If you're going to sacrifice your life to save mine, then I'm the one who ought to have the knowledge, not you."

John rolled his eyes and groaned. "Very well, brat. I suppose you're right. We'll work on it together in bed. Bollocks, your brother is going to string me up by my short hairs. You can't tell him any of this. Not before I have the chance to speak to him in private."

"Fine. You'll see him before I do, anyway." He was going to deposit her in Edinburgh and then take off for London. He might not make it there alive. Even if he did, she might not be alive by the time he returned to fetch her. Somersby had planned to use her to hurt someone dear to her. That wretched ledger wasn't the only reason he was desperate to find her.

Whom did he wish to hurt?

John stretched his big frame beside her. She curled up against him, resting her head against his shoulder, but otherwise leaving him free to turn the pages. Unfortunately, those rows of ciphers meant nothing to her. She tried to concentrate, but felt herself nodding off a time or two.

She must have fallen into a sound asleep, for she awoke shortly before dawn to the soft neigh of a horse passing close to Maeve's cottage. She tried to sit up, but realized she was turned on her side, facing the wall, and John's big body was half atop her, gently pinning her between the wall and mattress. One of his arms rested on her body, the weight of that muscled limb falling across her chest as she turned to face him. "John," she whispered, not certain whether he was awake and doubting that he was, for his breaths were calm and even. "I think—"

"Quiet, Nicola. Somersby's men are here. Damn it, I don't know how they found us." He rolled off the bed and grabbed his rifle in one smooth, silent motion. He tugged on his boots. "Stay here. Don't move. Let me take care of them."

"What if Sammy decides to betray us?"

"He won't. He and his boys may not know Somersby, but they've met men like him before. They understand what such a man will do to them if he finds out they've been harboring us. They know he won't spare Maeve either."

"What of Valor? He's in the stable and will give us away the moment they spot him."

John caressed her cheek. "He's hidden in the forest. I wouldn't dare leave him in the village stables for any passerby to see." He handed her one of his pistols. "Stay here. Don't poke your head out the window. Latch the door and don't come out until I tell you it's safe. And don't shoot that weapon until you're sure it isn't me you're aiming at." He paused a moment to stare at her, then leaned forward and planted a kiss on her cheek.

Not a quick peck, either.

It was a soft, lingering kiss. "Behave, brat. Don't shoot me."

Then he was off, somehow crossing to the door and removing the table that had blocked it without making a sound. If she hadn't been looking straight at him, she would not have known that he was moving about, or that he'd just opened the door and stolen out of it into the gray mist of morning.

She shoved on her boots and hurried to the door to latch it, then she crouched behind Maeve's rocking chair with John's pistol in hand and waited. And waited some more. And finally crept to the window when she could bear the suspense no longer. She heard Somersby's men haul Sammy out of his cottage and shove him toward the stable. "I told ye, no one's come by here all week. But ye're welcome to search the village if ye dinna believe me. Search the barn. Search the stables. Ye'll not find what ye're looking for."

"Shut up," one of Somersby's men ordered with a snarl. "If they aren't here, then you've hidden them."

"Hidden who? Ye aren't tax collectors, are ye?"

There were only three of Somersby's men that she could see. She doubted there were more, for Somersby would have needed a small army to patrol the vast area and still have men enough to send to Edinburgh and London. But those three were indeed ugly, scarred creatures whose faces were distorted with malice.

Sammy cast them a defiant look. "Who sent ye here?"

The biggest man slammed his fist into Sammy's face. "I told you to shut up. Open your foul Scottish mouth again and I'll kill you."

Nicola held tight to her pistol, wishing she had the ability to get off more than one shot. No wonder there was still tension between their two countries. Even English vermin such as these men believed themselves to be above any law-abiding Scot. Not that Sammy was law abiding by any stretch of reason, but he certainly wasn't bothering anyone now.

A fourth man suddenly came out of Sammy's cottage dragging a barely clad Maeve by her hair. "Tell us the truth, you lying scum or I'll slit your harlot's throat."

Nicola began to shake.

How long was John going to remain silent and allow these men to brutalize Maeve and Sammy? And where were Sammy's sons?

She closed her eyes and rested her head against the rough stone wall. "Keep out of this, Nicola," she whispered to herself. "John knows what he's doing."

But what if they'd caught John?

And Sammy's sons?

What if there were more than these four villains?

Her eyes were closed no longer than the equivalent of a few heartbeats, but she had yet to open them before she heard a pounding at the latched door. Startled, she almost fired her weapon in surprise. "Open the door, Nicola."

She recognized John's voice and hastened to obey.

He took the pistol out of her hand, grabbed the pouch he must have tucked under Maeve's bed last night, then gave a quick look around to make certain he'd left nothing behind. "We have to go."

"What happened? Where are Somersby's men?" Then she saw them, all four of them sprawled lifeless on the ground atop a widening pool of blood. "John?"

"They were about to slit Maeve's throat."

Sammy came in, nursing the bruise to his jaw from the punch he'd just received. "They would have slit mine next. Villainous scum. Thank ye, m'lord. Seems ye saved m'life again. I'm indebted to ye."

Sammy's sons, who had come in behind him, nodded in agreement.

"Not this time, Sammy. I led them straight here. I owed you no less than to keep all of you safe."

Nicola felt a loud hum between her ears.

She felt dizzy.

Somersby's men were evil, but to hear them growling one moment and then know they were dead in the next, was too much for her. And yet, she would have shot the man who intended to slit Maeve's throat. She would have fired at his head and prayed that she'd hit him between the eyes.

She took a step and swayed.

John wrapped his arm around her waist. "Nicola! Are you all right?"

"No."

"Bollocks." He led her, half walking beside her and half carrying her, away from the village toward a nearby stream. "Here, sit down."

He helped her onto a fallen birch. After making certain she was not going to tumble off it, he knelt along the stream's bank to dip his neckcloth in the rushing water. Nicola watched him wring it out. "I'm sorry you had to see that," he said, gently running the cloth across her forehead, then her cheeks, lips, and neck. He dipped it again and dabbed it against her lips, which felt as dry and cracked as her throat. "Any better?"

She shook her head. "Not yet. I still feel ill."

"Is she carrying yer child?" Angus asked, he and his brothers having followed them out from the village, gawking at her all the while.

"No!" Nicola shot back. "I'm just ill. I've never seen dead men before. Did you kill them all, John?"

He ignored the question, for he appeared to understand that she wasn't asking out of pride in his accomplishment, but out of horror. Angus wasn't nearly as insightful. "He killed the one threatening Maeve, then started on the other three who were holding Sammy. We helped. Couldn't let those beasts kill our own kin." His chest puffed out with pride. "He deserves it sometimes, but he's our pa. No one threatens him and lives."

It was a simple code of honor.

Protect your family.

Steal from everyone else.

John was still gazing at her with concern. "Can you walk now? We have to go."

She nodded. "I'll be all right in a moment. How did they find us?"

"I don't know. They may have put dogs on our scent, although I saw none with these men. Perhaps they noticed our shadows as we crossed the open meadow last night."

John took her hands in his to help her up.

She rested her head on his shoulder. "This is real," she said in a tremulous whisper and swallowed hard. "People die. I saw how they treated Maeve, dragging her by the hair and giving her no time to wrap so much as a shawl about her shoulders for modesty. They held a knife to her throat. They would have done the same to me, assuming they did not have orders to simply slit my throat."

"I wasn't going to let it happen."

"I know. But those men looked so cruel. I can't stop thinking about what they would have done if they'd found me. I think they would have hurt and humiliated me first."

"They can't do anything to you now." John's voice was exquisitely gentle.

Sammy brought Valor to the stream. He did not look happy. John took the reins from his hands, his expression as grim as Sammy's. "How is Maeve?"

"Shaken to the core, but unharmed. I'll tell her ye asked after her. But go now, m'lord. Look after yer lovely wife. My boys will escort ye to Loch Avon. It isn't far to Braemar from there."

Nicola gave Sammy a heartfelt hug. "Thank you sincerely, Mr. Fraser."

His anger seemed to dissipate and he cast her a lopsided smile. "Och, lassie. Ye take care of yerself. Listen to yer husband. He's a good man and will protect ye and that unborn babe ye're carrying."

Why did they all believe she was carrying John's child? "I'm not…"

Sammy patted her cheek. "If ye say so, but I've never seen a hungrier look in a man's eyes," he said, glancing at John. "If ye aren't carryin' yet, then ye soon will be."

John grinned.

Her cheeks caught flame.

She opened her mouth to respond, realized she had no words, and snapped it shut again.

John's child?

They'd have to marry first… well, unless she wished scandal to follow her for the rest of her days.

She felt a dull ache in her heart.

John was so close, looking gruff and divinely rugged with his days' growth of beard and his slightly too long hair curling about the nape of his neck. She probably looked like a cat just struck by lightning, her hair sticking out in every which way, an unholy, matted mess.

"You look beautiful, brat," John said, easily reading her mind as he led her to Valor and lifted her onto the saddle. He climbed up behind her and drew her against him.

"We have horses," she said, realizing Somersby's men would have no use for their mounts now. "I can ride one of those."

John growled. "The hell you will. I'll not have you anywhere near their beasts."

"Sammy will sell them at market," Angus said.

And keep the proceeds, Nicola realized. Well, that rascal had earned it. She leaned her head against John's shoulder as they rode off with Sammy's boys, needing the heat and muscled strength of him to soothe her.

She felt the cool wind on her cheeks and its sting against her eyes.

Her eyes began to water.

John kissed her on the forehead. "It'll be all right, brat. We had a close call, nothing more."

She inhaled sharply. "Nothing more? They would have killed Maeve and Sammy, and then killed us."

"Nicola, why are you falling apart now? We've been on the run from them since the night of Somersby's party."

"I know. I'm so sorry, John. I'll try to do better. I think it's all catching up to me this morning. And now Sammy's nitwit sons think I'm carrying your child and won't stop staring at me."

Suddenly, she understood the reason for her tears.

It wasn't the close call with Somersby's men that had her so overset. It was the fact that she wasn't carrying John's child. That she wasn't married to John. That he would leave her once this assignment was over.

She would never again feel the heat of his body against hers or the delicious warmth of his arms protectively circled around her, hugging her tightly to him.

How soon before this was over?

How soon before they encountered more of Somersby's men?

And where was Somersby?

# CHAPTER 9

JOHN KNEW HE had to tell Nicola what that ceremonial declaration performed in front of Sammy and his boys had meant. It was a handfasting and they were now considered husband and wife under Scottish law. Within the year, they had to decide whether to consummate the marriage and be permanently bound, or do nothing and quietly go their separate ways.

He wasn't proud of deceiving Nicola, but he'd had no choice. The gleam in Sammy's eyes and those of his boys signified that one of those rascals meant to take Nicola as his wife. John had to claim her first, for merely giving assurance that they were married hadn't been enough. He'd had to prove it, and this was the only way he knew how to accomplish it without spilling blood.

Nicola would understand, wouldn't she?

*Hell, no.*

She would come after him with the closest weapon at hand, for he'd stolen her dreams with that one action.

Since Sammy's boys were still riding with them until Loch Avon, John knew he'd have to wait until they had safely crossed the loch and were settled for the night in the village of Braemar before he dared confess his deed to her.

"How do you feel, Nicola? Any better?" he asked as the day wore on and the sun now shone directly above them. It was midday and he expected that she would be quite hungry since they hadn't eaten since last night.

She nodded. "Much. I'm so sorry that—"

"Don't be. You don't owe me any apology. I should have realized those men had picked up our trail and done more to keep you safe." He gave her hand a little squeeze, for he'd been holding onto it for much of this day's journey. One hand on Valor's reins, and one arm wrapped around Nicola with his hand resting over hers. "We'll reach Loch Avon soon. That's where we'll part ways with Sammy's boys."

He felt the rise and fall of her bosom in silent laughter. "My flock of admirers? I think I shall miss them, but I dare not tell them that or we might never be rid of them."

He gave a mock shudder. "Don't you dare give them any encouragement. They aren't above stealing a man's wife if they have a mind to do so. They won't care that you're married, carrying my child, or that we love each other."

Nicola immediately tensed at the mention of love.

He was a fool to even bring it up.

He felt the moment she turned within herself, for he'd robbed her of all her romantic dreams. She glanced up at him with sad eyes. "Perhaps they sense this is all a sham, that we aren't married, that I'm not with child, and… that you don't love me."

Fortunately, he had not the chance to respond before Archie, who had taken the lead on the narrow mountain trail, rode back to them. "Loch Avon is just around the next bend."

John allowed the Fraser boys to scout ahead while he remained behind with Nicola. They were so close to parting ways with these reivers, he dared not let Nicola out of his clutches for a moment. Angus was in lust with her, probably in love with her, and it showed. The boy wanted Nicola for his own. Would he attempt to claim her now?

John couldn't blame him if he did try. Nicola was beautiful, even more so because she had no notion of just how beautiful she was.

John felt disgusted with himself.

He'd known and loved Nicola for years. Even though she was his best friend's sister, why hadn't he simply told her—and Julian—that he loved her? And why had he allowed his need for revenge against those who'd killed his parents destroy his own happiness? He'd tempered his rage by joining the elite circle of agents for the Crown, never planning to be encumbered by a family, expecting to feel satisfied whenever he brought down evil. But he never had. When would it ever be enough?

Would there ever come a time when he overcame his anger and led a normal life?

He knew the girl he wanted.

He *loved* this girl.

When would he be man enough to admit it to her?

"John, look! It's so beautiful," Nicola said as they rounded the bend and the crystal blue lake came into view. Indeed, the sight before them was an exquisite explosion of colors. He drew Valor up a moment while they took in the splendid scenery.

He sensed that Nicola needed a moment of peaceful contemplation amid the chaos swirling around them.

The cloudless October sky was a deep azure. The surrounding hills were covered in purple heather. Beyond them lay mountains covered in emerald green forests. To the east lay a meadow dotted with rowan and bracken and shaded in hues of browns and vivid greens. In the center of it all was a shining, crystal lake.

The cool air carried the scent of heather and pine toward them.

The sun bore down on them with sheltering warmth. It shone upon Nicola's hair, highlighting the lush, red tones of her auburn curls. "I wonder if faeries come out at night to frolic here," she said in an awed whisper.

John laughed. "The locals think they do. Indeed, there are faerie glens all over Scotland. There's a well-known one on the Isle of Skye and another faerie glen not far from here."

Nicola's eyes rounded in delight. "Oh, how magical. I wish… never mind. It's too silly to think of such things when we're on the run for our lives."

"I'll bring you back here once proof of Somersby's treason is in safe hands and he's no longer a danger to you."

She cast him a wry smile. "John, you needn't indulge me. I know you'll never bring me back here. Perhaps my brother and Rose will take me here one day."

He said nothing, but silently promised himself that he would be the one to return here with Nicola.

They ate lunch beside the lake, careful to remain hidden within its shaded borders. Valor dined on sweet grasses and drank water from a rivulet that ran along the edge of their shady spot. Since they dared not light a fire, their repast consisted of fresh bread and cheese that Maeve had packed for them.

"Perhaps we ought to escort you to Braemar," Angus said, his young heart obviously breaking at the thought of never seeing Nicola again.

Archie cuffed him in the head. "And get ourselves arrested and hanged? Start thinking with yer head and not yer… can't say it in the presence of a lady." He cast Nicola an appreciative glance, then turned to John. "Best to keep to the outskirts of town. There's a quiet inn where the Uppity Ups like to go when they need to be discreet. Sammy's sister runs it. Her name is Adela Fraser. The inn is called The Fox's Lair. Just tell her that Sammy sent ye and he said not to charge ye for the room or the baths or the meals."

Nicola's eyes rounded in surprise. "That's quite generous of him."

Malcolm laughed. "No, it isn't. He took yer necklace."

Nicola's hand instinctively went to her throat. "My locket?"

"Aye, that's the one." Malcolm frowned lightly. "He apologizes for sorting through his lordship's pouch. I hope it dinna have sentimental value for ye."

Nicola shook her head. "No. None at all."

Archie folded his arms across his chest and grinned. "Good. He likes ye and would have felt some remorse for taking it from ye, otherwise."

John caressed her cheek. "I'll buy you another one when this is over."

Angus stormed off without saying a word.

His brothers said quick farewells and took off after him.

Nicola groaned in relief. "I don't think I shall soon forget any of these Frasers."

"Indeed, they are one of a kind. I'm surprised their Fraser laird hasn't hanged them all yet. Sammy and his boys aren't above stealing from their own." John gathered the remains of their lunch and tucked the last of the bread and cheese into his pouch. "Thank goodness," he said with a low, rumble of laughter, "the book is still here."

Nicola released her breath in a long, deep sigh. "Oh, dear. The possibility that they'd steal it never crossed my mind. I don't care about the locket, of course. But to lose that book would have been disastrous."

"Sammy wasn't going to take it. He can't read, so it holds no interest for him. But he likes shiny objects. Coins. Diamonds. He can't keep his sticky fingers off those. Yet, he does have a sense of fairness. He gave us a night at his sister's inn as his guest." He ran a hand through his hair in consternation. "You'll have to stay close to me while we're there. It isn't a respectable place and you're... temptation."

She stared at him in disbelief and laughed softly. "I haven't washed in two, or is it three, days? My hair resembles a hornet's nest. My clothes are shabby, to say the least. My—"

"Lips are sweet as nectar, and your body is what men dream of. So, stay close to me. And if anyone asks, you are my wife. I am your husband." He ran a hand through his hair once more. "And you are carrying my child."

Nicola scowled at him. "That again."

"Yes, that again." He stared at her breasts that were lush and full. Brazenly ogled them to get his point across. "Men will believe it. Everyone will believe it. Your breasts are what men dream about, too."

Her cheeks turned to crimson flames. "I... you..."

"Do you think I haven't noticed? Do you think holding you in my arms for days on end has been a chore for me? It hasn't." Indeed, it was exquisite agony. He turned away, knowing he'd said too much. What was wrong with him? He was worse than Angus. Far worse than that inexperienced lad, for he was not going to behave like a gentleman with Nicola tonight. He was going to explain that they were married and then claim his husbandly rights.

He strode to the rivulet and splashed cold water on his face.

He was a fool, a damned, stupid fool.

He'd never take Nicola without her consent. Nor would he ever take her without being fully committed to their marriage. She deserved no less.

She deserved love and happiness.

She did not deserve a tormented, hate-filled agent of the Crown.

NICOLA HADN'T EXPECTED The Fox's Lair to be as charming an inn as it was. She found it perfect in every way. The structure was a large, thatched roof cottage with cheerful flower beds along its stone walkway and a welcoming red door with a shining brass knocker in the shape of a fox at its center. Two footmen stood beside the door and a young groom stood at the ready to take whatever mode of transportation one arrived in off to the stables that were nestled deep in the nearby woods, out of sight of prying eyes.

Nicola closed her eyes and inhaled deeply. "I smell apple tarts."

John laughed. "I'll order us a dozen."

Within moments, the innkeeper, a plump, bright-eyed woman who could only be Sammy Fraser's sister, rushed forward to greet them. Indeed, she had the stout look of Sammy, and her round, dark eyes took everything in with avid interest. Her hair was a flaming red, no doubt enhanced by a good dose of henna dye. She cast them both speculative looks, her gaze ultimately resting on John with obvious approval. "Ye don't look like my usual guests. What brings ye here, m'lord?"

Of course, John could never be mistaken for anything other than a nobleman. He commanded authority and respect, even after days on the run, unwashed, sporting a rough growth of beard, fatigued and unkempt. Nothing could diminish his air of strength and power, or his appeal.

Nicola did not dare think about what she must look like to Adela Fraser. A half-starved rabbit, perhaps. She did not look fine enough to be John's paramour or even fine enough to pass for one of his servants.

"My wife and I ran into a spot of trouble. Your brother, Sammy, helped us out."

Her dark red eyebrows shot up at the mention of her brother. "That scoundrel? What did he steal from ye?"

"My diamond locket," Nicola said.

"Och, ye poor lass. That wretch! Did he tell ye that he'd share it with me if I gave you food and lodgings for the night?" She gave a hearty laugh when Nicola nodded. "He won't share, you know. That isn't Sammy's way."

"He won't?" She turned to John in panic.

He took her hand in his and rubbed his thumb along her palm to calm her.

She was exhausted and hungry, not to mention too filthy to be permitted to stand in the entry hall of this charming inn. "John..."

"We'll pay our way, Miss Fraser. I always pay my debts. I don't care about my comfort, but my wife needs to rest." He took out the last of their funds and was about to hand it to Sammy's sister, but the woman stayed his hand.

"Ye're not the sort of clientele I usually get, m'lord." She cast Nicola a surprisingly tender smile. "I'll not be tossing ye out, m'lovey. It's refreshing to see a young couple in love. Married to each other, no less."

She turned to John. "Nor will I take what is obviously the last of yer funds, though I have no doubt ye're a man of means as well as a man of honor and would repay me. It isn't yer blunt I want. My brother is a wretched scoundrel. No scruples whatsoever. I'll make him pay up."

As relief washed over her, Nicola felt herself about to turn into a watering pot. Oh, dear. She was never this weepy in all her life. Hunger and exhaustion, not to mention running for one's life, must have done this to her.

She and John followed Sammy's sister as she led the way to an elegantly appointed bedchamber that looked like heaven to her. A large, four poster bed with a red satin coverlet and a dozen pillows decorating the headboard dominated the room. A cozy settee stood in front of the hearth, and there was a small table with two cushioned chairs by the window.

Within moments, a footman came in to light a fire in the hearth. More servants entered carrying a tub and pails of heated water, scented soaps, a hairbrush, and a robe for her.

Nicola wanted to fling off her clothes and jump into the water. Her desire must have shown, for both John and Sammy's sister looked at her and laughed. "I'll leave ye in peace in a moment, lovey. Yer husband said ye enjoyed the scent of my apple tarts. My butler will bring some in along with a pot of tea for ye. It isn't the usual request. Most of my guests ask for Sammy's whisky, but I don't think it's wise for a lass in yer condition."

Nicola pinched her lips together in a forced smile. Why did everyone so easily believe she was with child? John must have whispered in the woman's ear. That she had accepted his remark without question was a bit unsettling.

After the tea and light repast had been delivered, Nicola turned to John and cast him a smile. "Our own little corner of paradise."

He looked pained and uncomfortable. "I'll check on Valor while you bathe."

"No, John." She paled at the thought of his leaving her. "Don't go."

He regarded her, confused. "I'll only be at the stables. I won't be far, nor will I stay there very long. I can't just... I don't want to make you feel uncomfortable while you undress."

She shook her head and gave a mirthless laugh. "Everyone believes we're married and I'm carrying your child. We've slept together in Maeve's bed."

"Fully clothed."

She nodded. "The point is, we've been together ever since we went on the run, our bodies in constant contact, our hearts attuned to the beat of each other's heart. You've killed to protect me." She sank onto the settee and gazed into the fire. "John, my soul has been laid bare to you. I have nothing to hide from you. Not now, not ever."

His groan sounded pained as he came to her side and knelt

beside her. "So be it," he said, his voice a husky rumble that sent tingles shooting through her body. He reached out to slip the shawl off her shoulders, his hands caressing her as he removed it.

Wordlessly, he nudged her to her feet and began to unlace the ties of her woolen gown. She closed her eyes as more tingles shot through her body when he began to lift the gown off her. His movements were slow and sensual, his big hands sliding along her legs as he grasped the hem of her gown to draw it up.

Suddenly, he stilled. Releasing the fabric, he gave a soft curse and took a step back. "Nicola, I have something important to tell you."

She opened her eyes, now curious to hear whatever it was he wanted to confess. He began to pace in front of her. He looked uncertain and pained. She'd never seen John look anything but sure of himself and in full command of his feelings. "You can tell me anything. Surely, you must know that by now."

He stopped pacing and returned to her side, his grip tightening on her shoulders. He released a long, deep breath. "Nicola, we're married."

She laughed and shook her head. "I know that's the story we're telling everyone. I'm also carrying your child. Never say you are starting to believe the lies?"

"It isn't a lie. We're married."

She frowned at him. "Stop saying that."

"We're married," he insisted. "The ceremonial declaration I had you make in front of Sammy and his family… well, we're in Scotland now… and what I had you recite is the equivalent of a marriage vow. When I took your hand in mine and recited those words, then had you do the same… that was a wedding ceremony. Our wedding. You're now my wife under Scottish law. But there's a catch."

The blood drained from her face and she suddenly felt dizzy. Angry, too. She'd wished to marry John. Her dreams had been filled with the magic of this moment ever since she'd first met him. But to have it stolen from her, taken from her like a thief in the night. To exchange vows with the man she'd always loved and not realize this is what she was doing? "What? Are you jesting?"

Theirs was a marriage of necessity. A marriage based on a lie.

"It's real. At least for the year. If we consummate—"

She gasped.

"If we consummate our vows, then we're married for life."

Her heart shot into her throat and lodged there painfully. She wanted to speak, but had trouble finding her voice. "Are you saying that I've trapped you into marriage?"

He gave an incredulous laugh. "You? I'm the one who trapped *you*. I've robbed you of the courtship you deserve. I've stolen the innocence and romance. But I want you to understand that I had no choice. Sammy was going to claim you for one of his sons unless I proved to him that we were wed."

"So you sacrificed yourself to protect me." She nodded. "And you're hoping that we can quietly end this once we return to London. I understand. I won't make it difficult for you."

Nor would she make matters worse by crying. She needed to be strong, to deny that her breaths were short and that her heart was as shattered as her dreams. So why was he scowling at her? "Nicola, you don't understand."

"Yes. Yes, I do. You only married me to protect me because that's what you always feel compelled to do. Once we're safely back in London and Somersby is no longer a threat, you'll expect to have your freedom back. I assure you, I won't give you a problem." Her brother might challenge him to a duel. Pistols at dawn. But she would make Julian see reason. After all, she'd brought this on herself. She was the one who'd allowed Somersby to court her and then she'd stolen his secret book.

John had merely done what he needed to save her life.

"Damn it, Nicola. When you put it that way…"

"How else must it be stated? I don't see you on your knees, declaring your undying love for me. What I see is a man trying to squirm out of a noose. And I'm trying to assure you that I will never tighten that noose around your neck. You'll have your precious freedom. I'll sign whatever document will grant you that." She frowned at him. "So why are you still staring at me with eyes blazing?"

Suddenly, it all felt too much.

She'd opened her heart to this man and all he could say was that their marriage was a sham. All he could do was look at her with rage and turmoil in his eyes.

Truly, what more did he want from her? The answer was so easy, all he had to say was *I want you, Nicola. I want you.* That's all she needed to hear from him. She wasn't asking for an *I love you.* But to admit even the slightest need for her seemed overwhelming to him.

She stormed over to the tub and began to undress, no longer caring whether he watched with eyes popping wide or yawned and turned away. He could do—or not do—whatever he wished. "I will not interfere with your hopes and dreams, John. What more do you want from me?"

# CHAPTER 10

"NOTHING," JOHN SAID, his voice raw and strained, wanting to press his lips to hers with a sweet, crushing urgency. "I want nothing from you. Just wanted to be clear about our… situation."

Nicola looked up at him, her eyes blazing. "You have been. Abundantly clear. Don't let me delay you." She turned away, sat down on a stool beside the tub, and began to roll the stockings off her legs. Long, exquisitely shaped legs.

John saw that her hands were shaking. Yet, she'd never let on. That was Nicola, too proud ever to admit she was hurt and vulnerable.

Her lips and chin were quivering.

He started toward her, wanting to take her into his arms. He loved how perfectly she fit in them. But he held back, for he wasn't in control of his feelings and was not certain where it might lead. "Nicola—"

"Go check on Valor." She refused to look at him. Instead, she stared at her stockings with enough intensity to bore a hole in them. "I'll latch the door after you've gone. Give me twenty minutes to bathe and then I'll let you back in. Take a tart with you if you're hungry. Take all the tarts you want. Make love to as many of them as your heart desires. That's what men do, don't they? Have their fill and walk away?"

Obviously, they were no longer talking about pies. "Nicola—"

"Just go, John. You needn't say anything more to me. I'd like to get into the tub while the water's still warm."

He could have cleared up the misunderstanding with ease. One kiss. One confession of love. Kissing her on Captain Grant's boat had been a mistake. Kissing her again would change everything.

He had murderers to hunt down. He still sought vengeance for his family.

He wasn't ready for his life to change.

Not that he had doubts about Nicola. Any doubts were about himself. Could he give up his quest?

His thirst for revenge defined him. It's what had turned him into one of the Crown's most effective agents. It's what had turned his heart to stone.

He left their quarters, waited to hear Nicola latch the door after him, and then took a quick walk around the inn. He scouted the common rooms and then the grounds, taking in the best routes of escape should the need arise. He walked to the stable and took note of several carriages and horses other than this own.

"M'lord, ye needn't worry about yer horse," the young groom said. "I've fed 'im and groomed 'im."

The lad appeared to have a natural love of animals. John had seen it in the way he'd handled Valor when they'd first arrived. "I have no doubt. But I rode him a long way and thought I'd bring him a treat." He'd picked up an apple that had fallen off one of the trees he'd passed along the path and now handed it over. "Care to feed him?"

"Thank you, m'lord!" The boy nodded and took off with it to Valor's stall. "Look what I have for ye," he cooed to John's massive beast and continued to stroke and compliment him while feeding him the apple. "Ye're the finest horse I've ever seen. Perhaps the finest in all of Scotland. But ye know it, don't ye?"

As though in response, Valor gently nudged the boy's shoulder. "Och," he said with a genuinely merry laugh, "ye do know it. No humbleness in ye, is there? Ye know ye're the best."

John could not recall when he had ever felt such youthful pleasure. It seemed odd that such innocence should flourish at this inn where everyone who stayed here harbored secrets and deceptions.

He returned to the quarters he shared with Nicola a short while later. She'd finished her bath and was now wrapped in the slightly too big robe that Adela Fraser had provided to her. She'd brushed out her wet hair so that it fell down her back in a glorious, red wave. He caught the scent of the lavender soap she'd used on her body. The fragrance lingered in the air and blended with the steam off the bath water and the smoke of the hickory wood fire.

By the open book of accounts on the table, he realized she had been studying its contents while waiting for his return. "The bath water is still warm, John."

She looked delectable.

He wanted to strip her out of her robe and haul her into the tub with him. He'd left to cool his ardor, but he'd no sooner taken a step into the room than it was back with full force. The thought of Nicola's silky, pink skin, still damp from its earlier washing, had him hot and aching.

He wanted to lift her into his arms and carry her to bed.

He would have done it, but he smelled worse than an unkempt stable, certainly worse than Sammy Fraser or his boys. He removed his jacket and shirt, and was about to toss them onto the settee when Nicola cleared her throat. He'd thought she'd gone back to deciphering Somersby's book. But she must have been slipping him glances whenever his back was turned. "Are you still angry with me?" He wouldn't have blamed her if she was.

"No."

He sank onto the settee beside the clothing he'd just removed and tugged off his boots. He wasn't certain he believed her, but anything was better than resuming that painful discussion and hurting her feelings again. He was glad that she'd distracted herself by attempting to decipher the book. "Find anything interesting in there?"

She nodded. "Actually, I think I did. These entries are written in some sort of code. That's why I couldn't make sense of them when we were sifting through the pages last night. So we just need to figure out what each letter represents and then we'll be able to read the words."

"I thought as much. Close your eyes."

"Why?"

"I'm about to take off my breeches. Not that I mind your looking at me, but I felt I ought to give you fair warning."

Her cheeks turned to crimson flames. "Um… oh… yes, I see. I'll shade my eyes and concentrate on this cipher."

"You do that." He shed the last of his clothes and sank into the tub with an *aaah*. The water had cooled, but was still warm enough to soothe the ache in his bones. Not that he was very sore, for he was used to riding over long distances. In truth, the only part of him that ached was his heart.

What was he going to do about Nicola?

He shook out of the thought and concentrated on washing the dirt off his body. Since they had only the one tub, and he had no wish to impose further on Adela's generosity by demanding a fresh bath be brought in, he'd used the same water that Nicola had rinsed in. It was fairly clean. And there was a full pail of fresh water beside the tub that he now used to wash his hair.

Their clothes had absorbed most of the road dust, and although he hated to leave them without clothing even for a few minutes, he decided to ring for a servant to take them for a quick cleaning. "Ah, Adela provided sandalwood for me. I was afraid I'd be forced to use one of your scented soaps. Not that I would mind smelling like a rose. Or a lavender cake."

"I used the lavender."

"I know," he said while scrubbing himself down. "I caught the scent of it on your skin when I walked in."

"It's divine, isn't it?" She glanced at him, realized he was naked in the tub, and hastily looked away.

He finished washing his hair and then ran his fingers through it to brush it off his face. Sparing a look at Nicola to be sure she wasn't peeking, he climbed out of the tub and dried himself off with one of the large cloths Adela had directed the servants to bring in along with the other comforts.

The woman knew her clientele and made certain to anticipate their every need.

He wrapped the cloth securely around his waist and then

strode to the bellpull to summon a servant. A young woman promptly arrived at their door. John gave her their clothing. "See that they're freshened and brought back to us within the hour."

She bobbed a curtsy. "Yes, m'lord."

He closed the door and turned back to Nicola.

She had the prettiest blush on her cheeks, and even from across the room, he could see that the pulse at the base of her throat was madly throbbing.

He strode to her side and pulled out the chair next to hers, taking a moment to serve himself a tart and pour himself a cup of tea before speaking. "Have you made any progress with these ciphers?"

Nicola was fidgeting like a ferret in her chair. "No. John, must you sit so close to me?"

He arched an eyebrow. "How am I to look at the book if I sit across the table from you?"

"You're *naked.*"

He glanced down at the drying cloth that was covering all of him below his waist. "Unless you've suddenly developed the ability to see through fabric, I would say that I'm as well covered as you are."

"Which is hardly at all."

He ran a hand through his hair. Less than an hour ago, she was ready to bare her heart and body to him. He supposed he'd hurt her very badly, allowing her to believe that this would not be a forever marriage.

Their marital state would have to be permanent. Her family would never allow him to walk away at the end of the handfasting period. Nor could the scandal of these days and nights spent together ever be taken back. It did not matter that they were running for their lives. It did not matter that he'd given her no more than a kiss up to now.

Her family would insist on their remaining married for that kiss alone. He glanced at Nicola, who was still fidgeting and whose pulse at her throat was still throbbing.

He needed to make matters right.

He took one of her small hands in both of his, surprising her with his touch. "I know we'd both rather avoid this topic, but I don't see how we can. Nicola, let's start this conversation again."

She eyed him suspiciously, but did not attempt to draw her hand away. "Which conversation?"

"The one where I left you believing that our marriage would come to an end once Somersby was brought into custody."

She emitted a ragged breath. "What are you saying? That it won't end?"

He stroked his thumb along her palm, loving the softness of her skin. "Not unless you want it to. I won't end it. I have no desire to end it."

"You don't?" She met his gaze and held it for an endless moment. "For my sake or for yours?"

"Does it matter?"

"Yes, it matters very much to me."

He sighed. "For both our sakes then. This Scottish marriage won't be recognized in England, but that makes it no less valid. I'll obtain a special license once we cross into England. We'll be properly married under English law as soon as possible after that."

"Wait, are you saying that you won't leave me behind in Edinburgh?" Her eyes widened in surprise as the realization sank in.

"I've decided not to."

"What changed your mind?"

A muscle twitched in his jaw. "Many reasons."

How could he explain these feelings roiling inside of him without baring his own heart and soul? Although it had been his original plan to deposit her with the regimental commander, he now knew that she would never be safe until Somersby and his operation was destroyed. That vile scum would come after her no matter how many soldiers were guarding her, no matter how thick the walls in the regimental garrison.

If Somersby was so obsessed with doing harm to someone in Nicola's family and using her to accomplish it—and if it was a case of vengeance, John knew all too well how strong the tug of that could be—then Somersby's compulsion might send him after

Nicola first. Not the book of accounts.

"Name one reason for your change of heart," Nicola said, interrupting his thoughts.

"You're mine to protect. It was a mistake on my part to believe that you'd be safer without me." Indeed, since nobody understood hatred and revenge better than he did, there was no one better able to protect Nicola than him.

She cast him a hesitant smile. "Name another reason, John."

"I won't have you shamed or made the subject of scandal. You're my wife and I mean to ensure you'll have the respect you deserve. And before you mouth off to me, which you will, because that's what you do," he continued with a grin, "I—"

"John!"

"I don't mind that you're not meek or biddable. If I wanted that, I could have chosen a wife from a dozen brainless debutantes who cared not a whit for me, but fancied my title. So, to be clear about who I want and what I want... it's you. Forever."

"Forever," she said in a whisper and released her breath in a frail shudder. But her lips began to twitch and tip upward in an almost smile. "That's quite the ardent confession. My head is spinning. I think I might swoon."

He winced. "I'm hardly one of those romantic poets who happen to be all the rage in London at the moment."

"No, not even close." She finally did smile, although hesitantly. "Thank you, John."

He did not deserve her gratitude. She was the one who was saving him from a life of angry solitude. She was the one who gave him hope that his life might become something more than a quest for revenge.

He released her hand to wolf down the last of the light repast sitting on a tray on the table. Nicola had eaten a little, probably not enough. He'd order a full supper brought to them later tonight.

He then drank his cup of tea, slogging it back as though it were a pint of ale. "Let's have a closer look at those pages. How are you at breaking codes?"

"I don't know. I've never tried before." But to someone with a mind as agile as Nicola's, he had no doubt she'd catch on quickly. "But before we start, there's something I must ask."

He nodded. "Go on."

"I couldn't help but notice the scars on your back. How did you get them? They look old."

"It doesn't matter. They aren't important."

Nicola must have caught the angry rise in his voice. She edged back in her chair, more irritated with him than intimidated by his scowl. "Not important? Something so trivial, you've forgotten all about it? I suppose those scars are what turned you into the jovial, outgoing man you are today. A Johnny-good-times. Always laughing. Always filled with good cheer for one and all."

"It's none of your business, Nicola."

She shook her head and sighed. "Fine. You'll tell me when you feel the time is right. Perhaps later this evening, after you take me to bed and we perform our expected mating dance, spawning like frenzied salmon in—"

"Bollocks! Who puts these ideas into your head?" He rose and strode across the room to stand before the fire blazing in the hearth. That's how hot his anger burned for those who had destroyed his family. But it was also how hot his desire burned for Nicola.

The blasted girl had a rapier-sharp mind and just as sharp a tongue. He liked that about her, but at times—such as now—he wished she was a simpleton. Lord, she knew just how to rile him. He wanted to be angry with her, but instead, he threw his head back and laughed. "Spawning like salmon? Where did you hear such nonsense?"

"In one of those scandalous novels no innocent young woman is ever supposed to read. But I think the author misused the term. Spawning one's eggs is what happens to a female fish after the act of... you know."

"The frenzied mating."

She nodded. "You do want that, don't you, John? I mean, if we're to have a real marriage. Is that what you had in mind when agreeing to a forever union between us? Because if it isn't, then perhaps we ought to rethink the matter."

He tossed another log onto the fire and watched the flames intensify. "No need to rethink. I'm… bollocks. I'm all in."

# CHAPTER 11

NICOLA WASN'T CERTAIN how she went from running for her life to jumping into bed with the one man she'd loved all her life. John had just told her that he was not going to end their Scottish marriage, that he was going to make it official as soon as they reached England. He was keeping her with him all the way to London, and keeping her with him forever afterward.

Before this night was through, he was going to take her innocence. At least, she hoped this is what he intended. For now, they were concentrating on the entries in the ledger and trying to decipher their meaning. Some were obviously numbers representing amounts paid or amounts owed. But the portions describing plans or listing names of buyers and shippers and goods transported were in an alphabetic code that made no sense. "Where are we to start, John?"

She tried to concentrate on the pages and not his body leaning so close to hers that she caught the scent of sandalwood on his golden skin. Although they were not touching, she felt a delicious heat radiating off him. "We look for words that seem to be repeating. Like these." He pointed to several on the page that used the same letters. "These are four letters long. Maybe they represent the word 'lord' since most of the buyers of contraband merchandise are likely to be wealthy individuals who demand quality goods and don't care if there is a war going on or that those goods must be smuggled into England."

Nicola pointed to the sheet of parchment she'd asked the maid to fetch for her and nodded. "Oh, I see. So once we're certain those ciphers represent L-O-R-D, then we can go through the page and figure out the rest of the ciphers. We can set up a coding chart on this blank paper. What if the sentences are written in French?"

John gave a snorting laugh. "Somersby spent his university days drinking and womanizing. His father had to step in to keep him from being tossed out of Oxford on his ear. I doubt he'll be so clever as to use a foreign language."

"Very well. I suppose it will become obvious to us soon enough." She set the book sideways so that they could both have a clear view of the pages. "Let me see if I can figure out this page. You work on the other page. This is so interesting." Almost interesting enough to make her forget that a barely clad John, his muscled shoulders and broad chest spiking her heartbeat to dangerous proportions, was seated within a hair's breadth of her.

John smiled at her, giving her one of the softest smiles she'd ever seen on him. His rare smiles were often polite and forced, and they looked more pained than heartfelt. But this one was different. It was a let-down-all-defenses smile that warmed her heart as nothing else could.

He arched an eyebrow. "You are looking at me as though I'm a strawberry cake topped with sweet cream."

"I can't help it. You're handsome and naked and seated so close to me that I can feel the little fuzzy hairs on your arm tickle along my skin. I'm washed and well-fed and working on something important for the Crown. This is my idea of heaven. If it weren't for a crazed beast ransacking the Highlands in search of us, I think this would count as one of the happiest days of my life. It will count as the happiest if you were to take me to that bed," she said, glancing at the large four-poster situated right behind her.

"If?" His smile turned appealingly wicked.

She cleared her throat and nodded. "I did not wish to presume that you would… you know."

"Frenzied mating?"

She laughed. "Yes, you wretch."

He cupped her chin and gave it a tweak. "Let's get back to

deciphering these pages."

Heat shot into her cheeks. "Of course, that's far more important. And there's no rush for the other *thing*, nor must we even think of doing such a *thing* when this is far more…"

"Important?"

She nodded vehemently. "I'm sorry that I got distracted. I suppose I'll never make a good agent for the Crown."

"Nicola, you're about to blow apart a smuggling operation that extends throughout Europe. I believe the culprits behind this scheme are using the proceeds from these smuggled goods to incite a rebellion that threatens the existence of the monarchy. Somersby is involved up to his eyeballs. Overthrow of the monarchy is really what he's interested in accomplishing. The smuggling operation is only a small part of it."

"It is?"

He nodded. "He means to bring down the king and turn England over to French control. Likely, he will then betray the French and keep England for himself, for he has the highest opinion of himself. But he made the unfortunate mistake of bringing you into his web of schemes. I don't know who in your family he means to destroy, but I have no doubt he is regretting his plan."

"I hope so."

"I know he is, for his means of acquiring the wealth and weaponry to accomplish his grand scheme is written down in this little book. It is in my hands because of you." He cast her an affectionate smile. "You will be a legend among the agents of the Crown, assuming we manage to decipher it. I know we will."

"A legend? John, that's so exciting. You're used to being important and serving a vital purpose, but I'm not. Women are often relegated to the home, left to tend to the household and the children. Not that those aren't important functions, but this… this is wonderful." She took a deep breath as she glanced at the page before her and a name suddenly leaped into her mind. "Look! There's an O, and this must be an apostrophe. And these are the rest of the letters except for the last, D-O-O-L. This name must be O'Doole. So we now have the E as well."

"Nicely done. And this name must be Oliver. We now have the I and the V."

She pursed her lips. "This isn't very hard."

"Somersby isn't very smart. But he's hungry for power. I don't think this cipher was ever intended to be difficult to break. He merely intended that anyone looking over his shoulder at a page would not be able to read it. He knows we'll figure out what he's written down. That's why he's so desperate to stop us."

"Do you think we'll find any indication of who in my family he wants to destroy?"

He frowned. "I hope so, but not likely. So far, this looks to be an account of his sales and purchases and contacts. Some of these pages must contain names of rebels and weapons suppliers. I'm sure one of those men, once they're rounded up by the king's guard, will talk in exchange for leniency. They might give us a clue as to Somersby's hatred for your family."

"I hope so."

They continued working side by side late into the evening. One of Adela's maids delivered a hearty supper for them. They broke away from their deciphering long enough to dine quietly in front of the fire. John had donned his trousers when they, along with all their clothes, were returned to them, freshened and pressed and the dirt beaten out of them.

Nicola remained in her robe, finding it quite comfortable and not looking forward to putting on her itchy, woolen traveling gown just yet. John did not bother to don his shirt. The room was warm and she'd already seen and commented on his scars and those bruises from his encounter with Somersby's ruffians. So there was no reason to hide them from her.

They'd resumed their decoding after supper, but when Nicola rubbed her eyes and yawned, John shut the book and placed it back in his pouch which was now hanging over the footboard. She understood that he wanted to keep it near while they slept. He also kept his knife, pistol, and rifle close. "Let's get some rest. I'd like to be on the road before sunrise."

She yawned again and nodded. "I think we've accomplished a fine day's work, don't you?"

"Yes, brat. An excellent day's work." He took her hand and led her to the bed, but John did not climb in beside her. He grabbed a few pillows and one of the coverlets, obviously intending to make a pallet for himself beside the fire.

Nicola scrambled out of bed and grabbed two pillows as well.

He eyed her quizzically. "What are you doing?"

"Sleeping wherever you sleep."

"Nicola—"

"I thought we had this conversation. If I'm to be your forever wife, then I want the benefits that come with it."

His chuckle ended in a groan. "I wanted us to get some rest tonight, for we have a long ride ahead of us."

"All the more reason to settle comfortably in that bed."

"If I'm in it with you, neither of us will get any sleep," he said with a husky timbre to his voice that shot tingles through her body.

Her eyes rounded in surprise. "We won't?"

He grinned. "Not a single hour."

"I'm not certain what you mean by that, but if your intentions are as wicked as those of the men in the scandalous books I've been reading, then I don't think I'll mind not sleeping a wink. Are you suggesting that I am irresistible to you?"

He sighed as he ran his fingers through his hair in obvious consternation. "Lord, you're a brat. Go back to bed."

"Not without you."

He groaned lightly. "Are you sure you're not one of Napoleon's agents sent here to plague me? Very well, I'll join you in a moment. You do realize that this marriage isn't proper under English law."

She tossed the pillows back on the bed and hopped on the mattress. "We're in Scotland now. I am your wife under Scottish law. There is a possibility we'll both be dead by tomorrow. I am not going to worry about propriety."

"Bollocks, Nicola. I'm going to have a talk with your brother when we reach London. He and your uncle have given you far too much independence."

She ignored his complaint and settled herself under the covers, determined to allow whatever might happen between them. The men in the stories she'd read seemed to be ruled by lust, but that lust also seemed to be spent rather quickly in the heat of satisfying themselves. Indeed, the act of love did not appear to be particularly comfortable or romantic, just fiery and fast.

Yet, it was precisely the wild intensity of it that intrigued her.

She plumped two pillows under her head and sank back against them, intending to close her eyes for just a moment. Would John be tempted? She meant to remain awake to find out, but her eyelids suddenly felt like leaden weights and within moments, she fell sound asleep.

JOHN WAS GOING to wait to the count of twenty before daring to turn back to look at Nicola. He did not think he could resist her, but running for their lives was no jest. They needed all the rest they could get, for they weren't likely to find such comfortable lodgings anywhere else along their journey. He had only counted to twelve before he heard her even breaths and soft snores.

"That didn't take long," he said in a whisper, although he was not surprised. Nicola was not used to the mountain chill or riding hard all day. Nor was she used to her life being threatened. The sight of Somersby's men lying dead at her feet, their blood spilled on the ground, must have frightened the wits out of her.

Also, he doubted she'd slept comfortably in Maeve's bed. It had been too small for both of them to fit. Even if it had been as big and soft as his enormous bed at Bainbridge Hall, her sleep would have been fitful. Visions of death and threats from Somersby's men would interfere with anyone's peaceful rest.

Somersby's men had meant to kill Maeve, Sammy, and his boys.

Those men also intended to kill Nicola.

Although she'd tried to hide it, he knew that she'd fretted about last night's incident all day long to the point of exhausting herself with worry.

He strode to the bed and looked down upon Nicola. The sleep of innocence. He felt a tug to his heart. She looked irresistible, curled like a kitten under the coverlet, only the auburn curls at the top of her head showing. He eased the cover down just the littlest bit so that her nose and mouth were no longer hidden.

"Sweet dreams, brat." He eased down beside her and planted a soft kiss on her forehead. He considered setting up a pallet once more by the fire, but changed his mind. He was exhausted, too. He needed a good night's sleep.

Unfortunately, it was something he rarely accomplished.

He stretched out beside Nicola and drew her body against his, telling himself it was for her comfort when, in truth, it was more for his. There was something oddly healing about having her beside him, her sweet, warm body curled against him.

She looked as innocent as an angel when asleep.

However, he liked that she was a hellion when awake. No helpless, frightened creature. Not like his mother. He cursed silently. He was not going to have that dream tonight, not while lying beside Nicola.

But he felt the darkness coming on the moment his eyes closed, that rage borne of frustration and terror. He fought against it, but it swamped his body as his deepening sleep began to tear down all of his defenses. The wall he maintained around his heart crumbled. *Grab the pistol. Shoot their leader.* That's what he remembered calling out to his mother when he was a little boy and they'd been attacked. *Grab the pistol.*

Even at that young age, he'd understood. Shoot the leader. The others would flee.

But his mother had been frozen in fear, leaving it to him to crawl across the room and pick up the pistol to fire at the big man who was beating and kicking his father even as he collapsed to the ground. John had meant to fire at the man's chest, but the pistol recoiled in his little hands and the shot went wide.

"John, is something wrong?" Nicola asked in a sleepy murmur, her caring voice penetrating his senses.

But thoughts of his past now had him by the throat. He tried not to think of that night, did not want to think of his father unconscious and bleeding, or his mother cowering in a corner and doing nothing to save herself. Nor did she do anything to save him, her only child.

It was left to him to try to save her, but he was a weaponless, six-year-old child and could do little to protect those he loved. He'd tried to stop the beast when he'd turned on his mother, but he had no way to reload the pistol.

*Fight.*

*Fight for your life.*

But his mother had merely buried her face in her hands and cried. She'd died quickly, putting up no resistance. John remembered the beast's hideous laughter filling the room as he'd then turned to John. He was waving a long, bloodied knife in front of him, his voice cruel when he spoke. *You'll be next, you filthy English spawn.*

He was little and quick, managing to slip between the beast's legs and escape out a window. The window had shattered atop him as the beast and his men fired shots at him. He'd run for his life, paying no heed to the shards of glass embedded in his skin. A hot, metallic ball tore through the fleshy part of his arm.

*You won't ever catch me.*

He'd ignored his wounds and crawled to his hiding spot in an ancient cistern that stood beside the ambassador's house. Only then did he give in to the pain and cry.

"John, please." He recognized Nicola's voice and felt her hands on his shoulders, gently shaking him.

He rolled onto his back, his forehead dripping with sweat and his heart pounding a hole in his chest. "Hell, sorry." He took her soft hands in one of his. "Did I hurt you?"

He worried that he'd lashed out and accidentally struck her. "No, John. But your body tensed and then you suddenly jerked and cried out. Are you all right?" She put her ear to his chest and hugged him. "Your heart's beating so fast."

He wrapped his arms around her and held her close. The softness of her body and the lavender scent of her skin now filled his senses with an overwhelming yearning. "I... it'll calm down." He didn't know what else to say. "Go back to sleep, Nicola. It's hours yet before dawn."

"Does this nightmare haunt you every night?"

He groaned softly. This was Nicola. Of course, she was not going to let the matter drop. "It doesn't matter."

"Of course, it does." She ran her hand across his shoulder. "Your skin is damp. I can see beads of sweat on your forehead."

He closed his eyes a moment and swallowed hard. "I'm not talking about it."

She sighed. "Not now, anyway."

"Not ever." Although his eyes were still closed, he felt her defiant scowl upon him. "I mean it, Nicola. Not. Ever."

She said nothing, merely curled against him, one arm across his chest and her head nestled against his shoulder. He knew that she was not going to give up until she had her answers, for that was Nicola's way. It was part of what he found irritating about her and what he also loved most about her. She fought for those she loved. She did not shrink back in fear. "Please let me in, John. I'll never hurt you."

"I know, brat." He ran his fingers through the silken waves of her unbound hair. Let her in? She was so deeply in his heart it scared him, and he was scared of nothing.

Perhaps not nothing.

He was scared of needing her.

He was scared of losing her.

He was scared of losing his whole heart to her.

# CHAPTER 12

NICOLA AWOKE SHORTLY before dawn, but dared not stir while still in John's arms. His muscled strength surrounded her in a delicious blanket of heat. His skin was warm despite the fire dying out in the hearth. While she needed to wrap herself against him to ward off the morning chill, he seemed unaffected by it. "John, are you awake?" she asked in a whisper.

She stifled her disappointment when he did not respond. In truth, she was also disappointed in not experiencing the pleasures of the marriage bed. She'd wanted her night of passion, but would never mention it to John. He had spent the night battling his inner demons and did not need her piling on more worries.

What had tormented him so badly last night?

For his sake, she needed to find out. What he'd experienced was no mere bad dream. This was a night terror that gripped him often. Ever since he was a boy? She knew he was an orphan raised by his aunt and uncle, the then Earl of Bainbridge. John had assumed the title upon the older man's death.

That was all she knew about his past.

How did he come to be an orphan? He had to confide in her, not to satisfy her curiosity, but to heal his pain. If he ever hoped to find happiness—and John clearly was not a happy man—he needed to share the overwhelming burden he carried in his heart before it consumed him. It mattered not that he was now a wealthy earl. This had nothing to do with wealth or title. It had everything to do with power, a dark and controlling one that had him caught like a fish on a hook.

It also had to do with his lack of power at one time, for it was his sense of helplessness that brought on those nightly terrors. From the few words he'd spoken, she gathered that his parents had died violent deaths and he'd been unable to save them. But he'd been a mere child when they'd died. He couldn't possibly have had the strength to save them at so young an age.

But this was John.

A man with an ingrained need to protect those he loved.

He had been born a fighter. His need to fight and protect explained why he was always wary and on the alert. He needed to save the royal family. He needed to save her. It wasn't merely a matter of duty. It was who he was.

Hunter. Predator. Protector.

Why hadn't her brother ever mentioned John's past to her? Did Julian even know? Or had John managed to hide his pain from everyone?

The scars she'd seen on his back were old, perhaps from childhood.

He must have carried this torment all his life and it had shaped him into the man he was today, one of the top agents of the Crown. He was also a man who hid his feelings, who allowed no one close to him. But she was in his bed now and had no intention of ever sleeping apart from him again.

"Nicola, stop wriggling."

"I'm sorry. Did I wake you?" She propped on one elbow for a better look at him. Oh, he looked so handsome even with the light stubble of a beard and the sleepy look in his eyes. Those entrancing gray-green orbs were now open and staring back at her.

He laughed softly and reached out to brush back a wayward curl on her forehead. "No. We have to get up soon anyway."

She nodded and collapsed back onto her pillow with a groan. "Is it awful for me to wish for more time here?"

He placed his hands behind his head and stared up at the ceiling. "Not at all."

"Our time here was a little moment of heaven, wasn't it?"

He frowned lightly, still looking upward and not at her. "Not quite heaven. I must have tossed and turned most of the night."

She sighed. "I was worried about you, John."

"I know. This is what my nights are, Nicola. I don't sleep well, as you've now found out. You'll have your separate quarters once we're back in London and Somersby is dealt with."

"Why would I want separate quarters? I don't ever wish to sleep apart from you."

He turned to look at her askance. "I kept you up most of the night."

"John, sleeping next to you is wonderful. You held me in your arms."

"When I wasn't thrashing about," he said, sounding disgusted with himself.

"I think that will subside in time. You'll grow used to having me next to you in your bed. Hopefully, you'll feel comforted by it." He frowned at first, but after a moment, his lips turned upward in a devastatingly appealing smile. It emboldened her. "Perhaps tonight you'll keep me up under more pleasant circumstances. You still owe me a night of... you know."

He laughed softly. "Frenzied mating? It doesn't have to happen only at night. Coupling can occur at any time of the day."

"Such as early morning?" She sighed when he failed to respond to her obvious proposition. "I suppose that means 'no.' Very well, if I'm not to experience passionate pleasure, I may as well fall back to sleep. But I want you to know that I am quite well rested and don't need to fall back to—"

He rolled her under him in one swift motion. "Nicola, stop talking. Lord, you're a brat." Then his mouth descended on hers with unexpected ardor, his lips warm and gentle as they pressed against her own. She felt the exquisite weight of his muscled body atop her, although he was careful to prop himself on his elbows so as not to bring his full heft down on her.

Not that she would have minded.

She loved his size and brawn. Their intimacy felt divine. "John, make me yours forever. I want to be your wife in every sense."

He kissed her again, this time plundering her mouth with a

possessive hunger, and at the same time, his hands worked to strip her out of her robe. She wore nothing now, hid nothing from his view.

He eased back and lifted his head to look at her. "Nicola, you're beautiful." His voice was raw and his smile devastatingly tender.

He kissed her again, the press of his mouth upon hers now feeling more urgent. She was feeling a similar urgency and ran her hands along his golden skin, slid them over his taut, muscled body.

Her heart began to race, not only out of desire—blessed saints, she felt so much love for this man—but also out of uncertainty. What was she supposed to do?

He seemed to understand her concern. "Just close your eyes and feel. Don't hold back."

His big, rough hands then began to stroke along her body, starting little fires wherever he touched. He cupped her breast and ran his thumb across its tip, evoking a gasp from her at the sudden, pleasurable sensation.

"So beautiful," he whispered and closed his mouth over her breast. She gasped again. In truth, she was having trouble catching her breath as he began to suckle and swirl his tongue in languid strokes across the tip of it, soon followed by intensifying flicks.

"John!" Mother in heaven, she felt everything. How could she possibly hold back when every pulse in her body was throbbing and her blood was on fire?

In no time, he'd ignited her desire so that her skin was molten and about to burst into flames.

She clutched his shoulders.

She arched her back, desperate to quell the scorching heat within her. But the touch of his lips upon her body intensified her wanton needs. The sensual roughness of his day's growth of beard caused her skin to tingle wherever he touched.

Then he moved lower.

"Open for me, Nicola," he said with a huskiness to his voice that shot more tingles through her body.

She did not know what he meant by the request until he gently nudged her legs apart and set his shoulders under them. Then his mouth came down upon her most intimate spot. She was shocked by the feel of his tongue on her, but the urge to protest died in her throat. A delicious heat began to build inside of her. How was it possible when she was already on fire? The blood coursing through her veins was a hot, thick pool of desire.

She was lost to him and he knew it.

He meant to claim her, to mark her as his, for he was no longer the protector, but the hunter capturing his prey. He captured her with the hot touch of his mouth and the gentle stroke of his fingers. She clutched the headboard, afraid she might float into the clouds if she did not hold fast to something solid.

His tongue swirled on her… thrust inside her. "John. Oh… my, heavens." She could feel the tug and strain of his muscles against her calves. This had to be sinful. It felt too deliciously wicked to be anything other than a forbidden pleasure.

Why had she never read about this in her scandalous books?

Obviously, she was reading the wrong books.

Heat built within her. Her heart pounded with a roar so that she heard nothing but its frantic beat. She felt nothing but the mounting pressure between her legs. Just as she thought she might explode, he moved off her to remove his breeches. She felt cool air against her most intimate part and then felt the hard length of him as he positioned himself over her. "Nicola…"

"Yes, I want you." Was that desperate, aching voice hers?

She held out her arms to him and felt the damp warmth of his skin as he enveloped her in his embrace. His sinewed heat and the strength of him surrounded her. She felt a moment's pain when he entered her, his thrusts cautious at first. He must have wanted her body to grow used to his before he allowed himself to lose control.

Would he lose control? She hardly dared believe that she held such power over him. He was guarded in everything he did. But she saw his iron control slipping, saw the wild heat in his hunter eyes, the feral strain of his body as he fully embedded himself inside her and began their wild mating dance.

The discomfort she'd felt now melted away.

She closed her eyes as exquisite sensations washed over her.

The feel of his chest rubbing against hers. The iron bands of his arms wrapped around her body. The gentleness and strength of his hands guiding her movements to match his.

She gripped his shoulders, her fingers digging in and afraid to let go, for he was carrying her along on a magical journey and she did not want it to end. Mother in heaven, the sensations he evoked! The slick heat of him inside of her. The rugged, masculine scent of him. Sandalwood and saddle leather. The salty taste of his skin.

The arousing touch of his rough, calloused fingers along her skin. He was making her feel him. Making her know him. Know his scent. Know the taste of his mouth on hers. Know his touch upon her skin.

An overwhelming pressure built inside her. She tried to hold down this unfamiliar feeling, but it was to no avail. She was caught in its powerful grip and carried on a scorching wave crest of desire. More waves followed, endless waves that swelled and crested, lifting her to shuddering and explosive heights. "I'm lost to you, John. I love you."

Had John heard her whispered revelation? Her voice sounded muffled, for her heart was pounding as loud as the roar of a lion and echoing between her own ears.

"John. John," she whispered, kissing his face.

She loved this man with all her being.

Her heart was his.

With a deep, grunting thrust, he experienced his own release. His liquid essence spilled inside of her. His eyes were smoldering embers. His big shoulders were taut and his muscles straining. He was a magnificent creature, wild and powerful, and wanting her.

She clutched his shoulders as he gave a final, shuddering thrust and collapsed atop her, his skin warm and damp from the exquisite heat of his pleasure.

He did not have to tell her that he loved her.

She knew it without words, for he'd spilled his seed inside of her.

He was no untried youth who could not contain himself. He knew what the consequences of their mating might bring. A child.

His child.

He could have held back. He could have withdrawn, but he hadn't. "I love you," she whispered again, knowing he would never repeat the words to her. But by his actions, she knew that he had given himself to her.

As their passion began to cool, their ragged breaths and gasps and moans of pleasure dying down, John carefully pulled out of her and then sank onto his back. After a long moment, he grinned at her, then reached out and drew her back into his arms. "How do you feel?"

She smiled at him. "Quite starry-eyed, if you must know. I never considered… I had no idea… I floated to the stars."

"So did I."

"Don't tease me, John."

He growled softly, a raw, predatory growl that shot tingles through her body. He rolled her atop him and kissed her on the nose. "I'm serious. You are an enchantress."

She playfully swatted his shoulder and laughed. "Now I know you're teasing me."

"Cross my heart, it's the truth." He kissed her once more, this time on the lips. "Come on, brat. Time to get up."

She scampered off him and out of bed, but paused to look back at him as he rose, splendid and naked, on the other side of the bed. He was the enchanting one, his body as magnificent as any Greek warrior god depicted in marble. "What is it, Nicola?"

She drew her robe on to cover herself, but she wasn't embarrassed so much as cold now that the fire had died, leaving only a few embers glowing in the hearth. "We're truly married."

He grunted. "Yes, for better or for worse."

She frowned lightly. "It will always be for the better. We have each other now. You are no longer alone, John. Although I will respect your privacy whenever you feel the need for it."

He shook his head and laughed. "Nicola, I know you too well. You will trample all over my privacy. I shall never have a moment's peace." He came around to her side of the bed and drew her into his arms. "But it isn't a bad thing. You grow on a man."

"Like mold on tree bark?"

He sighed. "Your description, not mine. There is nothing moldy about you. Wash up and get dressed. It's almost sunrise."

They used the last ewer of fresh water to wash themselves, then John helped her to dress and then dressed himself. "There are tarts left over from last night. Have one before we go."

He reached over and grabbed one for himself, devouring it in two bites. He checked his pouch once again to assure himself the book and rolled-up deciphering parchment was still there, then buckled it and tossed it over his shoulder. "We'll stop at an inn along the way and fill our bellies with something hot and nourishing. Hopefully, Somersby's men will be nowhere about."

She quickly finished braiding her hair and then grabbed her shawl. "I'm ready."

John opened the door, holding her back while he checked to see if anyone was stirring. "All clear."

He took her hand in his while they hurried outside to fetch Valor. John saddled him and led him out of the stable before assisting her up and climbing on behind her. She nestled against his chest and let the warmth of his arms encircle her, feeling a moment of contentment.

Did John feel the same?

She doubted it.

He was once again tense and alert, his hunter-predator instincts in full control as he spurred Valor to a canter. Within moments, they lost sight of the stable and were swallowed up in the gray mist that clung to the crags and valleys.

When the sun rose a short while later and burned away the mist, she noticed that they were riding eastward toward the North Sea. "We're going to Aberdeen," John said, following the direction of her gaze and easily reading her thoughts. "We'll secure a ship to sail us to London, or Edinburgh, if that's all there is to be had."

"Edinburgh," she murmured, suddenly worried that he might decide to leave her there after all. He'd planned to do so at first. But she would abide by his choice, whether it meant that he would take her with him or leave her behind. The book was proof of Somersby's treason and too important to ignore. If John felt it was best to travel to London alone, then she would accept his decision.

"Nicola, my intention is to keep you with me all the way to London."

He was quite good at reading her thoughts, she had to admit. She had yet to understand him at all. "I won't resent you if you can't. The safety of England is more important."

He firmed his hold around her waist and drew her toward him. "You're my wife now, in every sense of the word. Nothing is more important than you."

Her eyes widened in surprise. "John, that is nonsense. You don't even love me."

"Your life is worth more to me than a damn book."

"It isn't just any book." She eased against him, quite liking this sudden, oafish protectiveness about him. She was bound to him now under the eyes of the Good Lord—even if it was only the Scottish Good Lord—and he meant to keep her by his side forever. He'd told her so and he was a man of his word.

She had gotten what she wanted, but did John know yet what he wanted? She swallowed back a lump of sorrow. Once he figured it out, would his life include her? She did not wish to become a castaway wife. "Very well. I have no intention of arguing the point. I just wanted you to know that I'll abide by your wishes, whatever those might be."

He laughed. "Good to know. But I can hardly believe my own ears. Nicola Emory turned into a biddable, obedient wife? Is it possible?"

She playfully poked him in the ribs. "Yes, you dolt. It is possible. But only when your suggestions make sense. If your plan is idiotic, I'll be the first one to tell you so."

"Ah, I'm vastly relieved. Marriage hasn't changed you." His playful manner faded and he turned serious. "Don't ever change, Nicola. Stay the fighter that you are. Use your wits. Don't let anyone intimidate you. Promise me."

She turned in the saddle to face him. "What's this about, John? Is that bad dream you had last night still troubling you?"

"No. Never mind. Forget I said anything."

She sighed and turned to face outward so that her back was once again pressed against his solid chest. "You know I will find out the truth eventually. If you won't tell me, then I will find someone who will. But this is my promise to you. I promise to remain as stubbornly determined and headstrong as ever. I promise to give you not a moment's peace until there are no secrets between us. There, does that make you feel better?"

"Lord, you're a brat."

"Which is what you seem to like about me. Oh, and another thing. What have you done with your spectacles? You haven't worn them since the night of Somersby's party."

"They're tucked away in the pouch. I have no need of them now."

"I knew your eyesight was always perfect. You merely used them to appear scholarly and dull. Well, you don't know much about women if you think that ploy worked. In truth, few men understand us. Those spectacles made you look divinely attractive. Utterly desirable."

"Shows what little you know. Those spectacles kept the marriage-minded females at a distance. Everyone avoided me, except you."

"They avoided you because you frightened the wits out of them, and it had nothing to do with your spectacles. Some people smile when their thoughts are at rest. Others pout. Others look thoughtful. You look like a killer wolf about to rip the heart and guts out of anyone who gets in your way. Your spectacles actually softened you. But you have that killer look now." She tensed in the saddle. "What's wrong? Are we being followed?"

"Yes, brat. We've been followed ever since we left the inn."

She gasped. "Do you know by whom?"

"No, but I think it's time we found out."

# CHAPTER 13

JOHN SPURRED VALOR to a gallop as they reached the main road to Aberdeen. It was a well-worn path used by many travelers headed eastward toward the coast. The king's men routinely patrolled the area. Although the hour was still early, he hoped they might come across a garrison and seek temporary shelter with them.

He was troubled by the possibility they were still being followed. How many men did Somersby have at his disposal? How could he have every road covered and his men constantly on their trail?

Nicola had her head buried against his chest and was clinging to his waist as he spurred Valor to greater speed. The horse was rested and had yet to be taken on his morning run, so he was ready to let loose and fly over this flat terrain. But John dared not give him his full head, for Nicola was perched precariously and holding on for dear life.

He could have left their followers in the dust had he not been worried about Nicola. She knew it too. He could feel her frustration, but did not want her doing anything noble. She was well and truly his wife now, and he would not leave her behind.

Although the road was heavily traveled, it was not a straight path. It curved and wound its way eastward and there were several convenient places to hide, several sharp bends of the road. When the road curved along a particularly woodsy section, he reined Valor in and led him down a steep, densely wooded embankment. Once out of sight of the roadway, he jumped down and tethered Valor to a jutting branch. He then helped Nicola to dismount and turned to grab his rifle.

She placed a hand on his arm. "Give me a weapon, too."

He frowned at her, for he wanted Nicola to stay behind and remain safely out of sight, but there was a stubborn set to her jaw. Even though she'd just told him that she would obey, he wasn't certain that she would. What if she followed him? "Here, take my pistol. But don't you dare use it unless those men see you and begin firing. We're just scouting right now. The point is not to be seen and *not* to engage them."

She nodded.

He took her hand and led her up a small hill.

Within moments, a single rider came into view. "I'll be damned," John muttered and told Nicola to lower her weapon. "It's all right. I know her."

"Her? She's a lady? Riding alone?"

"Selena Baldridge is a marchioness, but she's no lady," John said, emitting an amused chuckle. "She must have seen me at the inn and wondered what I was doing there. She won't harm you." He stepped onto the road to acknowledge his presence. Lady Selena dismounted with the grace and agility of a swan, then put her arms around his neck and blatantly kissed him on the mouth. It was a hungry, I-want-you-in-my-bed kiss.

Nicola did not think her heart could sink any lower.

John not only knew her. He obviously *knew* her in the biblical sense of the word.

Perhaps Selena was not going to harm them, but this woman was not harmless. In truth, Nicola had never seen such predatory instincts in a member of her own sex before, and her sex could be quite predatory when it came to catching a husband. Even the wicked countess she'd thought had enthralled her brother appeared tame compared to this woman.

Was Selena hungry for any man? Or just John?

She quietly studied the beautiful redhead with aquamarine eyes. She was exquisite, truth be told. Her hands were all over John and he did not appear to mind. "Selena's a trained agent of the Crown," he said, introducing them. "Nicola is my wife. Lady Bainbridge."

That took Selena by surprise. "How long ago did this happen? You said nothing about her the last time we were together."

They were together?

In bed?

"Not long ago," John said. "We're recently wed. What are you doing in Scotland?"

She tossed her head back. "I heard you were on assignment up here and thought I'd come up and help you. But it seems you already have all the help you need."

"That was a foolish thing to do." John did not look pleased. "You might have blown my cover. Does Prinny know you're up here?"

"No," she said, now pouting. "He isn't pleased with me at the moment."

"I'm not surprised. Does anyone know? Anything might have happened to you on the ride up here. You shouldn't be on your own."

She shrugged and turned away from him, folding her arms across her chest in an obvious sign of indignation. "I am always careful."

"I might have shot you. You're fortunate not to be lying dead on the road now."

"That isn't your style. You always take pains to know your enemy. I was in no danger from you." She cast Nicola a sly grin. "But your wife isn't pleased to have me here. You'd better not tell her about our past or she might shoot me."

His frown darkened. "Stop causing trouble. You may as well ride with us to Aberdeen. We need to secure a boat to London, but the less we're seen around town, the better. You can take care of that chore for us."

One gracefully curved eyebrow shot up. "And why would I do that?"

"Because I need your help."

She emitted a trill of laughter. "You? Needing anyone's help? That's hilarious. But I suppose you're burdened now." She pointedly gazed at Nicola. "And what will I get as a reward for rendering assistance?"

"The gratitude of the Crown." He strode down the embankment and returned with Valor. He lifted Nicola onto the saddle and mounted behind her. "We've wasted enough time. Well, are you going to help us or not?"

"I may as well." She shrugged and climbed onto her magnificent filly. "It will amuse me to see you pretend to be married." Another merry trill escaped her lips as she rode off ahead of them toward Aberdeen.

John sighed. "Don't say anything, Nicola."

"I wasn't going to."

"You have flames shooting from your eyes and your hands are curled into fists." He sighed again. "She's a good agent. We've worked together on several missions."

"Worked rather closely, I gather."

He said nothing, merely urged Valor forward. They easily caught up to Selena's filly. Nicola wished she had her own mount to ride. They should have taken one of the horses that Sammy had claimed. Since she was not a good rider, it hadn't felt important at the time. Now, she felt like a useless appendage that only served to hold John back.

Selena was beautiful and a brilliant rider. She was an agent of the Crown. Until this very moment, Nicola had no idea that women were permitted to act as agents. Not that it would have mattered. Her brother would never have allowed her to undertake a dangerous operation. She was meant to marry and live a traditional life.

Well, the marriage part hadn't gone according to plan. She had a demented beau now desperate to hunt her down and kill her, and a husband who had married her out of an excessive sense of duty. *Well done, Nicola.*

They stopped at an inn around midday to rest their horses and grab a bite to eat. John told them to stay back while he made certain no unwanted characters were lurking about. He returned a few moments later. "It's safe."

"From whom?" Selena asked.

Nicola was about to respond, but John cast her a look of caution. Did he not trust this woman? But they were agents of the Crown, working toward the same purpose. Weren't they?

"John, darling, how am I to protect your lovely *wife* if you'll tell me nothing?" She sidled up to John, suggestively sliding her hand up his chest. "Surely, you can tell me something."

"Nicola was about to enter into a betrothal with the Marquis of Somersby, but that all changed when I declared my feelings for her and stole her away from him. He's enraged and determined to kill us both."

Selena cast her a skeptical glance and laughed. "Darling, she's lovely, of course. But exquisite enough to prod Somersby into a jealous rage? Don't be ridiculous. Why is Somersby really after the two of you?"

John took Nicola's hand as a precaution.

Nicola really wanted to smash her fist into Selena's perfect face. In truth, she knew that she wasn't an exquisite beauty. Selena was right about that. Nor did she have a sensual allure that would push any man into a jealous rage. But Selena had a mocking, disdainful way of stating the obvious that roiled her temper. The woman was purposely goading her.

John gave her hand a little squeeze, nudging her fist open so that his fingers gently entwined with hers while he spoke to their new companion. "Selena," he said with a note of impatience in his voice, "you don't need to know more. All that matters is that Somersby will kill us if he finds us."

Nicola knew that Selena had the same tenacity she had, although she hoped she wasn't as irritating as this proud beauty was. She ought to have admired the woman for her spirit and independence. Wasn't this exactly how she had responded to being denied the truth about the death of John's parents?

"John, darling."

Ugh, there was that annoying air of disdain again.

"John, darling. You need to tell me the rest of it. You are running to London for a purpose. What do you have that Somersby wants? And don't tell me it is your wife, because I know the man and his sexual proclivities. No woman is that important to him." She cast Nicola a sympathetic glance.

John frowned. "Perhaps I'll tell you when we reach Aberdeen."

He arranged for their mounts to be fed, and then led both of them into the inn and ordered a simple meal to be brought to their table. "At once, m'lord." But the innkeeper wasn't quite certain what to make of the three of them.

No doubt he assumed John and Selena were the married couple and she was Selena's maid. Which must have perplexed the man all the more when John settled beside her and proceeded to see to her needs first, leaving Selena to fend for herself.

"My wife would like some tea," John said, pointing toward Nicola.

"Yer wife, m'lord?" The innkeeper now looked thoroughly confused. "Yes, of course. And what would yer..." His voice trailed off, having no clue as to Selena's relation to John.

"Lady Selena will have the same."

Selena tossed her head back. "I'll have ale. Bring me a pint. No lady's portion served for me."

"I'll have the same," John said, looking none too pleased. At the moment, he must have considered Selena more of a liability than a help. Her beauty alone would have brought unwanted notice to them, but she was also loud and outrageous. Everyone would remember them here.

They finished their meal and continued toward Aberdeen. As night fell, they found shelter in an abandoned kirk and slept on the hard pews. Nicola missed falling asleep in John's arms and hoped that he missed having her beside him. His expression revealed none of what he was thinking. "Good night, brat," was all he said and kissed her softly on the cheek.

He took the night watch. Nicola knew he would not dare fall asleep and show his vulnerability to Selena. While Nicola's heart ached for the torment he endured when overtaken by those dreams, she felt warmed by the fact that he'd trusted her with this secret.

Whether he'd had relations with Selena in the past no longer mattered.

He'd given his trust and promise of forever to her.

They resumed their journey at sunrise, John not engaging either Selena or her in conversation. Fortunately, this day's ride proved uneventful, for even Selena was subdued. They arrived at their destination just as the sun was setting over the city of Aberdeen. Its gray granite buildings sparkled like silver in the fading sunlight, and Nicola thought the effect quite magical.

The severity of the granite was softened by the abundance of greenery in its parks and the rivers that flowed through the city. John found a modest inn for them near the center of town and obtained two rooms. They were close to the sea, and the scent of fish and salty water carried to them on the brisk wind.

Nicola breathed a sigh of relief when John engaged one of the rooms for Selena and took the other for themselves. There were times these past two days that she had needed the reminder they were truly husband and wife, for Selena had an insidious way of casting doubt on their marriage. John said little, but she sensed he was troubled by the beautiful marchioness' presence. Yet, he was reluctant to part ways with her. She'd heard the adage about keeping your friends close and your enemies closer, and hoped this was the reason he wanted Selena to remain with them.

"Why don't you trust her?" Nicola asked him once they'd settled in their room for the evening. "Do you think she's a traitor?"

"No, not Selena." He tossed his pouch over the bedpost. "She's loyal to England, but she must have done something foolish to anger Prinny. That's why she left London in a hurry. She needed to keep out of the way of his wrath."

"What do you think she did?"

He shrugged as he sank onto the bed and pulled off his boots. "I don't know. Perhaps resisted his advances. She was his mistress at one time."

Nicola's eyes widened.

He removed his shirt and then rose to pour water from the ewer on the nightstand into a basin. He washed the road dust off his hands and face, and poured some over his head to wet his hair as he continued. "But I think she must have done something more than simply reject his advances." He turned to her, looking quite handsome with pearly beads of water glistening off his shoulders and chest. "She won't betray us to Somersby, but you mustn't trust her."

"I won't." She hastily took her turn at the washstand, knowing that no matter how hard she scrubbed, she was not likely to look very tempting.

John helped her to unlace her gown, then strode to the hearth to stoke the fire before stretching out on the bed with a groan of relief. "Ah, feels good."

She knew he hadn't gotten much rest last night.

Since he still wore his pants, she kept her camisole on and climbed into bed with him. They would spend the night sleeping, no magical night of passion for them. But she was quite satisfied to be in John's arms. He wrapped them around her when she lay down beside him. "Nicola, I'll be heading out early to secure a ship for us."

"I thought Selena was going to do that for us."

He nodded. "She seems reluctant. I don't want to make a fuss over it. I'll do it myself. I want you to stay here. This isn't the finest inn, but it's decent. I'll return as soon as I've made the arrangements."

"All right. What about Selena?"

"I don't know what she plans to do. Nothing, I hope. But if she goes out, you are not to go with her. Somersby's men might see you."

"Assuming they're here."

"I hope they're not, but I can't take the risk. It's you they're after, not Selena. Anyway, she can take care of herself."

"And you think I can't?" She should not have felt insulted by the remark, for Somersby's men were dangerous. But it did rankle her to know that John had more faith in Selena's abilities than in hers.

"She's trained to fight," he said with a yawn that spoke of his exhaustion. "You're not. Get some sleep, Nicola."

Sighing, she tipped her head up and kissed his jaw. "You needn't worry that I'll disobey you. I'll follow your instructions to the letter."

He laughed softly at her remark, but the tension in his muscles seemed to fade away. She hoped her presence beside him would ease his tormented dreams. He'd stayed up all night yesterday and badly needed a decent night's sleep, and she wanted to be sure he would be alert when at the docks in the morning.

She wanted to wish him sweet dreams, but knew his dreams would not be. She considered telling him that she loved him, but decided to leave that for another time.

She was tired, too.

Closing her eyes, she nestled against John and soaked in the warmth of his body.

Within moments, she drifted off to sleep.

JOHN STOLE OUT of bed at sunrise, quietly dressed, and then hurried off to secure a vessel for their journey to London. He'd left Nicola contentedly sleeping and was eager to return to her, for his dreams had been filled with Somersby's men finding them, and he was worried that today might be the day they would. He was also worried about Selena. She was plotting something, but he did not know exactly what.

He did not think Selena had fallen so low as to betray him, but she was prideful and jealous, faults that had gotten her into trouble with Prinny before. Although John had never been intimate with Selena, she'd made no secret of her desire to have an affair with him. To now find him with Nicola, no matter that they were running for their lives, and learn that he'd married Nicola, must have riled her all the more.

He was never one to mix business with pleasure. It made for nasty entanglements. But Selena had no such misgivings. She was a sexual being and used her seductive powers to her advantage.

He groaned lightly and shook his head. He'd once thought her an excellent agent for the Crown. But now, he wasn't so certain. She was angry and unpredictable.

She was a dangerous wolf on the prowl, while Nicola—for all

her independent spirit—was a lamb.

He slowed his pace and proceeded carefully upon approaching the docks. This was an unsavory area no matter what time of day, certainly not safe to walk alone at this early hour of the morning. Thieves, often working in pairs, were always on the lookout for an unsuspecting mark. Somersby and his ruffians were not the only danger to him here.

Good fortune was on his side. He encountered no trouble in finding a suitable vessel and a captain willing to transport them to London. However, the captain's price was steep. That was the least of John's concerns. He booked passage for the three of them and space in the hold for two horses. Although reluctant to bring Selena along, he was concerned that she would do something foolish if left on her own while Somersby was lurking about.

He hoped it was not a mistake, for he could little afford the cost of bringing her along. Indeed, after paying for the inn and putting down earnest money for passage on this ship, he would have no funds left.

Of course, he would have no difficulty replenishing his pockets once they arrived in London, but that was still days away.

He returned to the inn as distant church bells pealed to mark the noonday hour. Nicola was seated in the common room having tea with the innkeeper's wife. The lively, older woman jumped out of her seat and rushed toward him the moment he stepped into the room. "M'lord, would you care for a cup? And some lemon cake?"

"Thank you, Mrs. Wilkins. I would." There had been an icy wind whipping through the docks and it had left him feeling quite chilled.

"I gather by your smile that you've had success," Nicola said once their hostess lumbered away, leaving them alone.

He nodded and settled beside her. "We'll sail with the afternoon tide. Where did Selena go?"

"Nowhere," she said with a shrug of her shoulders. "She claimed to be fatigued and retired to her room about half an hour ago."

John shot to his feet. "Blast, she lied to you. Her horse isn't in the stable."

Nicola rose along with him. "What?"

"I doubt she's resting." He raced upstairs and went straight to his pouch that was now tossed on the bed, its contents spilled atop the mattress. Everything was there but the book.

*Damn her.*

She'd figured out that it was somehow important and had taken it. But where did she go? Lord help them if she'd completely lost her mind and taken it to Somersby. No, she was crazy and unpredictable, but not a traitor. Was she?

Nicola hurried in after him, her eyes widening when she saw their meager belongings strewn across the bed and realized the book was missing. "John—"

"I have to go after her."

He started past Nicola, but she caught his arm to hold him back. "No, you needn't. She doesn't have it."

He shook his head and stared at her. "What are you talking about? It's gone."

"She stole a book, but not *the* book. It wasn't ours."

He continued to regard her without comprehension.

Nicola hurried to explain. "I switched it."

"You what?"

"I didn't trust her. Nor did you. So when I noticed a book with a similar binding on a shelf in the inn's common room, I replaced ours with it shortly after you left this morning. Our book is safely hidden under the bed slats." She lifted the mattress slightly and withdrew Somersby's ledger.

John shook his head and laughed. Had he worried that Nicola was no match for Selena? He lifted her into his arms and twirled her around, proud that his precious lamb had bested the wolf. He set her down gently but did not let her go. "Nicola…"

She grinned at him. "It felt good to outsmart her. She had the most irritating way of looking down her nose at me."

He kissed her soundly on the lips. "Remind me never to play chess against you."

"You'd easily best me. I don't know anything about tactics."

"Hah! Napoleon would be quaking in his boots if you were

ever appointed to our war ministry. Thank you, brat," he said with uncharacteristic feeling.

She reveled in his admiration for a moment before casting him an impish smirk. "We have the next few hours with nothing to do. Just how grateful are you?"

Laughing again, he strode to the door and was about to close it when he noticed Mrs. Wilkins hurrying down the hall toward him. "M'lord," she said in a breathless rush, "there are two men here asking questions about ye. I instructed my girls to say nothing, but I thought ye had better know. They dinna look respectable."

Nicola gasped and took his hand. "Oh, John!"

*Damn. Damn. Damn.*

Another few hours and they would have been aboard ship, sailing to London. "Is there a back way out of here, Mrs. Wilkins?"

"Aye, m'lord. Come quick and I'll show ye." She continued to chatter while he quickly gathered their belongings, stuffing them and the precious book in his pouch. "Not respectable men at all. And to be askin' about yer darling wife, too. I know quality, I told m'girls. Ye paid yer account without fuss and yer wife chatted with me, sweet as can be. And these men show up with a look of murder in their eyes."

"They are killers," Nicola said, her voice sounding frail. "They are as evil as they appear."

The older woman led them down the servant's staircase and out a side door hidden behind the inn's pantry. John realized these men must have spotted Valor. Mrs. Wilkins and her staff would be in danger if they lied about the horse. "Tell them that the stallion is mine and that I've left him here for safekeeping. Tell them that we acquired fresh horses and rode off earlier this morning for Edinburgh."

"Aye, m'lord. That's what my girls and I will tell them." She gave a satisfied nod.

He admired the woman's spirit, but was still concerned that she and her serving maids would come to harm at the hands of Somersby's hired scum. "Do not turn your back on these men. My wife is not exaggerating. They are hired killers."

She rolled up her sleeves to expose her beefy arms. "I'm used to drunken louts and their brawling ways. I keep a loaded shotgun in the taproom. I won't hesitate to use it on those scoundrels if they dare harm any of my girls. Get on with ye, now. I'll keep 'em distracted as long as I can."

John grinned. "If I weren't already married, I'd propose to you on the spot." He bowed over her hand, bringing a girlish blush to her plump cheeks.

"Aw, get off safely. That'll be reward enough for me."

He and Nicola had almost made it to the hired vessel when more of Somersby's men caught sight of them. Perhaps they were the same men who had called upon Mrs. Wilkins. No matter, they had been noticed. John thrust Nicola none too gently behind him.

"Ack! What are you—"

Her question was interrupted by a round of shots fired at them. An innocent passerby was grazed in the leg, but John quickly assessed that the man was not too badly harmed. "Run, Nicola. We're in sight of the Avalon. Climb aboard and stay there. Tell the captain to be ready to sail at once. I'll be along as soon as I take care of Somersby's men."

"But John—"

"They're busy reloading their weapons. Do as I say. Blast it, Nicola. Run!"

To his relief, she obeyed and made her way up the gangplank as fast as her legs would carry her. More shots rang out. He felt one bullet fly past his ear, a little too close for comfort. But it also meant they were concentrating their attention on him and ignoring Nicola for the moment.

He waited until she was safely aboard the Avalon, and then withdrew his knife from its sheath in the lip of his boot. He turned to face the villains. Although he'd served as an agent of the Crown for many years, he was not a man who ever took death lightly.

But these men would kill Nicola unless he stopped them.

So that's what he was going to do… kill them first.

# CHAPTER 14

NICOLA REMAINED ON deck, worriedly peering through the ship's railing and careful to keep herself out of harm's way. The whiz and pop of shots being fired had sent everyone on the dock scampering for cover and she could no longer see John. This latest round of gunfire seemed to be coming from one direction, all the shots aimed at the spot where she'd last seen him.

John wasn't firing back.

Had he been hit? Was he hurt?

She ground her teeth in frustration, wishing she could do something to help him. All she had was a thick wooden oar that she'd grabbed off a small rowboat strapped to the ship's prow. The vessel on which John had booked passage for them was a sturdily built northern whaler, one of many that regularly sailed out of Aberdeen. "John, where are you?" she whispered, knowing he'd be angry that she'd remained on deck instead of hiding below and angrier if she were to leave the vessel to find him.

She wouldn't leave for fear the captain might hoist anchor and sail off without them. So, she had to remain in her hiding spot, ready to crack the man's skull in two if he dared raise the gangplank before John was aboard.

But a wooden oar that was too heavy for her to lift did not make for an effective weapon. She'd seen several small harpoons stowed in the rowboat where she'd found the oar. Hurrying back to the rowboat, she grabbed two of them and then quickly returned to her hiding spot and tried to catch sight of John.

The sun shone brightly overhead. It took Nicola a moment to realize the flashes of gold that appeared to be moving among the crates lining the dockside were glints of sunshine reflecting off John's hair. "You're alive. Thank goodness," she whispered, and watched him slip between those crates.

He was quietly making his way behind the assailants. Those villains were unaware and still concentrating their shots in the direction they believed they had him pinned down. Nicola flinched when a burst of shots suddenly erupted, and then all was silent.

Where was John?

Had he been wounded?

She was about to go in search of him when he suddenly came into view. Several dock workers ran over to him, offering assistance. One of them had been struck in the arm. John took a moment to make certain the man's injury was not serious.

He then turned to the others and spoke to them briefly, but she was too far away to hear what he was saying to them. It appeared he was leaving them to deal with Somersby's men.

Nicola shuddered.

If Somersby's men were not dead, they would be by the time the authorities were called in. These workers were not to be trifled with. They'd seek justice for what those villains had done. They'd shot at least one of their workers as well as the bystander wounded earlier.

Retribution would be swift.

That gave Nicola no comfort. Somersby's men were everywhere, seemingly able to find them no matter which road they traveled. John must have been thinking the same, for his expression, as he gazed at the Avalon, was grim.

He ran a hand through his hair and began to walk toward the ship. Nicola stepped out from her hiding spot and was about to meet him on the gangplank, when Selena, pistol in hand, darted out from behind some crates and intercepted him as he was about to climb aboard. "I'll need that book, darling."

John's expression turned thunderous. "You told Somersby's men where to find us. You might have gotten Nicola killed," he said with a growl, ignoring the pistol she now had pointed at his chest.

The wind carried John's words upward so that Nicola could hear what he was saying. His concern warmed her heart. But Selena's response, filled with haughty disdain, left her cold. "So what? I ought to shoot her for the trick she pulled."

John made a choked sound and shook his head in disbelief. "The trick she pulled? And what about you? I ought to turn you over to the local magistrate for what you did. Do you realize what's at stake? You led those men to us. And for what? The sake of your vanity?" He took a step toward her. "Put down your weapon and climb aboard."

"No. There's no going back to London for me without that book."

John seemed to have ice flowing through his veins, for he did not so much as flinch when she cocked her pistol that was still pointed at his chest. "Enough, Selena. You're only making matters worse for yourself. Tell me what you did to infuriate Prinny. I'll do my best to smooth your way back into his good graces."

She shook her head and gave a laugh that sounded quite desperate to Nicola's ears. "It's too late, my darling. Prinny will have nothing more to do with me. My only hope is to bring him whatever it is that Somersby's desperate to recover. Forgive me, but I must have that book."

"I know you, Selena. If he refuses you, then you'll sell it to the highest bidder. I can't let you do that."

"I promise to return it to Prinny. There, satisfied? I don't want him to be angry with me anymore."

He shook his head slowly. "As I said, I know you too well. You'll auction it off and then disappear, leaving the monarchy in upheaval while you live in luxury off a fat purse somewhere out of Prinny's reach."

"I won't, John. I give you my word of honor. I'll return it to Prinny."

"If that's true, then put down your pistol and let me pass. You're not going to interfere with my investigation. That book stays in my hands. We'll turn it over together."

"No."

"Don't do this, Selena. Go into hiding and keep yourself out of trouble while I deal with Prinny on your behalf. You have *my* word of honor that I'll attend to it at once. But you won't get your hands on that book."

"Ah, my darling. I'm afraid that won't do." Her expression hardened. "Give it to me now, or I shall be forced to kill you and your simpering wife."

Simpering? Nicola sorely wanted to throttle this woman. No, that was too mild for what she deserved. She wanted to pound her fist into her elegant nose.

What could she do to help John? Selena still had her pistol pointed at his chest. The oar was too heavy to toss at her. It would fall straight into the water. But those small harpoons might be of use.

Nicola picked up one and was about to shoot it at her, when Selena suddenly lowered her pistol, gave it over to John, and flung herself into his arms.

Nicola still wanted to hurl those harpoons at her, but for completely different reasons now. Then she wanted to hurl one of those harpoons at John, for he was actually consoling Selena. Never mind that she'd threatened to kill him only moments ago. Her body was pressed so close to his that not a single ray of light could pass between them.

John did not seem to mind. Indeed, he did nothing to push the odious woman away, even when she boldly threw her arms around his neck and drew his head down to kiss him hungrily on the mouth.

Nicola resolved to skewer both of them when they came aboard.

Why wait? She was tempted to hurl the harpoons at them while they were still kissing.

To Nicola's surprise, John boarded the ship alone only moments later. She met him at the top of the gangplank. "I thought Selena was coming with us."

"No."

She could not tell whether he was disappointed or relieved.

"But the two of you put on such a tender display."

"Because she kissed me?" He shrugged. "That's what Selena does, and it's best to just let her do whatever she wants. Had I rejected her, she would have flown into a jealous rage and done something to harm you."

"So you were actually thinking of me while kissing her. How generous of you."

"She kissed me." His eyebrow shot up as he nodded cautiously. "Why are you holding harpoons?"

"I was going to use them to rescue you." She sighed. "Then I wanted to shove them between Selena's ribs."

He groaned. "And mine, too.

"The thought had crossed my mind."

He eased the harpoons out of her hands and set them back in the rowboat. "She's going to pick up Valor and bring him down to London for me."

Nicola's eyes widened in surprise. "And you trust her to do that?"

"No, but I don't want her on this vessel with us. I had to give her a task to keep her devious mind occupied. She knows I'm testing her loyalty. I'm not sure what she'll do. I've never seen her this scared. I hope she's ready to atone for whatever mischief she caused to infuriate Prinny. But as I said, one never knows what Selena will do."

"You sound so casual about it. She almost got us killed. How can you so readily forgive her?"

"I owe her. She's saved my life more than once. She was a loyal and effective agent at one time. I don't know what has happened to change that. Can we discuss her later? I want to get us out of here while we have the tide."

They stood on deck, out of the way of the ship's crew as they hoisted sail and quietly left port. "Only two of ye," the captain remarked in his thick, Scottish brogue once they were well underway. "Ye booked three passengers and two horses."

"And you'll have full payment once we reach London," John said with a casual confidence that belied his concern. But Nicola knew he was worried, for he'd spent the last of his shillings and they'd have no funds until they reached London.

Of course, since John was an earl, he'd be extended credit at any bank and most shops, inns, or other establishments along the way. But they were on the whaler now and every request, even so much as asking for a cup of tea, would be a negotiation with its tight-fisted captain.

Nicola was more than willing to sacrifice the silk gown she'd worn on the night of Somersby's party. She'd mentioned it to John several times before, reminding him that the silk and the pearl beading on it had to be of some value.

She was never going to wear that gown again, so why wouldn't he accept it?

John remained by her side, but they stood together in silence. She wondered what he was thinking about. In truth, she was afraid to ask. Likely, he was thinking of Selena. The woman was beautiful and smart, and could hold her own against any man. That she was also mad as a hatter did not seem to bother John. Most men were quick to overlook a woman's failings, especially if the woman was as beautiful as Selena. Indeed, sometimes that unpredictable nature intrigued them.

Sometimes it ensorcelled them.

John turned to her when she shivered. "You must be cold. Let's go below deck. The wind will be brutal once we're in open waters."

She made no protest when he took her arm to escort her to their cabin. The air changed the moment they descended the stairs. The scent of whale blubber permeated the ship's lower decks, overpowering her senses.

"It stinks, I know," John said with a grimace. "At least we're alive and Somersby can't hurt us while we're at sea."

She was too busy holding down the bile in her throat to respond. He mistook her silence for anger. Well, she was hurt and angry, and more than a little envious of the bond Selena and John obviously shared, one built over the years while working as agents for the Crown.

John cleared his throat. "How about we decipher the rest of the book that you so cleverly hid from Selena? She's still mad as blazes that you tricked her into taking the wrong one."

"How can you find any of this funny?" she asked, frowning at him when he dared to smile. That it was a gentle, affectionate smile did nothing to calm her down. "Her actions aren't cute. They almost got us killed."

"I know. I was thinking of your cleverness, not her demented antics." He opened the door to their cabin and led her inside, then shut the door and turned her to face him. "I've faced death too many times to count. Perhaps I've grown numb to it by now. But if you think I am not torn apart with worry over you, then think again."

"John, I—"

His hands tightened on her shoulders. "Killing a person is no easy thing, no matter how evil that person is. You tell yourself it's all right, that by taking an evil life you're saving hundreds of good lives, and perhaps that is how we keep ourselves from descending into madness. Obviously, Selena doesn't believe it any longer. Perhaps she accidentally killed an innocent. Whatever the reason, she's lost her solid footing and is frantically trying to find her way back to firm ground."

He released her and gave a heavy sigh. "She's been a good and trusted friend to me all these years. A friend, never a bedmate. Don't ask me to turn my back on her now."

Tears welled in Nicola's eyes. "I won't. But don't let your need to protect those you love blind you to the obvious. Stealing the book is one thing, but leading Somersby's men to us is quite another. I don't want to fight with you, John. I'm quite shaken from this latest attack and thankful we're both alive."

He took her back into his arms. "I know. You've been strong throughout this ordeal. Get some rest while I continue with those page entries. It wasn't my intention to force you to work on them."

"No, I'm fine. Or I will be once we start. I'd prefer the distraction." She eased out of his embrace and took a moment to look around their cabin. To her surprise, it was quite well appointed. The bed was in a nook against the wall and had a nightstand beside it. A small writing desk stood against the opposite wall and a shelf of books hung above it. The cabin also held two chairs made of sturdy oak that were placed near the desk.

Nicola crossed to the large porthole that could be opened if the heat and odors became stifling. She tugged on its latch and managed to nudge it just enough to allow the sea breeze in. They were high enough above the waterline that very little spray from even the strongest waves crashing against the ship's hull managed to spill in.

John lit the lamp that was perched atop the nightstand, and then withdrew the book from his pouch. He placed the lamp on the writing desk and pulled both chairs in front of it. "Ready, Nicola?"

She nodded and scampered to his side. "I'll take the entries on the right."

"We'll compare as we finish deciphering each page. Let me know if any name sounds familiar to you."

Nicola did not think more than an hour had passed before her eyes glazed over and she could read no more. She pushed away from the desk, her stomach now feeling queasy, so she rushed to the porthole and began taking in great gulps of sea air.

John rose along with her. "Are you all right?"

"My stomach… it's roiling with the pitch and roll of the ship."

He put his arms around her and held her steady until she calmed. "The delightful scent of whale blubber can't be helping."

She laughed. "It isn't. Quite nauseating, actually. But I'll survive."

"A little air will do you good. I'll escort you on deck, if you wish."

She nodded. "Did you recognize any of those names we deciphered?"

"A few, but nothing surprising."

"Nothing that surprised me, either." She looked up at him. "Most of those entries seem obvious. Dates recorded. Places of delivery. Names of recipients of the smuggled merchandise. Amounts paid. What if I've overlooked something?"

"We'll have several days to review those pages. Besides, there is a lot more in the book that we haven't deciphered yet. Longer passages that likely detail his plot to overthrow the monarchy, and the names of the Englishmen who support him. These are clearly not mere ledger entries."

"But what about Somersby's plot against my family?"

"I think you'll know when you come across what you're looking for. You've already figured out the most important part, that he intended to use you to hurt someone in your family. The answers will come in due time."

"I hope so."

The next few days passed quietly.

So did the nights. Once in bed, John took her in his arms and held her close, but nothing more. He didn't kiss her. He didn't touch her other than to hold her against his warm skin. Did Selena mean more to him than he was letting on? Was he regretting their marriage and preparing her for the day they would part company?

She was his wife. They'd consummated the marriage. Did he want out of it now?

The skies turned gray, as though reflecting the sad shadow cast upon her heart, and stayed that way until they sailed past Norwich and approached Harwich. Nicola was on deck, her shawl tightly wrapped around her shoulders, and the wind whipping her hair into a knotted mess, when John came to stand by her side. "We're going to be let off at Harwich. Somersby's men will be waiting for us in London. I think it is safer for us to travel the rest of the way over land."

"How? We haven't any funds."

The sun chose that moment to peek out from behind the clouds and beam down on them. John, of course, had a golden halo around him. He looked magnificently handsome, as always, quite rugged with the beard he'd let grow out. "I have an office in Harwich. I'm known there. We won't have trouble finding lodgings or a decent meal. We'll be off this whaler in a matter of hours."

She nodded. "I'd love a warm bath and a hot meal. Mostly, I want to be home and have this ordeal over. I want to hug Kendra and sweet little Emily. I want to chase fireflies with Robert and Callum," she said, referring to her younger siblings.

She clasped her hands and rested them on the railing as they began to shake. "I can't imagine what I was thinking to allow Somersby into my life. A fortnight ago, I was a silly debutante with not a care in the world. Now, I'm on the run for my life, married to a man who never would have offered for me if he weren't my brother's best friend, and chased by a deranged marquis who hates someone in my family enough to destroy my life. Oh, and he wishes to depose the king."

He covered her hands with one of his own. "We're almost done, Nicola. Another day or two at most and that book will be in Prinny's hands. We'll sort the rest of it out afterward."

She turned to face him. "Getting it to Prinny won't be easy. Somersby will have reached London by now. He'll have spies positioned everywhere, including around every royal residence."

"He won't stop me from gaining entry to the palace."

"I suppose not. You're the Crown's best agent. You can do anything."

He shook his head and stared at her. "Do I detect resentment in your tone?"

"No. Just fear." She emitted a ragged sigh. "What will happen to us once this is over?"

"Whatever you want to have happen. I'll obtain the special license in Harwich. We can be married by tomorrow... legally married under English law, that is. You're my wife, Nicola. Adding one more piece of paper to confirm it won't change how I feel."

"You're speaking out of a sense of honor and duty to protect. Those are noble obligations, but they are not the same as love. How do you feel about me, John? You haven't... you haven't touched me since we've been on this boat."

He frowned in contemplation. "I've held you in my arms each night."

"Yes, but you haven't *touched* me, not in a way that a husband has a right to touch his wife."

His eyes seemed to bore into her, the hunter-predator grays

and greens as bright and clear as crystals. "I slept. Did you not notice?"

"I did… but, I…" Her eyes widened in surprise. "You *slept*. I'm so dense. But in my own defense, I've been distracted."

He cupped her cheek in his palm and gently ran his thumb across it. "I was at peace while your body rested against mine. How do I feel about you? Ask me the right question, Nicola. Ask me how it is that I've slept through these past nights without waking in terror, my sheets and body no longer soaking wet, and my heart no longer pounding a hole in my chest? Ask me how it feels to finally experience that sense of calm."

He traced his thumb lightly across her lips and smiled at her. "Ask me how it feels to hold your soft body against me."

She swallowed the lump of sweet agony lodged in her throat. "I was so caught up in my own fears and doubts, I never once thought…" She shook her head and swallowed hard again. "I wish I could blame it on my nausea from the odious scent of whale blubber."

"We've both been on edge." He grinned and lowered his head to kiss her on the lips. "I'll attend to my husbandly duties this evening. It will be my pleasure."

She laughed. "It's my pleasure I'm concerned about."

His eyes had a sparkle to them, like sunlight gleaming on the water. "I'll make that a priority."

# CHAPTER 15

NICOLA'S LEGS WERE wobbling as she and John quickly made their way off the vessel to one of the dockside inns at Harwich. It was shortly after sundown, and after all these days at sea, Nicola's balance was off kilter. She felt the sway and tip of waves upon the water, her body seeming to rise and fall with each swell, even though they were now on firm ground.

She had expected John to take her to one of the run-down, noisy establishments frequented by seamen and ladies of ill repute that lined the harbor. But Nicola was delightfully surprised when John led her around the block to a modest structure with a weathered but genteel charm. The sign swaying above the door displayed three cups to designate its name, the Three Cups Inn.

It was not an elegant inn, but respectable.

As they walked in, Nicola noted that the furniture and carpets were of good quality. The sturdy, oak tables in the common room were wiped clean and set with serviceable bowls and dining utensils. The private dining room was a notch above the common room. The tables were also of oak, but of finer quality and highly polished, and set with crystal glassware, fine china, and silver utensils. The inn's library provided comfortable seating for guests wishing to spend a rainy afternoon reading.

Were she not worn down from the strain of running for her life, Nicola would have enjoyed these offered comforts. Since John had stayed at the Three Cups Inn before, no doubt on his way to fight on the Continent, or do whatever it was that he'd been assigned to do as an agent of the Crown, he was familiar to the innkeeper and able to secure them the inn's finest suite of rooms. More important, they were permitted to use the servant's entrance and back stairs, which allowed them to move about unseen by other guests.

The innkeeper was a burly woman by the name of Mrs. Finch who wore a perpetually indignant expression on her face, but appeared to adore John. Of course, who could resist him when he turned on the charm? He did just that as soon as they were settled in their guest chamber. The woman was fawning and giggling over him by the time he'd dropped his pouch over the bed's footboard. "Mrs. Finch, you are a treasure. Please have food and a warm bath sent up for my wife."

One of her graying eyebrows shot up in surprise. "Yer wife, is it?"

"Yes," John replied, choosing to act the besotted beau rather than use a tone of commanding authority that would have had the innkeeper quaking. Nicola's own knees would have been shaking had he chosen to use the cold air of authority that came so easily to him. Of course, being impertinent by nature, she would have shot back a smart retort to hide the fact that she was terrified.

"Yes, I have married," he said and turned to Nicola, gracing her with a devastatingly tender smile. "I was lost the moment I set eyes on her."

The soft way he spoke made Nicola's legs turn to butter, even though she knew he was spouting nonsense. He'd known her forever. He'd ignored her for years. But she couldn't help blushing at his remark. "It was a whirlwind courtship, but how was I to resist him, Mrs. Finch? He is such a merry soul. A tender romantic. Reciting poetry, lavishing me with chocolates and flowers. Insisting on walking my pet ferret."

John burst out laughing.

Nicola grinned impishly at Mrs. Finch. "He is none of those things, of course. He's aloof and often dour. But he's brave and honorable and divinely handsome. I love him with all my heart."

The woman cast her a nod of approval. "Aye, Lady Bainbridge. Ye've got the best man in England. We've seen many pass through here, most of them knaves and some like yer husband who are men of honor. The Earl of Hearts is what we call 'im, for we knew it would only be a love match for 'im."

"The Earl of Hearts," Nicola repeated in a whisper, quite liking the expression. John's heart was like Excalibur, the sword of Arthurian legend. People throughout England tried to draw it out of the stone, the rich and the poor, the young and the old. The strong and the weak. But only one could ever claim the sword, just as only one woman would ever claim John's heart.

She liked to think she was the one.

She knew he cared for her. But he'd also cared for Selena. And how many others before her? It was in his nature to protect those weaker than himself, to do the right thing no matter what he had to sacrifice.

But he'd married her in Scotland and was going to marry her again in England. Twice. Two marriages. And the Earl of Hearts, as Mrs. Finch had called him, would only marry for love. *Please, let it be so.*

John cleared his throat. "Are we done with the social niceties? I've much to accomplish this evening. Take care of my wife, Mrs. Finch. As you can see, we've come with nothing. The shops along High Street will be closing soon and Lady Bainbridge is in need of the basic necessities."

He turned to Nicola. "Sweetheart," he said with a casual intimacy that thoroughly surprised her, for the most loving term he'd used until this very moment was "brat." "Make a list of whatever you need and Mrs. Finch will take care of it."

She nodded.

He kissed her on the cheek. "I won't be gone long."

She nodded again. "Be careful."

He left without bothering to respond, for he was no longer the tender, doting husband, but the hunter-predator on the prowl, determined to destroy Somersby and whatever treasonous plot he and his fellow conspirators had conceived.

Nicola hastily made a list of what she needed and handed it to Mrs. Finch. "There's one more thing I need," she said as the woman tucked the list into her ample waistband. "A book with a cover similar to this." She withdrew Somersby's book from the pouch John had left dangling over the footboard and held it out for her to inspect.

Mrs. Finch scratched her head. "Any book?"

Nicola nodded. "As long as its binding is similar to this one. I know it is an odd request, but my husband will understand. Feel free to tell him, but it is vitally important that no one else knows."

The woman's eyes narrowed. "I can tell yer husband?"

"Yes, I have no secrets from him. Please, Mrs. Finch. We are obviously in dire straits and your discretion is of vital importance. If you must know, we are running from a spurned suitor of mine who is intent on killing us." It wasn't a lie. That Somersby cared not a whit for her and only wanted the book was not necessary to mention.

"Are ye truly married to Lord Bainbridge?"

She nodded. "In Scotland. He's gone off to obtain a special license so that we can be legally married in England. Not that our marriage isn't already legal. It is," she rushed to add, realizing the innkeeper might toss them out if she believed otherwise. "But he is an important man in England and holds a much coveted title. He wishes to remove all doubt that we are well and truly married."

A small smile escaped the woman's lips. "So he's marryin' ye twice?"

Nicola sighed, realizing she'd said too much and would never make a good spy. "Yes."

"Good heavens, he must really love ye."

AFTER MAKING CERTAIN no suspicious characters were lurking around the inn, John concentrated on where he was going and what he meant to accomplish in these next few hours. He tried not to think of Nicola, for she was safe and he needed to remain alert, his instincts honed to detect anyone following him or any attempted ambush.

His first stop was to secure the special license and make arrangements for a quiet wedding ceremony early in the morning. He then headed to the Bainbridge office, knowing it would be locked up for the evening by the time he arrived. Only Harry, their reliable night watchman, was on the premises. Harry's terriers were with him, two small dogs who served mostly as ratters but had also been trained to hold off attackers. Since John had helped to train them, he expected they would recognize him.

The dogs yipped with glee as he approached and furiously wagged their tails. He knelt down to pat them. "Horace. Mortimer. Have you lads behaved yourselves while I've been gone?"

"Lord Bainbridge, is that you?" Harry asked, lowering his pistol and setting it back in its holster. "Lud, it is you. No one told me you were comin' here. Forgive me, m'lord. I would never have aimed—"

"Quite all right, Harry. Glad to see that you're as diligent as ever." He strode inside and went to his office, opening the safe and removing sufficient funds to pay off the captain of the northern whaler and get that ship out of port before one of Somersby's cohorts made the connection and began searching for him and Nicola in Harwich. He took additional funds to purchase some niceties for Nicola for their travel to London, preferring to pay his way instead of leaving his name wherever they stopped. "Have you noticed anyone lurking around here recently?"

"No, m'lord. But I'll keep my eyes and ears open. The dogs would have barked wildly if any strangers had come near."

"If anyone does come around asking questions, you haven't seen me."

The guard quirked his head, but nodded. "Whatever you say, m'lord."

"It's important, Harry. The life of a very special young lady is at stake."

"And yers too, I expect." He ran a hand across his thick neck. "Ye have my word, of course."

John returned to the Three Cups Inn fairly late in the evening and used the servant's staircase to enter the room he'd obtained for him and Nicola. Nicola was still awake, curled up in a big chair beside the hearth, reading Somersby's accounts and sipping a cup of what appeared to be hot cocoa. By the look of the plate beside her on the side table, she'd eaten all of her supper. Her hair was washed and almost dry, tumbling in curly waves over her shoulders and down her back. She wore only her thin camisole, but the fire blazing in the hearth provided enough warmth to chase the October chill from the room. She looked soft and rosy and quite delectable.

He cleared his throat and made a little noise as he entered. "I'm back."

She gasped and stared at the latched door first, then realized he'd come in through the hidden door beside their bed. "Thank goodness." She jumped to her feet. "Did everything go as planned? Do you think anyone followed you?"

He removed his jacket and tossed it on the bed. "No, it seems this is the one town Somersby's men haven't thought to search yet. I expect he's concentrating his efforts on London now. He knows we can't be far away."

She sighed. "I can't wait until this adventure is over. I shall never complain about Lady Stafford's agonizingly dull musicales or those stiff Ladies Horticultural Society teas with all those bombastic matrons peering at me through their lorgnettes. I think I shall even hug that wretched snoop Lady Phoebe Withnall when I next see her."

John laughed as he sank down in a chair by the table, preparing to tug off his boots. "One gets used to being chased when you've done this as long as I have. But even I get weary of it at times."

Nicola set down her cup and came over to help him. "Oh, John. How thoughtless of me. You must be hungry and tired." She pointed to the platter on the table. "There's food for you and a bottle of wine. But I can ring for Mrs. Finch to bring up some ale if you prefer."

She glanced at the tub that was standing by the fireplace. "The water's cooled down by now, but it's clean and should be comfortable enough for you."

"Is that your polite way of telling me that I'd better wash up if I'm to touch you tonight?"

Nicola's eyes rounded in horror.

He'd meant it as a jest, but she'd taken the comment to heart. When he opened his arms to her, she came to him eagerly, offering no resistance when he drew her down onto his lap. "I'm teasing you, brat. I fully intend to wash. I must smell like the rankest back alleyways." He kissed her soundly on the lips, glad that she did not seem to mind the dust and grime that clung to his clothes.

"After all those days on the whaling ship and the permeating scent of blubber, I think you smell as sweet as a summer rose," she said, chuckling as she eased off his lap to allow him to finish removing his clothing. He quickly bathed, and once finished, put his pants back on for the sake of propriety. He wasted no time in devouring the leek soup and mince pie that had been brought up for him, for he was famished. He finished the ginger biscuits that Mrs. Finch had also left for them, and washed them down with a glass of wine.

The biscuits and wine did not go well together, and he realized too late that the pot of tea beside the biscuits was meant for that purpose.

Nicola grinned at him. "Remind me never to put my hand in front of you when you're hungry. But I wouldn't mind if you approached our… um, activities in bed with equal ardor."

"Ah, I promised you an unforgettable night."

She shook her head. "We have a lifetime for that. If you're exhausted—"

"Brat, no man is ever too exhausted." He took her hand and slowly lifted it to his lips. "I wouldn't pass up a night with you even if I were bleeding and had my guts spewing onto the floor."

Nicola rolled her eyes. "I'm quite swept away by your poetic words. Have I mentioned that I find you exceptionally romantic?"

He grinned at her sarcasm. "Perhaps my actions will please you more than my words."

He drew her close and proceeded to show her just how much he ached for her. He was determined to give her an unforgettable night. While there was much to be said for fast and frenzied, he wanted their coupling to be a slow, building pleasure. He took his time removing her camisole, his hands exploring and lingering on her body, his fingers caressing her skin and leaving a trail of heat wherever he touched her. She gave a soft, moaning shudder when he slipped the camisole off her shoulders and carried her to bed.

NICOLA WASN'T USED to being naked in John's arms or used to being a temptress. When John's gaze turned hot and smoldering, she buried her head against his shoulder and gave an embarrassed laugh.

He smiled as he set her down on the bed and smoothed her unbound hair off her face. Then his smile faded and he bent to kiss her with a hungry longing that reached deep within her heart. His kiss was magical, its gentle power stirring her senses so that she was aware of his every moment, the heat of his touch, the granite strength of his arms as he took her into his embrace.

He smelled of lavender, for that was the only soap they had been provided for the bath, but on him the scent was manly and rugged as it mixed with the saltiness of his skin.

He kissed her again, hot and exciting, so that every pulse in her body was thrumming and her heart was beating and leaping with rampant abandon.

When he settled his taut, muscled body over her, she practically mauled him with her frantic need. But he was intent on prolonging her pleasurable agony, so she closed her eyes and relaxed her body, allowing herself to take in every sensation that he was purposely arousing in her.

She loved the way he took his time exploring her body with his lips and hands, loved the wicked slide of his tongue along her most sensitive spots, so that by the time he entered her, she was slick and ready for him. Mother in heaven! She was so ready.

His thrusts carried her on a swirling tide of passion, her own hot, pounding need building ever higher, until she felt herself on the precipice. "John... John." She repeated his name with a desperate urgency. "John."

*I love you.*

He was a big man and strong, his powerful grip and granite arms able to crush anything or anyone who got in his way. And yet, he held her so lovingly that she wanted to cry. This was a man who'd suffered torment for most of his life. That he found peace with her, that he needed her and wanted her, was a gift she'd always cherish.

Perhaps he knew it.

She'd made no secret of loving him.

But with each kiss, with each caress, he was telling her that he'd chosen her, too. That he wanted her.

That he loved her?

He would tell her one day, and she'd accept his words with joy. But she did not need him to confess the words right now. They were both in the throes of passion, both reaching heights of ecstasy they were helpless to deny. They fell off the precipice together, reaching that hot moment of release at the same time, now both of them wild and moaning and clinging to each other as though they never wanted to let go.

After a long moment, John rolled off her and laughingly took her into his embrace. Her auburn curls were a tumbling, riotous mess and fell over her shoulders to rest upon his chest, but he did not seem to mind. "What's so funny?" she asked, smiling at him. "I suppose we did sound like a pair of wild boars just now, grunting and howling."

"Boars grunt. They don't howl." He laughed lightly again. "But you were howling. Squealing. Moaning. Sighing. I'm sure I heard a kittenish purr in there, too."

"Don't make fun of me, you beast."

His gaze turned affectionate. "Wouldn't dream of it, brat."

"Did you enjoy… what we did?"

"Hell, yes. I suppose I shouldn't admit this to you, but you've been in my dreams for quite a while now. Hot, wild dreams."

She rested her chin on his chest and stared at him wide-eyed. "Really? And?"

He cast her a wickedly seductive grin. "This was better than my wildest fantasies."

"Better? I'm glad." She kissed him and shot back an impertinent smile. "But do go on. I want to hear more."

"About how enchanting you are? Very well." He caressed her cheek and suddenly turned serious. "I never believed I could be happy until I had my revenge against the man who killed my parents. I had been living in a soulless abyss of my own making for too many years. But I'm with you now, about to marry you—"

"For the second time, I might add."

He nodded. "For the second time. I'd marry you a hundred times, brat."

Her heart fluttered. "Oh, John. That's a lovely thing to say."

"I mean it. For the first time, I understand why the missions I was assigned were given only to unmarried agents of the Crown. We were loners, cared for no one and were not distracted by the dangers we faced. If a mission turned sour and we were killed, we'd leave behind no widows or fatherless children. No one who cared."

Nicola found it hard to catch her breath. "John, I've always cared. You were never alone. I would have… I think I would have moved heaven and earth to save you."

"I know." He ran his hand lovingly through her tumble of hair. "Sometimes, the thought of you was all that kept me going."

Nicola held her breath, hardly daring to let it out now. John was confiding in her, allowing her into his thoughts and into his heart. Was he saying that he loved her? That he'd been in love with her all this time?

He sighed. "We're not out of danger yet, but I want you to know that you're not just an obligation to me. You're not a duty I owe to my best friend. You're the best thing that's come into my life and I'm so sorry that I almost let you slip away. Deeply sorry. It's my fault we're in this mess with Somersby. I should have said something to you and never did."

This was probably the time for her to say something sweet and soothing, but nothing like that came to mind. "Well, look on the bright side. We have a deranged villain after us because we've found the proof to collapse his evil empire and make England safe again. So there's that. It'll be a wonderful story to tell our grandchildren."

He rolled her under him and kissed her soundly on the lips. "I love you, brat."

Fireworks exploded and Nicola was certain she'd just heard a chorus of angels sing. All these days on the run, unwashed, usually hungry, and always in fear of their lives, suddenly seemed insignificant.

She no longer minded that he called her brat instead of something more affectionate. Sweetheart. My love. Darling. All these years he'd been calling her brat, he'd really been saying *I love you.*

"I love you too, John."

# CHAPTER 16

JOHN DREW NICOLA closer so that they were hot, damp skin to hot, damp skin. Hip to hip. The weight of his chest lightly crushed to her soft bosom. They were still entwined so that he felt the male part of him stir whenever Nicola rubbed her long, silky legs against him *there*. Lord have mercy! Did he have no control over himself when it came to this luscious girl?

She cast him a devilish smirk as she purposely rubbed her thigh against his throbbing member. "There's life in you yet."

He kissed her impudent mouth. "Lord, you're a demanding brat." She was also a beautifully irresistible mix of innocent and wanton. "Shall I make you howl with pleasure again? I'm sure your moans and breathless cries were heard as far as London." He propped himself on one elbow, feeling quite smug and proud of himself, but also overwhelmed by the intensity of feeling she evoked in him.

The girl of his dreams.

She buried her face in his shoulder. "Don't tell me that! Was I truly that loud?"

He stroked her curls, slowly running his fingers through her thick mane of hair. "I'm teasing you, brat. Although my ears are still ringing from your shouts of ecstasy."

He was jesting, but the rapid knocking at their door quickly stilled his laughter and put his hunter-predator instincts on alert. In the blink of an eye, he was off their bed, knife in hand, and poised at the door, ready to subdue anyone who attempted to enter. "It's Edgeware," a muffled voice called softly from the other side.

John muttered an oath as he eased his stance and lowered his weapon. He glanced at Nicola, who was naked in their bed and staring at him in wide-eyed horror. She'd drawn the coverlet up around her body, but he wasn't about to open the door and casually allow his friend in.

Nicola was his wife.

Although Ian Markham, the Duke of Edgeware, was a man he would trust with his life, a man who would protect his family and worldly possessions without question or hesitation, he couldn't bring himself to open the door. "Your timing leaves much to be desired, Your Grace. Give me a moment. I'll meet you in the smaller private dining room."

"Very well. Don't take too long."

John hastily donned his pants, shirt, and boots and then turned to Nicola, who was staring at him in consternation. "If he saw us and knows we're here, who else knows?"

"Hopefully, no one. I'll go down the back stairs. It should be safe enough." He needed to talk to Ian. In addition to being a wealthy duke, Ian was one of the Crown's best agents. He would catch on quickly to their situation and lend some much needed assistance.

But it was troubling that Ian had spotted them. He needed to find out how. They'd been discreet, or so he'd thought. He sighed. Ian would tell him if he'd noticed anyone suspicious lurking close by.

"John," Nicola said, scrambling out of bed to stop him as he was about to open the hidden door and make his way downstairs, "I switched the books again."

"What?"

She gathered the sheet around her body as she spoke. "I had Mrs. Finch send up a book with a similar leather binding. It worked the first time, so I saw no harm in using the trick again."

He shook his head and grinned, watching her still fussing with the sheet around her gloriously tempting body. She was the oddest mix of sweetly innocent and sharply clever. "Where's the real book?"

"Under the mattress. I thought for sure you'd feel the lump under you."

His grin turned to laughter. "The only lump I felt under me was… you."

She gave a huff of indignation. "You're going to give Somersby's accounts to the Duke of Edgeware and have him deliver it to Prinny, aren't you?"

"Yes." The girl was truly clever, her mind always working. She really would have made an excellent agent. "It's for the best."

He'd worked with Ian several times over the years and had great respect for him. In truth, he also had a growing respect for Nicola's quick wit and intelligence. It hadn't taken her long to consider all the alternatives and realize his intentions.

She nodded. "I think it's a good plan. Somersby won't be looking for him or grow suspicious if the duke pays a call on the royal family. I suppose you'll give him the deciphering code parchment, too."

"Yes." He reached under the mattress and grabbed the book. After opening it to make certain he now held Somersby's book and not the fake one Mrs. Finch had delivered to Nicola, he shut it again and tucked it under his arm. He dug into his pouch for the parchment. "I may as well take these down to him now. Our work is done, brat. All we have to do is stay in hiding until it's safe for us to return to London."

She frowned lightly. "By 'safe for us' I suppose you mean safe for me."

"Yes." She knew little about handling weapons and was too soft-hearted to hurt anyone. He was the one with years of training and experience. It wasn't merely his duty to keep her safe. He meant to grow old with her. He meant to share his life and heart with her. "Prinny is likely to put the Duke of Edgeware in charge of hunting down Somersby and rounding up every man named in the book."

"But some of them may be innocent, merely engaged in harmless smuggling of French goods. My aunt is particularly enamored of French chocolate."

John grinned as he reached for the hidden door used by the servants. "Ah, she packs pistols and purchases smuggled goods. Your aunt is quite a shady character, isn't she? Edgeware will use his discretion. He's one of the smartest men I know. Stay in bed and keep those covers up around your shoulders. Lord, you look beautiful. I'll be back shortly to worship and adore you."

He quietly made his way to the small dining room and was relieved to find Edgeware alone. "What's going on, Bainbridge?"

"Plenty. How did you know I was here?"

Edgeware shrugged. "I've been asked by Prinny to hunt down a rogue agent. I wanted the room and was told I couldn't have it. Nor would Mrs. Finch reveal who occupied it. I grew suspicious and kept watch on the servants' door figuring its mysterious occupant would try to sneak out at some point. When I realized it was you, I knew I had to warn you. I think that rogue agent may be after you."

John frowned. "Go on."

"I've put some of it together, for Julian Emory's sister is also missing. Is she with you?"

John nodded. "She accidentally got herself mixed up in the middle of something big." He related all that had happened, leaving out only the most personal details of his time spent with Nicola, which Ian would fill in for himself. "Get this book and deciphering code to Prinny as fast as possible. Guard it with your life."

"I will, but not until I witness your wedding ceremony. I'll leave immediately after that."

John frowned. "Don't you trust me to marry Nicola?"

"Of course, I do. But if anything happens to you, there must be no doubt of her legitimate status as your wife. No one will question my word, especially not her brother, who will come at you with a broadsword when she tells him of all your adventures on the run, which she will do. Sparing no details. That's the difference between men and women. Women share. Men don't."

"When did you turn into England's greatest philosopher?" John did not like the delay in Ian's leaving Harwich, but he also had Nicola's good name to consider. He nodded. "Thank you."

Ian laughed. "Just tell me where and when to show up. Or will you bring the minister here?"

"St. Mary's Church, right after matins."

"Good, that's only a few hours from now. The sun won't be up yet." He took the book and parchment from John. "I'll sign the wedding register and then head straight off for London."

"Send word to me as soon as possible."

"Count on it. I'll return to deliver the good news about our progress myself." His smirk was insufferable. "I'm determined to know Nicola better. Any woman able to get you willingly to the altar is a woman worthy of my respect. You'll have your hands full with her. Was she not in the thick of the plot to abduct her own brother?"

John groaned. "She and Rose Farthingale almost destroyed a year of our meticulous work on behalf of the Crown. But it was our fault. We never realized how… enterprising she and Rose could be."

"Hmm, hard-headed and determined. She'll need to be that in order to match wits with you. But I think that's what appeals to you most about her. She doesn't simper. She isn't helpless."

John flinched at the remark.

"Ah, I've struck a sensitive chord." Ian held up his hand when John opened his mouth to protest. "We're all driven by demons that haunt us. We wouldn't be agents of the Crown, serving in this particular unit, if that weren't true. Julian found his Rose, the woman with strength and love enough to turn him into a proper husband. Marriage is the best escape from this elite unit. Now, you've found your Nicola. I'm happy for you, John."

"I still have unfinished business," he said with a grunt, surprised by Ian's moment of sentimentality. Ian never let on what he was feeling. Never. In truth, there were times John suspected the icy duke had no feelings. Obviously, he was wrong. "I don't know what might happen next. What about you?"

Ian gave a wistful laugh. "I'm afraid there isn't anyone with the strength to pull me out of my haunted past. Too many of my demons are still alive and thriving."

Having said more than he probably intended to share, Ian rose and quietly left.

John remained seated, finding comfort in the darkness. He was used to the solitude. He was not used to handing over important missions. He always finished whatever he started. But the proof of Somersby's treason was now out of John's hands and it felt strange.

Of course, it had been the right thing to do. The need to protect Nicola had not influenced his decision. Somersby was hunting for them and that book. Giving it over to Ian was an easy choice. The Crown would take quick action. Perhaps offer him a reward for his good work. He knew what he wanted. It had nothing to do with wealth or stature.

He was a wealthy earl.

He wanted the name of the man who'd killed his parents.

NICOLA SENSED JOHN'S unease the moment he returned to their room. She'd donned her camisole and was sitting beside the dying fire, warming her hands over the glowing embers when the hidden door opened and John strode in. "It feels strange. Doesn't it, John?"

"Very." He came to her side and knelt beside her. "Edgeware insists on witnessing our wedding ceremony. We'll go to St. Mary's at matins. After that, it's just us. Here. For the next few days."

She nodded. "With nothing to do."

He grinned. "We'll think of something to occupy our time. Edgeware will send word once it's safe for us to return to London."

"Life will seem quite tame after this."

"I know, brat." He ran his knuckles across her cheek in a gentle caress. "But we'll be married. And since we're both stubborn and opinionated, I'm sure life will not be all that quiet for us."

She laughed softly. "I'll do my best to make certain it never gets dull. Nor will I truly rest easy until Somersby and his band of ruffians are captured and brought to trial."

"They will be. Prinny and Edgeware will make certain of it. But there's something else." He cleared his throat. "I intended to hold off mentioning it until after our wedding, but I think you ought to know. I don't want any secrets between us."

Was he going to mention Selena? Admit they were more than fellow agents?

"The night my parents died…"

Nicola's heart tugged. Of course, this wasn't about Selena. John was the Earl of Hearts. One love. One woman.

He took a deep breath. "I vowed to avenge their deaths. I will not break that vow."

She didn't quite understand his point, so she kept silent and simply nodded to encourage him to continue.

"I've been investigating that crime for years now and haven't turned up a single clue as to the identity of their killer."

"I'm so sorry, John. That beast put those scars on you, didn't he?"

He nodded. "I don't care about those. What I care about is the conspiracy of silence that's surrounded their murders. I think the royal family knows who did it. I think Prinny is ready to tell me now. That's the reward I will ask of him, assuming there is any reward offered. That's the truth I will demand from him."

Now she understood. "Then you will go off and kill this man. You won't seek a trial. You will be his judge and executioner."

"Justice will be done."

She cupped his cheek in her hand, needing to touch him as she spoke. His pain was so evident, it shattered her heart. But that pain would not allow him to think clearly on this extremely important matter. "John, why would Prinny suddenly do this after all these years of silence? Be careful. Things may not be as they seem."

He drew away from her side and began to pace in front of her. "What are you suggesting?"

"The Prince Regent knows that if he gives you a name, that man will be dead before the week is out. What if he gives you the wrong name? What if he and the royal family are merely using you as an unwitting assassin?"

"I'd know if they were. That man's face is etched into my nightmares. I see the burning evil in his eyes. I see his vile grin as he wields his knife. I hear his demented laughter. He showed my parents no mercy." His voice began to shake with anger and so did his hands. "I've said enough." He crossed to the table and poured himself a glass of wine from the bottle remaining from their supper.

He gulped down its contents in one swallow and was about to pour himself another when Nicola came to his side and took his hands in hers. "Leave it, John. I know how painful reliving those moments must be for you. Wine won't dull your pain."

He glanced at the bottle and then shrugged. "Those memories go away when I'm drunk."

"Always?"

"No. Sometimes they do."

"But they come roaring back when you're sober again."

"What's your point?"

"Your pain is not about being drunk or sober. Indeed, I've rarely seen you drink more than a pint of ale or a glass of wine. I doubt you drink when on assignment unless you're trying to fool someone, in which case, you probably spill the contents of your glass into a potted fern or some such useful vessel. This is about your thirst for revenge. Plain and simple."

"You won't talk me out of it." He frowned at her, obviously angry. "Beg out of the marriage if you want. But I'm going to kill that man as soon as Prinny gives me his name."

"I can't beg out. Not that I would ever want to. I love you. I could be carrying your child, for all we know. And if I am, then why are you determined to do the stupidest thing imaginable?"

"I made a vow and I'm going to see it through." His eyes were still blazing, but she knew him well enough to understand that her words had struck home.

"To whom did you make this vow? To yourself in memory of your parents? The best revenge is not administering death. The best revenge is happiness. Your happiness." She ignored his continued glower and put her hands on his shoulders. She felt the ripples of tension coursing through him like a dangerous ocean undercurrent. "Do you think your parents want you to be just like the man who took their lives? Or do you think they want to look down from heaven and see you holding your own son in your arms and smiling with joy?"

"Damn it, Nicola. I didn't ask for your opinion."

"Yes, you did. When you took me into your heart the first time you kissed me. When you gave me your heart the first time we… you know."

Despite his obvious turmoil, he managed a grin. "Made love?"

She cleared her throat. "Yes. That. And when you confided in me just now. You wanted me to talk you out of it. Deep in your heart, you know it isn't right. This isn't who you want to be."

He stared at her for the longest time, his hunter-predator eyes boring into her. "You think our first child will be a son?"

She laughed as she let out the breath she'd been holding. "Or a daughter. There's a solid chance it will be one or the other."

"I'll think about what you said." He took her in his arms and held her in a remarkably gentle embrace. "Let's go to bed. We have a wedding to go to in a couple of hours."

"You still want to marry me?" She had forced these horrid and bitter memories out of him, and he couldn't be pleased with her right now. But he'd kept his heart wrapped in darkness for too long. It was time for him to heal.

"Yes. Even more so now." He scooped her into his arms and carried her to bed. "But you're still an irritating brat."

# CHAPTER 17

THE CHAPEL WAS a beautiful, stone structure with stained glass windows and graceful archways, but there was no heat in the place, so Nicola was glad she'd worn the plain woolen gown John had purchased for her on their first day on the run. Perhaps some of the new purchases would arrive for her today, but her only choices when dressing this morning had been this sturdy, brown wool or the delicate, beaded silk she'd worn at Somersby's lodge.

There was no question.

She was never going to wear that silk gown again.

"You look lovely," the Duke of Edgeware said, seemingly sincere as he politely bowed over her hand. But his gaze was sharp and assessing, no doubt trying to figure out what charm she held for John, for it could not have been apparent.

John said nothing, looking more like a man who just wanted to get this nuisance of a wedding out of the way. But when it came time to exchange their vows, he took her hand in his and his gaze turned soft and tender. "I take thee, Nicola Jennifer Emory…"

His voice held steady and there was no hesitation as he repeated the holy vows.

She did the same.

When the brief ceremony was over, the witness registry signed, and Edgeware off to London, John grinned at her. "You're Lady Bainbridge now. Legal. Official. Unbreakable. How does it feel, brat?"

"As though I ought to be wearing a lorgnette and looking

down my nose at everyone." She shook her head and laughed. "I didn't think it would feel different from our Scottish handfasting, but it does. I'm respectable according to English law. It is truly final and irrevocable. But it feels good, John. It feels very good."

"Mutual, brat," he said and kissed her lightly on the nose. "Now, to get us back to the inn without being seen."

She sensed the moment his demeanor shifted from doting husband to hunter-predator again. Well, John was never the sort to dote. A smile. A squeeze of the hand. Those little gestures were the equivalent of fawning over her. But at night, when he took her in his arms, she knew he loved her.

What would these next few days bring? They weren't like most newlyweds. There would be no wedding breakfast. There would be no family around to congratulate them. There might be a lot of lovemaking since they'd be confined to the inn for days. She couldn't be sure, for John was just as likely to behave like a caged tiger, growling and pacing, and wearing a hole through the carpet.

"The sun's up," John muttered, regaining her attention.

She glanced up at the blue sky and the sun glistening off the sea. The waves and whitecaps, visible from the church steps, shone like silver. The harbor was filled with ships of all sizes, their masts still and bells lightly clanging with the ebb and flow of the water.

They weren't far from the inn, only needing to turn a few corners and walk down a few streets that ran parallel to the dock. She held on to John's arm as they walked along the narrow alleys, but noticed that he had his free hand poised on his weapon.

He suddenly stopped. "Get behind me, Nicola."

They were in sight of the inn.

She wanted to ask a thousand questions, but this wasn't the time. She obeyed and hurriedly moved behind him. "What do you see, John?"

"Nothing, but it doesn't feel right."

If John's instincts were on alert, that was good enough for her. She held her breath. She made no protest when he nudged her into a shadowed doorway, understanding that he meant to hide her from view. "Stay here. Don't move." He handed her a pistol.

"If more than one man approaches you, aim for the leader's chest. It's a bigger target."

"What?" But he was off before she could protest, leaving her scared and worried, and holding his pistol in her inexperienced grip.

He'd told her not to move.

She meant to obey.

But as the minutes wore on, she grew concerned.

The streets were fairly quiet, for the hour was still early. Most villagers were not yet up and about. Suddenly, several men ran past her. They'd come from the direction of the Three Cups Inn. Another man ran past her. They looked like frightened locals.

A woman stopped another man as he ran by and asked what was happening. "There's a fight. Some blokes are killing a man."

John!

Nicola ran toward the inn. Her heart was pounding so hard she couldn't hear her own footsteps pounding on the cobblestones. She rounded the corner and saw nothing. Where was the fight?

A barrel rolled toward her from a nearby alleyway. She hopped over it and ran to the alley. Six men had John. Another six lay on the floor unconscious. Mother in heaven! Twelve altogether. Who was their leader? Shoot him and the others will run. That's what John had told her.

Which one was the leader?

Then she knew, for the coward stepped forward only after his cohorts had pinned John down. He raised his knife to stab John.

She was not going to be a widow on her wedding day.

"Let go of my husband," she ordered, aiming the pistol John had given her at the villain's chest. She closed her eyes and heard a loud burst emanating from its barrel. It echoed off the alley walls. She quickly opened her eyes again and saw the man she'd fired at turn to her. His eyes widened in astonishment. She lowered her gaze to his chest. Blood seeped from his shirt and dripped onto the ground.

He fell to his knees.

Her own knees began to buckle.

Mother in heaven! She'd just shot a man.

Two of his cohorts fled past her, making no attempt to disarm her. They simply ran. But others remained. She shook her head to clear her thoughts and began to shout. "The dragoons have been summoned. Over here! Over here, Captain!" Nicola began waving her arms frantically.

The remaining men fled, leaving their leader sprawled on the ground in a pool of blood. The men John had managed to knock senseless before she'd arrived were also motionless on the ground. But they weren't dead. She ran to John, knowing she had to get him out of the alley before any of those men revived. She also couldn't risk those other fleeing scoundrels realizing she'd tricked them and returning.

There was no regiment of soldiers coming to save her or John.

"John!" She knelt beside him, afraid to move him, but she had to get him away from here fast. Her eyes began to cloud with tears. She wasn't certain that he was still alive. Then he moaned. "Thank goodness. Can you walk? Lean on me."

"Damn it. I told you to stay put."

"Shut up, you big oaf. Shout at me all you want afterward. Let me get you to safety. You look wretched. Is your nose broken?"

"Nothing's broken. Somersby's here. He went in search of you. I have to kill him first."

"You can't even stand on your own. Forget Somersby for now. We have to hide you and treat your wounds."

"But Somersby—"

"He's desperate to get his book back. He thinks we still have it. Let him waste his time ransacking our room at the inn. You know this town. Where can we go?"

"Bainbridge offices. Hampton Street."

Nicola flagged down a passing cart. "I'm Lady Bainbridge. There's a fifty pound reward in it for you if you can get us to Hampton Street at once."

The driver stared down the alley and then back at her. "And who's that bloke limpin' toward you?"

John looked awful, but he was up and moving, so she breathed a sigh of relief. "He's my husband. The Earl of Bainbridge."

"I'm not gettin' m'self mixed up in—"

He abruptly stopped talking. Nicola didn't understand why until she turned around and saw that John was pointing his pistol at the man's head. It was empty, of course. She'd already spent the shot. But the cart driver didn't know it. "You heard my wife. Take us to Hampton Street."

The man swallowed hard. "Hop on, m'lord."

Within the quarter hour, they drew up in front of a stately building that had a fenced-in rear yard. A big, burly guard ran forward to assist John out of the cart, two dogs lapping at his heels. "Yer lordship! Let me help you down. What curs attacked you?"

"Never mind about that, Harry. Just get my wife inside."

The driver raised his fist as the guard hurried to obey John's command. "What about m'reward!"

Nicola blushed. "I promised him fifty pounds."

John groaned. "This is turning into a perfect day. You could have offered him two shillings and he would have taken it."

She tipped her head up in indignation. "Your life is worth more than that." But she was relieved that he was cantankerous enough to complain about the expense. "Let's get you cleaned up and your injuries treated."

He hopped off the cart on his own, told the cart driver to wait, and then grabbed Nicola's arm and limped inside.

The guard he'd called Harry followed after them.

John led her to an expansive office that she knew must be his. The desk was of solid mahogany, as were the bookshelves. His chair was of finest brown leather. There was a safe embedded in the wall. He went to it and withdrew the reward money. "Harry, give it to the driver. Tell him I'll come after him if he dares tell anyone he saw us."

He sank down in the chair the moment Harry ambled off.

Nicola took a step toward him. "Let me see—"

"Don't." He rubbed his hand along the back of his neck and scowled at her. "You might have been killed."

"And you were definitely going to be killed. I saved your life. A thank you is in order."

He glowered at her. "You disobeyed my orders."

She arched an eyebrow. "Are you surprised? Did you seriously expect me to hide and do nothing?"

She expected a surly retort from him, but he buried his face in his hands and didn't move for the longest time. "John," she finally said in a ragged whisper and hesitantly moved closer to him.

He wrapped his arm around her waist and drew her onto his lap.

He still said nothing.

"John, I'm so sorry. But I couldn't let you die. I had to fight. I couldn't stand by and do nothing. Let me see your injuries. Is your hand broken? How about your ribs? Let me see your eye."

But when she tipped his head up, she caught her breath. There were tears in his eyes.

She started to edge off his lap, but he stopped her. "No, brat. Stay."

She was going to ask if she could wet his handkerchief to wipe the blood off him, but he started to talk first. "I was six years old the night my parents were killed."

She drew in a breath.

"We'd been living in Ireland all those years. My father was the king's emissary and in charge of the daily communications between Dublin and London. Something important was going on, so my parents and I were invited to stay at the ambassador's residence that evening. Men broke in. I still don't know whether my father was the intended target. I don't know if they cared. If you were English, you were going to die."

Nicola's hand was shaking as she set it gently on his arm.

"They killed him brutally while we watched. My father's pistol had fallen out of his coat pocket and lay at my mother's feet. She wouldn't pick it up to shoot the villain. So I picked it up, but the shot went wide. I was too little and the pistol recoiled. All I could hear was their laughter. All I could see was the blood. First my father's and then my mother's."

"John..."

"I'm not angry with you, Nicola. I'm relieved that you're not helpless. I'm relieved that this morning did not turn into a tragedy similar to the night my parents died. But this latest encounter has shaken me to the depths of my soul. I can't lose you. I'm going after Somersby before he hurts you."

She wanted to protest, but he was right. Somersby was too close. He was desperate. If Somersby succeeded in harming her, it would be John's nightmare come to life again. "All right. But you have to let me tend to your wounds first. I love you. I would like this marriage to last longer than a day." She eased off his lap and found a basin and ewer of water on the bureau that stood along a side wall. After dipping his handkerchief in the water, she returned to his side and began to clean him off.

Most of the blood was not his.

But he had a bloodied lip and sported the makings of a black eye. "Take off your shirt. Do you need my help?"

"No. I can do it. They only got in a punch or two."

She rolled her eyes. His entire right side was black and blue. "Any broken ribs?"

He moved his arms and twisted his upper torso to the right and then to the left. "No. All good."

"And your hands?"

He shrugged. "Knuckles are a little swollen. Nothing broken."

"You were fortunate."

He tossed her a lopsided grin. "I had you on my side."

She kissed him gently on the lips. "Always."

IT WAS JUST after nightfall when John left the Bainbridge office to go in search of Somersby. He hadn't discussed his plan in detail with Nicola for fear she'd follow him. She had been lucky this morning, but he would not put her life at risk again.

He'd left her in the care of Harry, his two terriers, and ten trusted workers whose duties were now to guard Nicola and make certain no one harmed her. Of course, he'd also instructed them not to allow her to leave, but that had been done out of her earshot. Obviously, he'd turned into a coward.

In truth, she did not appear determined to disobey him.

What also preyed on his mind was the possibility that Selena had led Somersby to them. She knew the vessel they'd sailed on. She knew he had offices in Harwich and also knew of the Three Cups Inn, for it had been used by agents of the Crown on several occasions. Perhaps Somersby would have figured it out for himself, but he thought it unlikely.

Selena had led the marquis here.

Which meant she was here as well.

He'd just turned the corner and was about to make his way down to the Three Cups Inn when he heard Mortimer's sharp bark. Horace quickly joined in, his yips and yaps slightly deeper, and now sounding fierce.

Someone had seen him leave and was now going after Nicola. He turned back in time to catch a shadowy figure running toward the building. He gave chase, slowed only slightly by a limp from this morning's fight. One of Somersby's men had stepped on his booted ankle during their assault, but it wasn't serious. The villain would have broken it if he had intended to.

He caught up with the shadowy figure within a matter of steps and reached out to grab his collar, but realized at once he'd just caught hold of a woman. Selena. Which meant she was armed and dangerous. He grabbed her hands and squeezed them until he heard a pistol clatter to the ground. It wouldn't be the only weapon she carried. "Let go of me or I'll scream!"

"Open your mouth again and I'll slit your throat. You've gone too far this time, Selena."

She struggled against him, but he had no intention of letting her out of his grasp. "You don't understand. I'm trying to help you."

"How? By leading Somersby and his hired scum straight to me?"

"You should have given me the book."

John laughed in disbelief. "You were working with Somersby all along. Prinny must have caught you stealing Crown documents and meant to have you hanged. That's why there's no going back for you. You backed the wrong side."

"You forced me to it."

"Don't blame your mistakes on me. You and I have nothing to do with each other. We were in the same line of work, that's all."

"I loved you. I offered you my heart. I offered you all of me, but you only wanted her."

"You joined Somersby's rebellion before I married Nicola."

She shook her head. "It was always that Emory girl. I saw the look in your eyes whenever she was mentioned. I saw you at *ton* parties, the way you looked at her whenever you thought no one was watching. You hurt me, John. So I had to hurt you back. Somersby and I thought it would be fun to see your precious Nicola snatched from you. He was going to marry her, take her money, and then stage an accident before the month was out."

Selena's words were like knives slashing straight through his heart. He'd been the target of their revenge. He was the one who'd put Nicola in danger.

JOHN DRAGGED SELENA back to his office, hating that she was under the same roof as Nicola, but there was no help for it. Neither the Harwich magistrate nor the local regimental commander was equipped to handle assassins and spies. Selena would have broken out of their meager prison within a matter of hours.

Nicola jumped out of her seat when she noticed that he'd already returned. "John, what happened?" Her eyes widened when she caught sight of the person struggling beside him.

"Keep away, Nicola. I haven't searched her for weapons yet. She's been working with Somersby all along. You suspected it." He was furious with himself as much as with Selena. He was spitting, fiery mad. "I should have paid closer attention."

"She used your friendship against you. She knew the loyal, honorable friend you were."

He began to run his hands over Selena's stiff and bony body.

He found three small knives and a garotte. "There's probably more."

He tossed Selena's cape to Nicola. "Take this next door into my clerk's office. Search along the seams."

"Ugh, her cape smells like whale blubber." But she held her breath and left the room to do as he'd requested.

John then called for rope and used it to bind Selena's wrists and ankles. "Harry, guard her. Don't get close. She's dangerous. Probably still hiding weapons. Keep Mortimer and Horace with you."

He then sent two of his men off to fetch the magistrate and regimental commander. "Have them bring guards. Somersby's still on the loose and I don't know how many men he's brought with him. Lady Bainbridge will explain to them what's happened."

Nicola had heard him give the order and her eyes rounded in surprise. "Aren't you going to wait for them?"

"No. I know where Somersby's hiding."

Nicola placed her hand on his arm to hold him back. "How can you possibly know?"

"What did you do with her cape?"

"I did what you asked. I stretched it across your clerk's desk and ran my hands along the satin lining. I found nothing. But the odor was making me ill, so I opened a window and stretched the cape across the sill to air it out."

He nodded. "I can feel the cool wind blowing in."

"Don't close the window yet, John. I can't tolerate the odor. But that isn't important. You said you knew where Somersby was hiding."

He nodded again. "You just told me. You smelled it on Selena's clothes."

She quirked her head in confusion, and then her eyes lit up in understanding. "They're hiding out in a storage barn beside the whaling ships. All the more reason to wait for the authorities. Let them help. You can't take on Somersby and his men all by yourself. Six was your limit," she said, reminding him of how many he'd taken down this morning. Unfortunately, Somersby had brought along twelve men and Nicola was never going to let him forget it.

He grumbled and paced, but waited for reinforcements.

After what seemed like an eternity but could only have been half an hour, he and a garrison of soldiers surrounded the dock area where several whaling ships were moored for the evening. Most of the seamen were ashore, imbibing at the nearby pubs.

John waited until the soldiers were in place and then entered the simple wooden structure that served as the whaling storage. Pots filled with whale blubber were boiling. Two whale carcasses were stretched across one of the long walls.

Somersby sat at a table with three of his cohorts.

"Put up your hands," the regimental commander ordered.

Somersby leaped to his feet, overturning the table in his haste, and withdrew his pistol. As he raised his weapon and aimed it at the regimental commander, John shot him between the eyes. "Bloody hell! The man almost got me. Who is that vermin, my lord?"

"No one important. A traitor."

The commander spit on the floor. "He's the one who ransacked Mrs. Finch's inn this morning. Poor woman, she barely escaped with her life. Traitor. Vermin. It's all the same. Glad he's dead."

John cast the commander a mirthless smile. "So am I."

# CHAPTER 18

JOHN STOOD IN silence as his best friend, Julian Emory, angrily paced across the elegantly carpeted floor of John's study. He and Nicola had returned to London almost a week ago and had quietly settled into the Bainbridge townhouse, but this was their first meeting with her brother and it did not appear to be going very well. "You went into the Highlands to hunt grouse and came back married to my sister," Julian accused.

His wife, Rose, merely smiled at her husband. "Why are you so surprised? He has always loved her. Haven't you, Lord Bainbridge?"

John grinned. "Indeed, Lady Chatham."

Julian scowled. "Stop being polite to each other. This is serious, Rose."

"I know, my love. But it doesn't change the fact that Lord Bainbridge has long been in love with Nicola."

"Love? Hah!" He eyed John suspiciously. "He is jokingly known as the Earl of Hearts because no woman has ever claimed his heart." Julian turned back to the window to stare out into the garden. John joined him, his heart beating a little faster as he watched Nicola—no matter that she was a countess, *his* countess—playing with her younger brothers and sisters. Kendra and Robert were racing from one end of the garden to the other, trying to avoid young Callum's tag. The boy was blindfolded and running around in circles.

Nicola was running back and forth with them, but careful to

stay close to their youngest sister, Emily. When Callum was about to clamp his grubby paws on Emily, it was Nicola who sheltered her and pulled her out of the way.

"She's my sister. You're my best friend. You're not supposed to… act upon your carnal urges with your best friend's sister."

Rose cleared her throat. "How is that any different from what you did?"

Julian growled. "It is completely different. You were my sister's best friend. Not at all the same thing." He sighed. "Damn it, Rose. Nicola's my sister."

"I know, my love." Rose joined them by the window. "And she couldn't have found herself a better husband, don't you think?"

"Maybe. Where are my aunt and uncle? And Jordan Drummond? I need allies. It's obvious my own wife won't support me."

"You know very well that Mr. Drummond has returned to Aberdeen to fetch Valor." Rose turned to John. "I hear he's a beautiful stallion. My sister, Laurel, is quite knowledgeable about horses. She's eager to have a look at him."

John's expression darkened and he turned away from the window. "I hope he's safely stabled where we left him. Selena might have done something to him."

Julian ran a hand raggedly through his hair. "Damn, that woman did a lot of damage."

Nicola walked in just then, arm in arm with John's elderly aunt, the other Lady Bainbridge, who would now be referred to as the dowager countess. "She didn't succeed. That's all that matters." Nicola cast him an impudent smile. "She didn't stand a chance. John and I made a good team."

John kissed her cheek and then drew back with a warning arch of his eyebrow. "But it's our last adventure. We fully intend to lead a very dull life from now on, don't we?"

Nicola mimicked his arched eyebrow. "I suppose. But hopefully not in the bedroom."

Julian groaned.

Rose and Lady Bainbridge laughed.

John shook his head and sighed. "Lord, you're a brat."

All talk of their adventures was dropped when Lord and Lady Darnley arrived with the other guests he and Nicola had invited to their home for afternoon tea. John detested these social affairs but it was necessary to properly introduce Nicola as his wife since their "elopement" was a scandal and all that the London elite were whispering about. The town's most notorious gossip, Lady Withnall, set her sights on him the moment she entered the parlor. "Bainbridge, I'll have a word with you."

He cast her a lethal glower.

"Stop frowning at me. I only mean to offer my congratulations. You've married a lovely girl. I was beginning to despair that you'd ever come around to it. You are obviously as dense a man as ever existed. But that's what you men are. Slow-witted when it comes to matters of the heart. You are no exception."

Despite his annoyance, John laughed.

"I expect you'll be deliriously happy for the rest of your days." She tapped him on the chest with her fan. "Be happy. Don't be a fool. Let go of the past and look toward the future. Now, bend down and kiss me on the cheek."

He gave an impatient shake of his head, but complied.

She tapped him on the chest again. "Be happy, Earl of Hearts."

Later that night, once the guests had all gone home and his staff had cleaned up and retired for the evening, John returned to his bedchamber knowing Nicola would be waiting up for him. She wore a thin nightrail and was seated on the carpeted floor, brushing her hair in front of the fireplace. The long strands tumbled loosely over her shoulders, the shades of red in her auburn hair illuminated by the firelight.

She turned to him as he approached. "Lady Withnall seemed to have had a lot to say to you. What was that about?"

He knelt beside her. "Confirming a decision I'd already made."

"And that is? John, you have such a serious look on your face. An incredibly handsome face, I might add." She placed her hand upon his cheek.

"Glad you're not tired of me yet, brat." He kissed her open palm and then settled beside her, drawing her into his arms. "I love the feel of your body against mine."

She smiled. "Feeling is mutual, Lord Bainbridge. I spent so much time in your arms while we were on the run. Every moment of it felt perfect. Felt right. Now we're back in London and I almost wish we were back on the run in the Highlands. My body misses the constant touch of yours. I suppose I will get used to it. We've only been in your home for a week."

"It's your home, too."

She nodded. "It feels like home to me. I think my home shall always be wherever you are."

"Hmm."

"John, the party was lovely, but your mind seems to be so far away right now. What's the matter?"

He sighed. "Prinny gave me a name."

She gazed up at him, startled. "What? Of the man who killed your parents? Oh, my heavens. What are you going to do?"

"Nothing." He held her against him, needing to breathe her in and soak in her vibrant warmth. "They killed the man within days after he murdered my parents. He was an English duke who expected that the brutal act against my parents would set off a rebellion throughout the land. He was just another Somersby, a greedy nobleman with aspirations to overthrow the monarchy and take his place as king. The royal family hid the truth from me, from everyone, just as they'll hide the truth about Somersby now."

Nicola rolled to her knees and curled her hands into fists. "And they waited until now to tell you? Shame on them. You gave years of service to the Crown and they used your rage to—"

He pulled her back down into his arms. "They used it to turn me into the man you love. They used it to protect the country we love. And used it to bring down Somersby, who was their latest threat."

"How can you condone their actions?"

"Because these threats are real and it is important to stamp them out before they can amount to anything. It is vital to the protection of England."

"But you've suffered so badly all these years."

"Perhaps some of it was of my own making. Who knows what I would have become had I known earlier?" He kissed her lightly on the lips. "It no longer matters. I have you. I don't know if we would have ever met if not for the path of my life. But now that we're married, I'll no longer be permitted to serve in that elite unit. I may be called on from time to time to assist wherever I must, but no more dangerous assignments for me."

"Thank goodness for that, but it all seems so unfair. Can I be angry for you?" She curled her hand into a fist around the hairbrush she was still holding.

"No. Set down your brush and come to bed. I need to hold you in my arms tonight." He rose and brought her up beside him. Firelight shone upon her hair and outlined her slender body. "I need to hold you in my arms every night of my life."

She sighed. "It isn't fair. You know I melt whenever you say such things."

"Then I must make it a habit to say these things to you more often." He furrowed his brow in thought. "You once asked me if vengeance is what my family would have wanted for me, and now I know it isn't. They would have wanted to see me carry my noisy children in my arms and laugh in the sunshine. They would have wanted to see me happily married, and that is what I shall always be with you. I'm sorry it took me so long to come around. I love you, brat."

Nicola reached up on tiptoes to kiss him. "I love you too, my Earl of Hearts."

## THE END

Dear reader, if you enjoyed *Earl of Hearts*, I would really appreciate it if you could post a review on the site where you purchased it. Also feel free to write one on Goodreads or other reader sites that you peruse. Even just a few sentences on what you thought about the book would be most helpful! If you do leave a review, send me a message on Facebook because I would love to thank you personally. Please also consider telling your friends about the FARTHINGALE series and recommending it to your book clubs.

Up next is The Viscount and the Vicar's Daughter, a humorous and heartwarming romance between Alexander Dayne, third Viscount Ardley, and the lovely vicar's daughter, Viola Ruskin, who steals his heart. Alexander is Gabriel Dayne's handsome older brother and a widower now under pressure from the family to find himself a bride. He reluctantly sets about the chore with the help of the very sensible vicar's daughter, Viola. But the more *ton* diamonds he meets, the more he realizes the only woman who will ever make him happy has been in front of him all along, and that is Viola. The problem is, Viola is also being courted by the local squire's son who everybody agrees is a more suitable match for her. Can Alexander, heir to an earl, convince Viola to ignore nonsensical class distinctions and follow her heart?

Keep reading to enjoy the first chapter of *The Viscount and the Vicar's Daughter*, and don't forget to grab your free Farthingale novella after the sneak peek.

# SNEAK PEEK: THE VISCOUNT AND THE VICAR'S DAUGHTER CHAPTER 1

*Ardley, England*
*June, 1823*

ALEXANDER DAYNE, THIRD Viscount Ardley, emitted a roar as someone dumped a pail of cold water over him while he lay flat on his back in...where in blazes was he? *Blast*. He was beside the vicarage house of St. Martin's Church again. He coughed and sputtered, trying to clear his fogged brain as he sat up with a groan and raked his hands through his hair to brush back the strands that had fallen over his eyes.

When he looked up, all he saw was the pale blue sky of breaking dawn, soft white clouds, and the highly irritating Miss Viola Ruskin casting her slender shadow over him. Her presence boded no good for him, but at least her lithe, little body shaded him from the glare of the early morning sun as she hovered close. "Do you have a death wish, Miss Ruskin?"

"No, my lord. But obviously, you do," she said, her voice as soft and lovely as a summer breeze despite her irritation.

He wiped the last of the droplets from his eyes and glowered at the pretty perpetrator who happened to be the local vicar's daughter. She was also known as the Ardley Angel, not only for her good deeds but also for her exquisite looks. However, she was quickly becoming the devil's bane of his existence.

"What have you to say for yourself?" she asked in a schoolmistress voice that sounded soft to his ears because there really was no evil in this girl, just an irritating primness that he, much to his horror, was finding quite to his liking lately. Her stunning, brandy-colored eyes were ablaze as she shook her head in disapproval. A lock of her dark brown hair had fallen over her forehead and her cheeks were flushed as though she had just exerted herself.

"Need I remind you that I am a grown man and do not need you to act as my mother." But he sank back onto the soft grass and groaned again, for the sky and ground seemed to be spinning around him and tossing him off balance. "Did you move me off the roadway?"

"Yes, my lord. It is the third time this week."

It galled him to be obliged to the girl, but he hadn't sunk quite so low yet as to deny she had now saved his hide more than once. For a sprite of a girl to drag his big body safely aside was no small feat. "Thank you."

She knelt beside him and put a soft hand on his shoulder. "I do not need your gratitude. What we all need is for you to come to your senses and behave in accordance with the honor of your title."

*Behave?*

Other than drink himself into oblivion, he thought he had held himself together fairly well in the two years since his world fell apart. Hardly misbehaved at all. Which probably explained why he was suddenly noticing Miss Ruskin's lush, pink lips within dangerously close reach of his.

They were incredibly attractive lips even when pursed, for she had a lovely, generous mouth.

Her bosom was also generous.

She must have noticed the lowering direction of his stare and gave him a disrespectful push before scrambling back to her feet. "This is exactly what I mean."

He rolled to his feet, ignoring the jolt of pain that shot into his skull as he did so, and took brief hold of her hand before she could storm away. "If I wish to drink myself into a stupor every night, that is my business and none of yours."

The impertinent sprite was not in the least intimidated by him even though he now stood a full head taller than her modest height. She wasn't small, but of average height, and yet there was something in her appearance that reminded him of a kitten, something small and worthy of a cuddle.

He was not about to cuddle this pillar of innocence as she stood there tossing daggers at him with her eyes.

"None of my business?" She gave a huff that raised her chest magnificently. "It is entirely my business when you insist on passing out in front of the vicarage like some destitute vagrant for all the parishioners to see."

He did not care what he looked like.

It was the way she looked that troubled him, so much beauty wrapped up in so much innocence. He groaned inwardly, irritated he had been studying her and inexplicably finding her fascinating.

This wasn't like him at all.

Why her?

And why now?

"There is no danger of your father's parishioners seeing me. It is early yet, not much past dawn if the glint of sunlight is any indication. You are the only one out here at this hour."

"Fortunately for you. But you may not be so fortunate next time." She shook her head and emitted a sigh of exasperation. "You are Viscount Ardley, lord of the big manor overlooking our small enclave. Most of the villagers are dependent on you for their livelihoods. How do you think they would feel if they were to see you passed out in a ditch? Well, what have you to say for yourself?"

He arched an eyebrow and gave a careless shrug. "Since I seem to be landing in that ditch with some regularity, I suppose it is a good thing for me we've had no rain to drown me."

She placed her hands on her hips and once more gave a magnificent huff. "This is all you have to say?"

He looked down at himself, realizing he wore no jacket or

vest...or cravat, for that matter. Indeed, he had on nothing but a white shirt of good quality lawn that he hoped had not been ruined by the dowsing she had just given him, and buff breeches that were relatively dry since she'd dumped most of the water on his head.

The soaked shirt was plastered to his body and made a *thwacking* sound as he peeled it away from his skin. "No rain," he said with a fierce frown, "and yet I seem to have gotten drenched."

"And I will do it again if I catch you inebriated in front of the church again. Do not be glib about this situation. You were stretched out in the middle of the road and might have been run over by a passing coach. Would serve you right...meaning no disrespect, my lord."

He burst out laughing. "No disrespect? You have insulted me in every way possible."

"Hardly. There is a lot more I would say to you if I were given leave to do so."

He ought to have been furious, but Viola Ruskin had a way with people. Everyone liked her, even though she was the most buttoned up, self righteous little thing, and always the first to comment on his bad behavior.

So what if he was drinking himself into oblivion nightly?

Did he not have good cause?

He stared at her, for no reason other than she had the most beautifully vibrant face. An alive face is what he would call it, for this is how he thought of everything now...as either alive or dead.

She was the sweet breath of life.

He was dead inside.

And yet, not quite as dead as he thought since he could not seem to tear his gaze away from her.

The little apple in her throat bobbed. "Let me help you inside," she said more gently. "I'll put the kettle on to boil."

"For tea? Do not trouble yourself. I'll take a brandy."

"You will do no such thing. You already reek of it, and your eyes are so bloodshot it is a wonder you can see anything out of them. Indeed, you are so soaked in spirits, I'm afraid to light a flame anywhere near you for fear you will spontaneously burst into flames. It shall be tea for you and nothing stronger."

"Do you dare contradict me?" He was a bloody viscount, after all. He could bloody well do any bloody thing he wanted…especially to himself.

"If by 'contradict' you mean save your life…then yes, I dare it." She tipped her chin up in defiance, but he could tell by the little bob of the apple of her throat that she was not as confident as she wished to appear.

He had a sudden urge to kiss her slender throat, but he would never do it. Was it not enough of a betrayal that he was lately having these lustful feelings for this girl?

Viola Ruskin was an infuriating mix of prim and sultry, and this seemed to hold an insane appeal for him. He could not understand why, especially since it was the last thing he wanted to feel. In truth, he meant to spend the rest of his days completely numb to all sensation. He wanted nothing but ice in his veins and steel in his heart. Indeed, he needed to be rid of this raw and incessant ache in his heart before it drove him to ruin.

Viola pursed her plump, pink lips in disapproval, then sighed and led him into the vicarage kitchen. The vicar's residence, a small but stately manse, was built of ancient stone and situated immediately behind the church which was also built of this same ancient stone and had magnificent stained glass windows and a soaring spire.

The kitchen was not very large, but there was sufficient light coming in through its windows and the open door at this hour of the morning to give the room a golden glow. She motioned for him to sit on a stool beside the long table.

He stumbled to it and sat heavily, letting out a breath. When he inhaled, he caught the scent of freshly baked bread…or pie…or something delicious that made his stomach growl. Perhaps it was her delicate, fruity scent that was so tempting. But he said nothing and merely watched as she added water to the kettle and then put it on to boil.

She cast surreptitious glances at him while she worked, next frying up eggs and slices of ham with practiced ease. They sizzled in the pan, releasing a heavenly aroma that made his mouth salivate and caused his stomach to growl again. "Do you not have a cook to attend to this chore for you?"

"Mrs. Bligh will be here shortly, but you need nourishment now. Besides, I am not ashamed to know my way around a kitchen. It is quite a useful talent."

"What do you mean?"

She turned to him with a wry arch of her eyebrow. "You really have no idea, do you?"

"No idea about what?"

She turned her back to him a moment to put the eggs and ham onto a plate for him. "What do you think will become of me once my father passes? You know his health is failing. I am doing my best to tend him, but nothing seems to help. He will be gone soon," she said with a soft tremor to her voice, "and another vicar will be appointed to take his place. He is all I have in the world. When he is gone, I shall have no one. Nor will I have a roof over my head, for the new vicar's family will certainly push me out when they move in."

He inhaled with a gut-felt ache. "Forgive me. I was callous and did not think."

"Why should you concern yourself with me?" She set the plate before him and added a scone from the basket sitting on the table and covered in a cheerful cloth. A heavenly aroma drifted toward him as she lifted the cloth. Those scones were obviously freshly baked. She must have been up quite early to have already prepared this batch.

Yet it could not have been something she did regularly, for her hands were delicate and not at all roughened by this sort of labor.

"I know you are too caught up in your own misery to think of anyone but yourself." She sighed and took the stool beside him. "I'm sorry. That was harsh of me and unfair. I know how dearly you loved your wife and daughter."

"Do not mention them," he said in a low growl.

"I'm sorry," she repeated, but he caught the edge of irritation in her voice. "We all lose loved ones. Do you think I am not struggling with the impending loss of mine as well? I never even knew my own mother. She died giving birth to me."

He was about to reach for her hand to give it a light squeeze in apology, but she moved away to pour him a cup of tea. She now set the cup down beside him and settled once more on her stool.

He still wanted to take her hand, but the moment had passed, so he picked up his fork instead and began to eat. "This is delicious."

"Thank you. I am hoping to find a position for myself as a cook...when the need arises."

He glanced at her in surprise. "Why would you bury yourself in a kitchen where no one can see you?"

She cast him a wry smile. "It is the safest place for me, surely that is obvious. One of the few positions for which I would be hired. No wife will take me on me as governess for her children or as maid for her household."

He nodded. "Because you are far too pretty."

*Blast.*

He hadn't meant to let that slip, but she did not appear to be taking it as anything more than a factual comment.

"I am not blind to the way men look at me."

"You could use your appearance to best advantage and find yourself a husband."

"Yes, I could. But I cannot bring myself to do it, at least not yet. I wish to make a love match, if possible. I do not wish to marry merely for the sake of convenience. I am not afraid of hard work. My life does not have to be easy, but it does have to be happy."

He gave a disdainful snort. "Happy?"

If only he could remember what that felt like.

"And what is wrong with wanting this? Why should I have to cringe every time my husband reaches out to touch me? Any man would expect rights to my body in exchange for providing a roof over my head and food on the table. But I am not made this way. I...I cannot give myself to someone I do not love." She blushed furiously. "Oh, this is more than you wanted to hear. Much more than I should have said."

She moved away and pretended to busy herself putting away supplies.

"Miss Ruskin, do not be afraid to come to me if ever you are in need of assistance. I may be wretched in many ways, but not to the point I would ever forget my duty to those who reside in my village." He set down his fork and stared at his empty plate, for he had devoured every last crumb.

She stopped fidgeting about the kitchen and turned to regard him with a thoughtful expression. "You would help me?"

"I know I have not been worthy of any of you these past two years, but I do understand what you mean about happiness. I have felt the loss of it acutely ever since Jillian passed. Then to lose my little Molly to the same illness mere days later. It was more than I could bear."

He saw tears form in her eyes. "I know, my lord. If I am severe with you, it is because I know that the man I have been finding drunk in the ditch outside the vicarage this past week is not who you are or were ever meant to be."

He snorted. "Pretty wretched, I know."

"We are all very proud of you...a war hero, a loving father and husband, a good and kind man who cares for those under his protection. But you've lost your way so badly at the moment. I have every confidence you will set yourself right and find your true path."

In addition to being physically beautiful, Viola was also intelligent and compassionate. He had behaved poorly, especially toward her, and now felt quite contrite. He was not an ogre but had been taking out his grief and frustration on others for too long. "I thank you for an excellent meal. I promise to do better for all of you."

She shook her head. "It is most important that you do this for yourself."

"I know. It has been two years now, and yet I feel as though I am getting worse instead of better."

"Because you are not permitting yourself to move on. May I speak my mind, my lord?"

He cast her a wry grin, for Viola was an opinionated little thing. Perhaps this is why he had been stirring awake only to find himself in front of St. Martin's Church these past few days. Was he seeking her out? "Go on."

She took a deep breath and returned to the seat beside his. "A part of you is ready to move on and this angers you."

"Why should it anger me? In truth, I am desperate for it."

"Yes, but you also believe moving on is a betrayal of Lady Jillian's memory. Yours was a love match and her loss has left a gaping hole in your heart. You want to find someone who will fill that emptiness, but at the same time you hate yourself for even considering someone else. You think it will somehow diminish all that Lady Jillian meant to you."

She was right, but it did not make him less angry to hear the truth from her lips.

He rose and raked a hand through his still wet hair.

*Blast.*

Droplets still streamed down his neck and into his chest thanks to her dumping that water on him. "Thank you for breakfast, Miss Ruskin. I shall endeavor to pass out in the village green next time rather than disturb you," he said with an icy sarcasm that was completely unprovoked on her part.

But the truth hurt and he was not yet ready to hear it.

She was right, but it did not mean he had to accept what she was saying. Nor was she the only one shoving this obvious dilemma in his face. His father's letters had been filled with pleas to stop living in the past and find himself a wife. His father was the Earl of Trent and he was the earl's heir.

No one was letting him forget this.

Everywhere he turned, his duty as eldest son was being flung in his face.

She placed a hand on his arm as he started to turn away. "If you are going to rant and rage at me, then you may as well address me as Viola. Why maintain formality when what you really want to do is forget I exist?"

"That makes no sense."

"Let us not keep up a polite pretense. You are in a very bad way and slowly killing yourself. I am glad if I make you angry because it is time you dealt with this problem that is plaguing you. You cannot stay buried in this dark well of misery you have dug for yourself. At least try to poke your head out and see what a little bit of sunlight might have to offer."

"Such as?"

"You are a viscount and heir to the Earl of Trent," she said, repeating his own thoughts. "Your estate is well-managed and healthy, and you are still young and handsome. Why not venture in–"

"Do not dare say the marriage mart! I have no interest in remarrying." Which is what he had told his family as well and received much the same reaction as he was now receiving from impertinent Viola.

Her father was the vicar.

She was just the sanctimonious vicar's daughter.

What right did she have to pass judgment on him?

He groaned inwardly, knowing he was being a complete and utter ogre to her.

She placed her hands on her hips and frowned at him, ignoring that he towered over her and was twice her strength. "You know I am right. This is precisely why you are angry at yourself...in addition to barking at me. Stop behaving like a trapped and wounded dog. Bark all you like, but it will not fix your pain. Only moving forward will ever help. Start slowly. Do not venture onto the marriage mart until you are good and ready. I am not suggesting you dive into those waters right away."

"Merely dip in a toe?"

She nodded. "You have friends, do you not?"

"I don't know. I've chased most of them away by now."

"The true ones will return upon your invitation. You still have your brother and parents, too."

He did not know why he was listening to her. Perhaps because she was making sense. And yet, the last thing he wanted to do was be sensible. "Your point?"

"Throw a weekend house party."

"Have you been corresponding with my mother?" he muttered with the same icy sarcasm in his tone as before.

"No, but your family has obviously been imploring you to do this or else you would not be looking at me as though you wish I would disappear into Hades along with the other demons burdening your soul. But this is my home and you are the trespasser here, not I. So it is you who should be on his way. And what is so wrong with the suggestion? It is just a party and need not be anything more. Your brother's wife and your mother will gladly help you make up an invitation list."

His groan was more of a low growl. "My mother? And Daisy? I am not a little boy who needs their guidance."

She looked him up and down. "You are certainly not a little boy. But you are behaving like one. Is it not obvious you desperately need a woman's hand in this?"

"If you are suggesting my mother and Daisy are to decide upon which sweet young things to invite, then forget it."

"Fine, then you select them. I'm sure you will make a catastrophic and disastrous mess of it."

"Will I now?" He lifted her up and held her up at his eye level.

He saw the sudden panic in her eyes, for he must have looked like something wild and unmanageable at this moment.

She grabbed onto his shoulders for support and her eyes widened a little more. "Put me down, my lord. This isn't funny."

"Neither is your suggestion." But he set her down because he did not need her shrieking in his ear. His head was still pounding like a hammer being swung atop a nut to crack it. "I will do it…hold a house party, but under two conditions."

"What are they?"

"That you spend the weekend cooking for me. I shall pay you handsomely for your trouble."

"But you have a cook. Mrs. Stringer has been in your service for almost a decade."

"She is not up to the task of preparing meals that require flair and delicacy. I shall give her the weekend off to visit her sister and let the staff know you will be assuming her role while she is gone. It is you…it must be you, Viola…or you can forget about the house party."

She sighed. "Gad, have you always been such an ogre and did we just not see it? All right, if Mrs. Stringer is amenable, then I shall do it. This will also be helpful to me in gaining your recommendation regarding my cooking abilities when the time comes. I'll need your word that I shall have your letter of recommendation."

He nodded. "If your meals are half as good as the scones, ham, and eggs you whipped up for me just now, you have my oath on it."

She let out a breath. "What is your second condition?"

*That you share my bed for the weekend.*

Oh, blessed saints! No! This was the brandy in him talking.

He quickly suppressed the errant thought.

The last thing he would ever do is hurt someone as kind as Viola. It was not her fault she was also luscious and lively, not to mention far more pleasant company than anyone outside of his own family. Nor was it her fault that he – when drunk and obviously delirious – desired her in this crass way.

Jillian would be so disappointed in him.

In truth, he was disappointed in himself, and quite detested himself for having such thoughts about the girl whose only intention was to help him. But he was a man, and had deprived himself of those needs far too long. There was no explanation for it other than his grief had gotten jumbled up with his anger and frustration. To put it in mathematical terms, grief plus anger and frustration had somehow equaled lust.

But why for Viola?

She was not the sort of girl he would ever touch.

"My lord? What is your second condition?"

Indeed, she was the decent sort he ought to be protecting, especially from him.

"That you help me select the young ladies to be invited." He studied her as her lovely eyes widened in obvious surprise. "It must be you, or I will not go through with it. Are you willing?"

**GET THE VISCOUNT AND THE VICAR'S DAUGHTER NOW!**

I would love for us to get to know one another! I hope you'll find me on my Facebook page, subscribe to my monthly newsletter, or connect with me on other social media channels that you enjoy. You can find links to do all of this at my website: mearaplatt.com.

—Meara

**Sign up for Meara Platt's newsletter
and you'll receive a free, exclusive copy**
of her Farthingale novella,
*If You Kissed Me.*

Visit her website
to grab your free copy:
*mearaplatt.com*

# ALSO BY MEARA PLATT

FARTHINGALE SERIES
My Fair Lily
The Duke I'm Going To Marry
Rules For Reforming A Rake
A Midsummer's Kiss
The Viscount's Rose
Earl Of Hearts
The Viscount and the Vicar's Daughter
A Duke for Adela
If You Wished For Me
Never Dare A Duke
Capturing The Heart Of A Cameron

THE BOOK OF LOVE SERIES
The Look of Love
The Touch of Love
The Taste of Love
The Song of Love
The Scent of Love
The Kiss of Love
The Chance of Love
The Gift of Love
The Heart of Love
The Promise of Love
The Wonder of Love
The Journey of Love
The Treasure of Love

The Dance of Love
The Miracle of Love
The Hope of Love (novella)
The Dream of Love (novella)
The Remembrance of Love (novella)
All I Want For Christmas (novella)
Tempting Taffy (novella)

De WOLFE ANGELS SERIES
Nobody's Angel
Kiss An Angel
Bhrodi's Angel

DARK GARDENS SERIES
Garden of Shadows
Garden of Light
Garden of Dragons
Garden of Destiny
Garden of Angels

THE BRAYDENS
A Match Made In Duty
Earl of Westcliff
Fortune's Dragon
Earl of Kinross
Aislin
Genalynn
A Rescued Heart
Earl of Alnwick
Pearls of Fire (also part of Pirates of Britannia)

THE LYON'S DEN SERIES
The Lyon's Surprise
Kiss of the Lyon

A Lyon in the Rough

MOONSTONE LANDING SERIES
Moonstone Landing (novella)
Moonstone Angel (novella)
The Moonstone Duke
The Moonstone Marquess
The Moonstone Major

PIRATES OF BRITANNIA
Pearls of Fire

# ABOUT THE AUTHOR

Meara Platt is a USA Today bestselling author and an award winning, Amazon UK All-star. Her favorite place in all the world is England's Lake District, which may not come as a surprise since many of her stories are set in that idyllic landscape, including her award-winning paranormal romance Dark Gardens series. If you'd like to learn more about the ancient Fae prophecy that is about to unfold in the Dark Gardens series, as well as Meara's lighthearted, international bestselling Regency romances in the Farthingale Series and the Braydens Series, please visit Meara's website at www.mearaplatt.com.